# JIMMY SWAN,
# THE JOY TRAVELLER

# JIMMY SWAN,
# THE JOY TRAVELLER

## NEIL MUNRO
(HUGH FOULIS)

Edited by
BRIAN D. OSBORNE
&
RONALD ARMSTRONG

**Birlinn**

This edition first published in 2002 by
Birlinn Limited
West Newington House
10 Newington Road
Edinburgh
EH9 1QS

www. birlinn.co.uk

First published in book form in 1993
by Birlinn Limited as
*Erchie & Jimmy Swan*

Introductory material and notes
copyright © Brian D. Osborne and
Ronald Armstrong 1993 and 2002

ISBN 1 874744 203 4

British Library Cataloguing-in-Publication Data
A catalogue record for this book is available
from the British Library

Typeset by Koinonia, Manchester
Printed and bound by Nørhaven Paperback A/S, Denmark

# Contents

| | | |
|---|---|---|
| *Neil Munro* | | vii |
| *Introduction* | | xv |
| | | |
| 1. | Stars to Push | 1 |
| 2. | On the Road | 4 |
| 3. | The Fatal Clock | 10 |
| 4. | A Spree | 16 |
| 5. | His "Bête Noir" | 21 |
| 6. | From Fort William | 26 |
| 7. | Jimmy's Silver Wedding | 31 |
| 8. | A Matrimonial Order | 37 |
| 9. | A Great Night | 42 |
| 10. | Rankine's Rookery | 48 |
| 11. | Dignity | 53 |
| 12. | Universal Provider | 57 |
| 13. | The Commercial Room | 62 |
| 14. | The Changed Man | 66 |
| 15. | Vitalising the Gloomy Grants | 70 |
| 16. | Blate Rachel | 76 |
| 17. | Rachel Comes to Town | 80 |
| 18. | A Poor Programme | 84 |
| 19. | Broderick's Shop | 87 |
| 20. | Gent's Attire | 91 |
| 21. | Keeping up with Cochrane | 95 |
| 22. | The Hen Crusade | 99 |
| 23. | Linoleum | 104 |
| 24. | The Grauvat King | 107 |
| 25. | Jimmy's Sins Find Him Out | 112 |
| 26. | A Wave of Temperance | 115 |
| 27. | Country Journeys | 119 |

28. Raising the Wind                                        124
29. Roses, Roses, All the Way                               128
30. Citizen Soldier                                         131
31. The Adventures of a Country Customer                    135
32. The Radiant James Swan                                  141
33. Jimmy Swan's Germany Spy                                145
34. Jimmy Swan in Warm Weather                             149
35. The Tall Hat                                            153
36. The Groveries in Retrospect                            156
37. Selling Shoes                                          159

    Notes                                                  163

# Neil Munro

NEIL MUNRO was born on 3rd June 1863 in Inveraray on Loch Fyneside, Argyll into a Gaelic-speaking family from a crofting background. His mother, Anne Munro, was an unmarried kitchen maid; no father's name was recorded on his birth certificate, which also registers the birth of a stillborn twin sister. In an age when the stigma of illegitimacy was still considerable, such a start in life was not propitious.

One of the minor mysteries of Munro's biography is that he consistently provided an alternative but entirely false birth date to works of reference such as *Who's Who*. This alternative date 3rd June 1864, was diligently copied by every standard reference work and is still given wide currency despite evidence for the correct date appearing in the present editors' editions of *Para Handy* in 1992 and *Erchie and Jimmy Swan* in 1993. Even more surprising is the fact that the monument to Munro in Glen Aray, unveiled in 1935, bears the correct birth date while his gravestone in Kilmalieu Cemetery, Inveraray, perpetuates the false date, but this inconsistency does not ever seem to have entered into the consciousness of literary historians, librarians and compilers of reference works.

Another mystery is the question of his paternity. Persistent legend suggests that a member of the ducal House of Argyll was Munro's father. While such stories are hard to prove, and equally hard to disprove, one later incident in the young Munro's life does tend to suggest a certain degree of well-placed patronage being shown in his favour.

In the 1871 census returns for Inveraray a one-roomed dwelling at McVicar's Land, Ark Lane, Inveraray was

shown as being occupied by Angus McArthur Munro, a
66-year-old former crofter, his daughter, Agnes an unmarried domestic servant aged 38 and his grandson, Neil,
aged seven. In 1875 Neil's mother Ann married Malcolm
Thomson, the governor of Inveraray Jail. In the 1881 census
returns Neil is shown living in Crombie's Land, Inveraray,
with his great-aunt, Bell McArthur, a 77-year-old retired
field worker, and Bell's daughter Lilly McDougall, a 44-
year-old laundress, while Munro's mother, then 51, was
living with her 76-year-old husband Malcolm Thomson
and his 41-year-old son, Malcolm Jnr.

From about 1869 to 1876 Munro attended Inveraray
Burgh School, where he was taught by Henry Dunn Smith,
a significant influence and later a friend.

After leaving school at the age of thirteen or fourteen he
was, to quote his own later words: "insinuated, without
any regard for my own desires, into a country lawyer's
office, wherefrom I withdrew myself as soon as I arrived at
years of discretion and revolt." (*The Brave Days*)

Munro's comment glosses over much that is significant.
The lawyer's office in Inveraray into which he was "insinuated" was that of William Douglas. Douglas was an
extremely well established lawyer in the county and had
been clerk to the Commissioners of Supply since 1864 and
was appointed clerk to the Lieutenancy of Argyll in 1873.
These posts brought Douglas into close contact with official
Argyll, and when one recollects that the lord lieutenant of
Argyll was the duke one may legitimately speculate about
the source of the influence that placed a youth from such a
disadvantaged, poor, working-class background in a
position which would normally be eagerly competed for by
the sons of the middle classes. Munro's fellow clerks in
Douglas's office included the son of the local doctor, and
the son of Douglas's managing clerk.

Munro seems to have found the work uncongenial and,
as he wrote later, was dismayed to find "I could earn in an
afternoon for my employer far more than the £5 per annum
I was getting as salary." In the 1881 census Munro is

described as law clerk (apprentice), but there is no evidence of his actually completing indenture papers as an apprentice. Munro was to leave Inveraray, more or less on his eighteenth birthday, in June 1881. It seems quite probable that the timing of his decision to move to Glasgow, with the eventual aim of taking up a career in journalism, was motivated by a desire to avoid committing himself to a five-year apprenticeship. Inveraray was however to remain central to his life and writings — he later had holiday homes there and in 1903 became the tenant of the house in the High Street once lived in by William Douglas, his former employer. He said on one occasion that "he never apparently could keep Inveraray and the romantic district of Argyll out of any story of his, and possibly he never would."

He and a friend, Archie McKellar, sailed on the Glasgow & Inveraray Steamboat Company's *Lord of the Isles* for Glasgow. Here he worked for two years as a clerk in a wholesale potato merchant and in an ironmonger's store, occupying some of his spare time improving his shorthand, a vital prerequisite for a career in journalism.

While at home in Inveraray he had read widely and had written essays for local publications. In the early years in Glasgow he developed his literary skills, submitting material to various publications. His first documented poem "The Phantom Smack: A Lochfyne Fisher's 'Bar'," appeared, under the pen name of "Bealach-an-Uaran" (a place-name near Inveraray), in the widely circulated *Oban Times,* on 3rd February 1883. Other poems have been traced in *The Lennox Herald* in June 1883 and the *Oban Times* in July 1884. By the time of this last publication Munro had found a place on the *Greenock Advertiser,* which however closed a few weeks after he joined it. He then got a place on a morning daily paper, the *Glasgow News* (not to be confused with the *Glasgow Evening News* with which he was so long associated. The *Glasgow Evening News* was re-titled the *Glasgow News* in 1905).

In July 1884 Munro married Jessie Ewing Adam, the daughter of Hugh Adam, a mechanic living in Braid Street,

Glasgow. Jessie was the same age as Munro and is described in the 1881 census as a clothfolder. In November of that year they moved to Falkirk, where Munro took up a post on the *Falkirk Herald*. Their first child, Annie, was born there, but died of meningitis aged two and a half.

In April 1887 the Munros returned to Glasgow and Neil resumed work as a reporter on the *Glasgow News*. In February 1888 the *Glasgow Evening News* absorbed the *News* and Munro became a sub-editor, very swiftly becoming Chief Reporter. Over the next few years Munro worked hard at journalism, submitting articles to a wide range of newspapers and magazines in Scotland and England; his activities included such curious and diverse tasks as reporting sermons for the *Scottish Pulpit* at fifteen shillings a time. In the early 1890s he was having sensational thriller fiction published in English newspapers and articles accepted by increasingly prestigious national magazines. By 1892 he had written a short story, a West Highland sketch, "Anapla's Boy", and submitted it to *Blackwood's Magazine*. Although this was rejected, a later submission, "Shudderman Soldier", was accepted, and over the next couple of years further "sheiling tales" based on West Highland themes were accepted by Blackwood until 1896, when they were able to bring out a small volume of eleven short stories under the title of *The Lost Pibroch*. This was enthusiastically reviewed and seen as the work of a new and fresh Scottish voice.

In 1897 Munro's career took a major move forward when *John Splendid,* his first historical novel, a work of broader appeal than *The Lost Pibroch*, was accepted for serialisation in *Blackwood's Magazine* and subsequent publication in book form by William Blackwood & Son. In October of that year, having sold his next novel, *Gilian the Dreamer*, for serialisation in *Good Words* and subsequent book publication by the London publishing house Isbister, he felt secure enough to resign his staff appointment on the *Evening News,* while retaining the Thursday literary column "Views and Reviews" and the Monday column "The Looker-On".

Munro's career, despite his abandoning the security of full-time journalism, flourished. A steady production of fiction, his *Evening News* work, regular columns for various other newspapers and magazines, occasional features and reports for London newspapers all made for a very considerable income and a substantial reputation. A rival newspaper, the *Glasgow Herald*, wrote in its obituary tribute to Munro: "No man exercised a more subtle literary influence on the West of Scotland than Neil Munro. His discriminating praise was sufficient to set aglow the heart of the young writer."

Nor was Munro's influence and literary connections confined to the west of Scotland. His diary and correspondence show links with such major literary figures of the period as Joseph Conrad, J. M. Barrie, John Buchan, Arnold Bennett, Andrew Lang, John Galsworthy, and R. B. Cunninghame Graham.

His income, although suffering the inevitable variability of the freelance author, was very substantial. In 1901, for example, his diary records earnings for the year of £1,243 — equivalent in modern terms to around £77,000. By this time the Munros and their five surviving children had moved out of Glasgow, first of all to a house at Waterside, near Busby, Renfrewshire and then in 1902 to a house in Gourock. So successful had Munro become that he was able to send his eldest daughter, Effie, aged seventeen, to finishing school in Switzerland in 1907. A final move, in 1918, brought him to an elegant Regency villa in Helensburgh, which he promptly renamed Cromalt, after a stream in his native Inveraray.

The theme of much of Munro's serious fiction was process of change and the decline of the old order in the Highlands. His continuing reputation centres on the three most famous historical novels, *John Splendid, Doom Castle* and *The New Road. The New Road*, published in 1914, confirmed his position as the pre-eminent historical novelist of his day. A review of it by John Buchan for the *Glasgow News* enthused, "It is a privilege to be allowed to express my humble admiration of what seems to me one of the finest romances written in our time. Mr Neil Munro is beyond question the foremost of living Scottish novelists, both in regard to the scope and variety of his work and its rare quality."

Sadly *The New Road* was to be the last great work of fiction from Munro's pen. During the First World War he was recalled to work on the *Glasgow News* and edited it for a number of years during and after the war, as well as going to France as a war correspondent on three occasions. Munro lost his eldest son, a medical student turned infantry subaltern in the Argyll & Sutherland Highlanders, on the Western Front in 1915 and felt the loss keenly. A sequel to *The New Road* featuring the enigmatic central character Ninian Macgregor Campbell and set in the aftermath of the '45 was planned. It was first mentioned to Blackwood in 1915 and in 1918 he was able to say that he had made a start on it — but as late as October 1928 George Blackwood was still patiently enquiring after it: "a real Munro novel for 1929 would be the very thing..." It never materialised, although eleven intriguing chapters remain among Munro's papers in the National Library of Scotland and are being published by Birlinn in a Munro Anthology prepared by the present editors. Munro's post-1914 work consisted of *Jimmy Swan: the Joy Traveller* (1917), a 1918 short story collection, *Jaunty Jock*, which collected together a variety of short stories he had published in various places over the previous decade, a third collection of Para Handy stories, *Hurricane Jack of the Vital Spark* (1923), to follow the two earlier collections in 1906 and 1911, and, rather bizarrely, a *History of the Royal Bank of Scotland 1727–1927*.

After Munro's death all his humorous fiction appeared in an omnibus edition under his own name and his friend and protégé George Blake edited two delightful collections of his journalism, *The Brave Days* (1931) and *The Looker-On* (1933) — these collections suggest the charm and variety of his newspaper columns and also afford some valuable biographical details. Munro never wrote an autobiography, although among his papers in the National Library of Scotland is what is described as his diary. This was probably started around 1905, with the aim of retrospectively recording the principal events and developments in his life and was presumably intended as an aid to biography or autobiography.

Munro was honoured in his lifetime by the award of the freedom of his native burgh of Inveraray in 1909 and the honorary degree of Doctor of Laws from Glasgow University in 1908. In 1930, two months before his death, Edinburgh University, as part of the installation ceremonies for their new chancellor, J. M. Barrie, also conferred a Doctorate of Laws on him.

Munro died at Helensburgh on 22nd December 1930 and was buried at Kilmalieu Cemetery, Inveraray. A memorial service was held in Glasgow Cathedral, attended by his many Glasgow friends, representatives of the university and the Church.

His own old newspaper made his death their lead story under the triple-decker headline:

DEATH OF NEIL MUNRO

PASSING OF A GREAT NOVELIST

GENIUS IN JOURNALISM

and the *Glasgow Herald* obituarist observed that although in later years he had published but little: "he had already accomplished his life's work — of taking up and wearing the mantle of R.L.S."

The connection with Stevenson was frequently made in tributes. The Rev. Lauchlan MacLean Watt, a noted literary authority of the period, and minister of Glasgow Cathedral, implicitly placed him above Stevenson when he described Munro as "the greatest Scottish novelist since Sir Walter Scott, and in the matter of Celtic story and character he excelled Sir Walter because of his more deeply intimate knowledge of that elusive mystery."

Five years after his death a monument was erected to him on a hillside in Glen Aray, overlooking the home of his ancestors. The initiative for the erection of the monument was taken by An Comunn Gàidhealach and it takes the form of a pyramid of local stone crowned with a Celtic book-shrine and bears Munro's name, the correct date of his birth and death, and the Gaelic inscription *Sar Litreachas* — " matchless literature".

# Introduction

IN SEPTEMBER 1913 Neil Munro wrote to George W. Blackwood, at his Edinburgh publishers William Blackwood & Son to ask:

> Are you in the mood for another shilling "Hugh Foulis" volume?
>
> For some time back I have been running a series of humorous sketches in the *Glasgow Evening News*, dealing with the character and road experiences of a pawky old commercial traveller, "Jimmy Swan". They have been exceedingly popular in the paper, and I'm confident they would do well as a book, with the title
>
> Jimmy Swan<br>The<br>Joy Traveller.

"Hugh Foulis" was the pen-name under whose thin disguise Munro had already published a collection of his newspaper tales of Erchie MacPherson, waiter and kirk beadle, and two collections of the adventures of Para Handy and the crew of the *Vital Spark*. Munro used this device to distance these, his seemingly ephemeral comic creations, from more serious literary fiction such as the historical novel, *The New Road,* which was, even as he wrote to George Blackwood, being published in the firm's long-established monthly *Blackwood's Magazine* — "Maga" to generations of authors and readers.

George Blackwood wasted no time in accepting Munro's offer and an early publication date was clearly envisaged, but at the end of December 1913 Blackwood was asking,

"What has come over *Jimmy Swan*?" Munro, always a shrewd judge of writing and sensitive to the commercial handling of his work, replied, "About *Jimmy Swan,* on further reflections I thought it better not to bring it out this winter; the stuff is all ready, but I think that between now and Spring I can substitute better sketches for some that I have."

However the stories were not submitted in spring 1914 and in June 1915, with Munro back in full-time newspaper work for the duration of the war, he again wrote to George Blackwood: "By the way, are you still in a humour to do a 1/- *Jimmy Swan: The Joy Traveller*? I think I wrote to you about it a year ago, but then came chaos, and I haven't had the heart to think of it since. But the stuff's all ready."

For various reasons, including no doubt Munro's emotional distress at the loss of his elder son, Hugh, on the Somme in 1915, the collection did not finally appear until April 1917. The *Glasgow Herald,* reviewing it, commented, "The sketches, written with the simple charm that distinguishes Mr Foulis in his lighter moments, are full of humour with an occasional touch of sentiment that is never maundering, and contains much shrewd observation of character."

The Jimmy Swan character had been introduced to the readers of Munro's "The Looker-On" column in the *News* in May 1911 with a delightful story, "The Adventures of a Country Customer" (number 31 in this edition), which showed Jimmy working at home in Glasgow, entertaining a customer who had come up from Galloway hoping to combine his business trip to the city with pleasure in the shape of a visit to the 1911 Scottish Exhibition of National History, Art and Industry in Kelvingrove Park. Probably because of the very topicality of this story, attractive in 1911, but obviously dated and inappropriate in 1917, Munro did not use it in his collection of twenty-nine Jimmy Swan tales, and its first appearance in book form came in 1993 in the present editors' omnibus edition of Munro's Erchie MacPherson and Jimmy Swan stories. This edition presented seven previously uncollected Jimmy Swan stories dating from 1911 to 1926, and these are again made available to contemporary readers in this new, separate edition of *Jimmy Swan: the Joy Traveller*. A set of notes to the stories, glossing any particularly obscure expressions or topical references, is provided at the end of the volume.

Although specific topical references, such as the 1911 Kelvingrove Exhibition, are less frequent in the Jimmy Swan stories than in the Erchie and Para Handy tales, there are still quite a few of the stories which take a newsworthy event — a royal visit, the census, the World War — as the point of departure for Jimmy's reflections, and all the tales delightfully reflect the opinions, tastes and moods of their period.

While Jimmy Swan made his newspaper debut in May 1911 in "The Adventures of a Country Customer", his coming was foreshadowed a year earlier in Munro's "The Looker-On" column in an article entitled "Knights of the Road." Here Munro reflected on the changing status of the travelling salesman, drawing a comparison between the new breed of down-trodden, bicycle-pushing, commercial traveller and the old-style salesman, represented by one John Swan — "the gorgeous Swan", "the Bashaw of Bagmen." Between this first incarnation and his fictional realisation in 1911 Swan has changed his Christian name from John to Jimmy, and his employer from Arthur's to Campbell & Macdonald's — but in all other respects the 1910 figure is the much-loved Joy Traveller of 1911.

Munro's 1910 essay is printed here for the first time since its original appearance in the *News*.

### THE LOOKER-ON    21st February 1910

KNIGHTS OF THE ROAD

One wet day last week I saw a young man ride into a small coast town with a tin box fastened on the handlebar of his bicycle, and another behind the saddle. A short, thin waterproof cape sent the rain pouring down in runnels on his legs; his shoes and stockings were caked with mud; his Donegal hat had shrunk to a size too small for him; his face was scourged to purple by the weather. A doleful spectacle! He drew up in front of a grocer's shop, dismounted stiffly, and unstrapped the two tin boxes. There were customers in the shop. While they were being served he stood at the door with the boxes at his feet, and wrung the rain out of his Donegal hat, pathetically patient, waiting with humility till the grocer had time or inclination to attend to him. The grocer condescended to give him a curt nod of recognition and without a word went on tying up parcels. "I am not in a hurry," said one of the customers, with a significant nod at the cyclist in the doorway. "Neither is he," replied the grocer; "he's only a commercial." Twenty minutes later, the weather-beaten ambassador of trade had his boxes open on the counter, and was doing his best to book an order for the very latest, cheapest line in fancy biscuits. His sample biscuits, arranged in trays, were pink-sugared, crimped, fantastic, fragile things that appeal to children; the grocer looked at them with depreciatory eyes, and gave brusque responses to the traveller's most cheerful efforts at that kind of conciliatory small talk which is hard to maintain by even the most heroic soul when one is drenched and physically miserable. "Nothing doing!" at last said the grocer, stiffening his jaw, and turning to his day-book. The traveller just said "Thank you Mr ——"; put the lid on his boxes and carrying them in one hand, while he pushed his bicycle with the other, went a little way along the street to another grocer's. Humble, obsequious, and inured to discouragement and affront — such is the new Knight of the Road.

THE GORGEOUS SWAN

And I remembered Swan. I remembered Swan of five-and-twenty years ago, the august and splendid Swan, whose advent in this very town was always marked by dignity and importance, whose Spring and Autumn journeys were a kind of royal progress. Swan, if you please, was Arthur's (or was it Stewart & Macdonald's?); when a draper shook hands with Swan, the draper thrilled with pride, for he felt himself in touch with vast affairs, imperial dominions of the soft goods trade, of which the splendid Swan was worthy viceroy. Swan looked the part, and carried about with him the proper atmosphere; I cannot for my life imagine Swan pedalling through the rain from town to town, and meekly accepting cold rebuffs from twopenny-ha'penny village shopkeepers. I see him now step off the steamer, large, rubicund, and leisurely, wrapped in the most expensive kind of overcoat, with the thickest, fleeciest kind of travelling rug upon his arm. He looks around the quay, complacent, genially expansive. "I've come!" he seems to say. "Here I am again, you see — John Swan of Arthur's. I'm glad to see you all, and you know ME. Now, what can we do for one another?" The boots from the best hotel takes off his cap to him, and relieves him of his handbag. Swan moves magnificently to the inn, with a dozen enormous wooden cases coming in barrows after him. The innkeeper receives him at the door, he gives him the effusive welcome that innkeepers today reserve for Dukes or the owners of forty-horse-power Panhards, and Swan, lordily shaking hands with him, hopes (in a deep, sonorous, statesman's voice) that Mrs Landlady is prospering. A great fire is burning jovially in the Commercial Room; a fire is set and ready to light in the great man's bedroom; lunch is ready. Swan goes to the sideboard and decides on a cut of this, a little off the breast of that, and expresses his willingness to honour the landlord by accepting an "aperitif" from the landlord's private bottle. The waiters respectfully bow to Swan; the chambermaids warmly smile when he greets them on the stair with a friendly, "Well, Margaret, back again, you see," or "Number 12, I suppose, as usual." An air of bustle, business, prosperity and portent has come into the hotel in the wake of Swan of Arthur's.

## OLD SCHOOL

I see him sally forth in the afternoon — not to sell; no, no, not to sell, but to pass some purely friendly and disinterested hours in the shops of his old acquaintances. They are happy to see his burly form, and his ringing laugh is, of course, infectious. He has six new stories, or he is prepared to take up the argument about the Irish question exactly at the point where they broke it off on the autumn journey. The prospects of a trade revival, the cause of the slump in woollens, or the rise in silk; the tendency in moirés or English blanketing; the catastrophe to Meek & Marshall, and the unpleasant rumours about Macpherson Brothers — on these and a thousand cognate subjects Swan conveys, with an air of exclusive confidence, the very latest sentiments of the city. Incidentally he refers to the old account just settled. "Over forty years your name had been on our books," he remarks with feeling. "The firm appreciates the connection. It began, I remember, with your father — ah! he knew the trade, none better! Our Mr James was speaking about him to me yesterday. 'Arthur's,' he said (these were his very words), 'Arthur's wouldn't be Arthur's but for the loyal support of the country trade and men like Peter Grant. And his son.' 'That's true,' I said to Mr James, 'but Arthur's wouldn't be Arthur's, and the Grants would not be forty years in your ledgers if Arthur's hadn't the character and the goods.' Ha, ha! I had him there Mr Grant, I think I had him there!"

## BASHAW OF BAGMEN

And so the grandiose Swan, with his infectious affability, goes from shop to shop with a not too ostentatious note-book, jotting down the handsomest orders with the calmness of a gas inspector; his enormous sample cases diverting the traffic of the pavements; his parcels cluttering the counters; his goods speaking for themselves, all the more eloquently since they have a guarantee behind them in the solid weight of the traveller's personality and the name of the mighty Arthur's. It is a pleasure to give orders to the gracious Swan. Look at his cases — built like ammunition wagons, clamped with iron; they have come through twenty years' commercial campaign without a dent; they symbolise the sterling, stable character of the Glasgow house, old Arthur's! And look at Swan, himself, too! — tailored like a duke, with a gentlemanly signet-ring, his fob-chain with its massive antique seals, his presentation watch — gold hunter — £40 – "after twenty-five years faithful service"; his cigars! It is an honour to have anything to do with Swan. Perhaps he has to continue his journey down the coast by road, to cover other towns and villages; then the roomiest vehicle and the very best pair of horses aren't a bit too good for him; the horses stand for hours with their harness on; and the uncomplaining driver hangs about the stable-yard waiting till the Grand Bashaw of Bagmen pleases to conclude his conversations with the shopkeepers, or his tea.

THE COMMERCIAL ROOM

Or perchance it is a two-night or a Sunday town, and there are other commercial travellers in the inn; then you shall see the old-time drummer in his state and glory. There is a venerable, sacred ritual for the Commercial Room. No loud professional disputation; no vulgar display or competition; every man is Mister; the proper tone is one of suavity, politeness. There is a Chairman — It is Swan. His years, his status, his Firm, and his long experience on this particular journey render that inevitable. It is he who suggests that Silverside would be nice for tomorrow's dinner; it is he who solemnly adjudicates upon the wine. For wine — a sound old port, or a favourite sherry, is the beverage of the Commercial Room; the decanter circles decorously round the table. "Gentlemen," says Swan, standing in the attitude of the late John Bright (his favourite statesman), "we have with us today for the first time our young friend Mr Jones, who represents the well-known house of J. & P. Campbell. I drink wine with you, Mr Jones, and on behalf of the other gentlemen bid you welcome." And Jones, very red and nervous, but very proud of his Knighthood bows to the compliment as to an accolade. And then the Sunday dinner! The cuisineric skill of Britain has been for a hundred years preserved solely by the influence and fastidiousness of the Commercial Room.

SIC TRANSIT

But Swan is gone, and though he may have a successor as important as himself, the dignity of the Commercial Room has considerably departed, too. The Knights of the Road are no longer what they were; a thousand mushroom little firms have flooded the country with a new kind of Knight of whom the dripping wretch with the biscuit-tins and the bicycle was typical. Inexperienced in life, ill-paid, hurried, cadging, cheap wares for cheap concerns, with no traditions behind them, and no prestige to lend them dignity, they have earned the contempt of the small retailer, and spoiled the Commercial Room. Even the Swans of the profession now have, by the influence of a class which must meekly bear all snubs, and be severely frugal in the matter of expenses, lost something of the prestance almost every bagman had in other days. The innkeeper's smile is less effusive; the fire is apt to be out in the Commercial Room.

If there is, as seems highly probable, a factual basis to this 1910 essay then it is possible to identify the "small coast town" where both the modern bicycle-borne bagman is seen following his unrewarding occupation and where the gorgeous Swan called and put up at the best hotel. The timing of the story, twenty-five years before the present, takes one back to the 1880s. Until June 1881 Neil Munro was still living in his native Inveraray, working as a lawyer's clerk. In 1910, as indeed throughout his adult life, he was a regular visitor to his birthplace, with a holiday home in the burgh. It thus seems very likely that the pathetic sight of the biscuit salesman was noted in Inveraray and that the prototype of Swan of Arthur's was a well-known figure in the Inveraray of Munro's teenage years. It will be noted that Swan arrives in the town by steamer — which would have in those days been the natural route for a Glasgow-based traveller to work Inveraray and the towns and villages of mid-Argyll.

Munro's elegy for the lost glory of the commercial traveller informs the whole atmosphere of the thirty-seven stories now presented in this volume. If Para Handy represents the Highland *seannachie*, telling tall tales around the stove in the *Vital Spark's* fo'c'sle, but with a child-like willingness to get up to any "high jeenks" that present themselves; and if Erchie MacPherson combines the wisdom of the street, Glasgow gallusness and the requisite degree of dignity called for by his twin callings; then Jimmy Swan's prevailing characteristics are his warmth, his proper sense of the worth of himself and the firm he represents and his awareness of his place in the scheme of things. This, essentially Scottish, guid conceit of himself is combined with an innate modesty and decency. As he remarks in "Country Journeys" (number 27 in this edition): "We might be better ourselves... It's a conviction of that kind that keeps me from kicking a lot of folk I meet."

Jimmy lives in a tenement in Gower Street, to the south of Ibrox, on the south side of Glasgow. Gower Street in 1911 was an eminently respectable address, inhabited by such pillars of the community as teachers, insurance clerks, master mariners and draughtsmen. He is the travelling representative of the great drapery and soft goods firm of Campbell & Macdonald, probably modelled on the real Glasgow drapery warehouse of Stewart & Macdonald (who later, in a curious case of life imitating art, changed their name to Campbell, Stewart & Macdonald.)

The Glasgow in which Jimmy lives and from where he sets out on his commercial travelling was then perhaps at its peak. The Second City of the Empire, as it delighted to call itself, was a vast, sprawling metropolis of over a million souls. The scores of shipyards on her river were unrivalled for scale, output and technological innovation. As the first Jimmy Swan stories were appearing, great ocean liners, such as the majestic *Aquitania,* were under construction on the Clyde; Glasgow-built railway locomotives were being shipped from the city's miles of docks to power railway systems from India to South America. The Scottish engineer, trained in the Clyde's shipyards and engine-shops, was a familiar and dependable reality from the Irra-waddy to the Rio Plate, and had become a literary convention which has lasted from Rudyard Kipling's MacAndrew to Star Trek's Scottie — indeed the convention has, with the twentieth-century decline in shipbuilding and heavy engineering, very largely outlasted the reality.

Nor was Jimmy Swan's Glasgow just a place of industry and commerce. It was a city possessed of confidence and self-esteem whose self-image was at a peak. The energy and vision of its citizens and City Council were exempli-fied in a host of ambitious civic projects — in the grandeur of the City Chambers, opened by Queen Victoria in 1888, in a sweeping programme of slum clearance, tramway building, gas and electricity supply schemes. Nor was the city's cultural life neglected — Glasgow patrons were among the earliest and most enthusiastic purchasers of the work of the French Impressionists, as the legacy of their gifts to the city's art galleries gloriously testifies. Indigenous talent was also supported — Mackintosh's School of Art, his Hill House for the Glasgow publisher W. W. Blackie, the sup-port for the works of the Glasgow Boys all speak of a vigorous and bustling city in the arts as in commerce.

Much of the literature of Glasgow has been polarised between a description of the life of the affluent upper middle classes and highly-coloured accounts of the horrors of slum life. Both are indisputably part of the Glasgow story, but Jimmy Swan's Gower Street flat with linoleum on the lobby-floor, his essential ordinariness, quiet decency and warm humanity are just as valid, and statistically rather more significant, than razor-gangs and captains of industry.

All Scotland seems to be Jimmy's sales territory but many of the stories are set in the fictitious, and curiously varied, town of Birrelton. As with John Swan of Arthur's, Jimmy Swan of Campbell & Macdonald's arrives by train or boat with a street-full of sample cases, a wagonette booked to take him from call to call — not for him the indignity of the bicycle and the tin box on the handle-bars. To these little towns Jimmy comes, bearing joy in the shape of the latest in Glasgow fashions:

> "That's joy," said Jimmy. "Youth and a new frock! I ran over a' my samples in my mind, and there's no' a one that's no' a swatch o' something meant for comfort, consolation, the pleasure o' the eye, or the pride o' life. What would life in Birrelton be without me, or the like o' me?" ("Stars to Push")

Nor are Jimmy's importations from Glasgow confined to the new season's lines in Shantungs and cottons. He brings news of the city, a fine bass voice to fortify and inspire the local choir, the latest stories to enliven a Masonic meeting or a Church social, and he even manages to find a new minister for Birrelton when the congregation couldn't see their way to agreeing on a candidate. Jimmy modestly explained away his success at this unusual form of trade: "I'm only a business man. You can get any mortal thing you like in Glasgow if you have the business experience and the ready money." ("Universal Provider".)

Business experience is what Jimmy has in abundance, and he is always willing to give a young salesman the benefit of his advice, or to look back on the great days of the trade with an old colleague or a friendly landlord. In "On the Road" he advises Watson, a young salesman starting out with a head full of notions of psychology and scientific salesmanship:

"Get it out of your head that you're out to sell and then to hook it; you're out to make friends for yourself and the firm. You can't make friends by any process of philosophy, though you may get casual customers."

"And how can I make friends?" asked Watson humbly.

"By being sure that you need them more than they need you," said Jimmy. "That's the start of it. Another way is to live, like me, to the age of five and fifty. And then your friends are apt to be far too many."

Just as the puffer and its Para Handy figure have vanished from the West Highlands, so too has the old-fashioned salesman vanished from the small towns and villages of Scotland. The stories of Jimmy Swan remain as a delightful evocation of a now vanished world, a world where every little town had at least one draper's shop, where the wagonette waited for the traveller and his sample cases at the pierhead or railway station, where hotels had Commercial Rooms, where Commercial Rooms kept slippers for Commercial Gentlemen, where a Jimmy Swan-like figure was a welcome link with the outside world, bringing as he said "wholesome human joy" as he went about his business with a Mazeppa cigar in his hand, a flower in his buttonhole and a pound a day for expenses.

Although eclipsed in fame by Para Handy, and indeed by Erchie, this should not obscure the real merit of these tales. Written by Munro over fifteen years of his literary maturity they are finely crafted work by a considerable artist working in a field he had made very much his own. Munro may have used the pseudonym of "Hugh Foulis" to distinguish these stories and the other series of newspaper tales from what his publisher called his "dignified works of fiction," but the modern reader is not bound to follow him in taking this distinction too seriously. The same artistic spirit and talent that went into the novels was, surely, not turned off when Munro sat down to write about Jimmy Swan or Para Handy.

It is indeed remarkable how these three series of comic stories have held their place in public esteem for close on a hundred years. Little of the humorous fiction from this period has shown anything like the same enduring quality; and when one considers the authors of comic fiction from the early years of the twentieth century who have stood the test of time both critically and in the market-place (and the list is distinguished if not long, Jerome K. Jerome and P. G. Wodehouse being perhaps pre-eminent), one can perhaps begin to judge Munro at his true worth.

Many connoisseurs of Munro's comic fiction rate Jimmy Swan ahead of his better-known contemporaries Para Handy and Erchie MacPherson: readers can make up their own minds about this vexed question, but can be assured of very genuine pleasure along the way.

# 1.  *Stars to Push*

MR SWAN, the work of the day accomplished, stood smoking at the Buck's Head door, and the sky was all a-glee with twinkling stars which are quite irrelevant to the story, and are merely mentioned here to indicate that it was evening. And yet, when I come to think of it, the stars deserve this mention, for their shining, so serene, and cool, and joyous, had some influence both on Jimmy and the story. They set him wondering on the mystery of things and on the purpose of his being and his life.

Behind him, in the hall of the hotel, the Boots, old Willie, piled his sample-cases ready for the boat at six o'clock next morning. The billiard-room seemed full of villagers; the sound of chaff and laughter and the clink of tumblers came from it occasionally. But Jimmy scarcely heard it — wrapt in contemplation of the stars.

From out the billiard-room, at last, there came a man who seemed to have decided, not a moment too soon — indeed, unfortunately, too late — that it was time for home. He fumbled for his top-coat, hanging with a dozen others on a stand, and he was forced to stretch himself a little over Jimmy's cases, piled up very high about the stand by Willie.

"A fine night, Mr Sloan," said Jimmy, who knew even recent incomers to Birrelton;[1] and he helped him to put on his coat.

"There's naething wrang wi' the night," said Mr Sloan, "except for thae damn bags o' yours — Perf'ly rideec'lous! A body might as weel be on a steamer — Shouldn' be allowed!" He was at that particular stage of fermentation where the scum of personal temperament comes bubbling to the top.

"Sorry they should be in your road," said Jimmy, affably. "They're often in my own. It's yin o' the chief drawbacks to bein' what the papers ca' an ambassador o' commerce."[2]

"Ambass'or o' commerce!" hiccoughed Mr Sloan. "Nonsense! Jus' a common bagman!"[3] And two younger men who had joined him laughed at this brilliant sally.

"Right ye are!" said Jimmy. "Just a common bagman! That's what I was thinkin', standin' here and takin' my bit smoke, and lookin' at the stars. Just a plain auld bagman sellin' silks and ribbons! I wish my line was traivellin' for stars. My jove! if I had stars to push, I could get orders! A line like that would gie me scope; I'm sometimes sick o' wastin' words on Shantungs[4] and on down-quilt patterns."

Mr Sloan was feeling nasty — distinctly nasty, having barked his shin on a sample case, and having an uneasy sense that he had forgotten something, and that he should have been home to his wife a good deal earlier. He wished to work himself into the proper spirit for a lively domestic altercation.

"What hae ye got in a' thae cases?" said he.

"Joy," said Jimmy, rappin' out his pipe upon his palm, and pursing up his mouth.

"Oh to bleezes!" said the man, "you're drunk."

"Just touched a wee, perhaps, wi' drinkin' starlight," said Jimmy. "But still I'm tellin' ye, I'm a traiveller for joy, and there's my samples. If I was openin' up my bags to ye, it's likely ye would only see dry-goods. I saw them last mysel' as dry-goods when I packed them, but it just came on me here in lookin' at the stars I was mistaken; there's naething in my bags but human joy."

The young men roared with laughter.

"'Scuse me, Mr Swan," said Mr Sloan, a little more agreeably, "I've often seen ye gaun aboot, and thought ye were in the drapery line; how was I to ken ye were traivellin' for beer?"

"No," said Jimmy, solemnly, "not beer! Wholesome human joy. Glowerin' at the stars there, I was tryin' to find some excuse for my paltry and insignificant existence, and then I minded I was an essential bit o' the mechanism for providin' dresses for the lassies o' Birrelton for next month's Territorial ball. Do ye think ye grasp me, Mr Sloan?"

"But what aboot the joy?" said Mr Sloan.

"That's joy," said Jimmy. "Youth, and a new frock! I ran over a' my samples in my mind, and there's no' a one that's no' a swatch o' something meant for comfort, consolation, the pleasure o' the eye, or the pride o' life. What would life in Birrelton be withoot me, or the like o' me? Man! that's one o' my ties ye're wearin', Mr Sloan! I wish ye would learn to put a better knot on't and gie the stuff a chance."

"Wha's tha' got to do wi' stars?" asked Mr Sloan, vaguely. "You said ye were sellin' stars. Or was it beer? I forget which."

"No," said Jimmy. "I'm not at present sellin' stars, though maybe that's in store for me if I could be a better man. I only mentioned stars because they set me wonderin' if an auld bagman was ony use at a' in that big scheme that put them twinklin' yonder... Good night, gentlemen! I'm aff to bed."

When they were gone, he watched the stars a little longer, finishing his pipe, and then went to the stand to take his coat upstairs with him. Instead of it he found the errant Sloan's.

"By George, I must get my coat," he said to Willie. "I have a pair o' gloves and a box o' chocolates for the wife in't."

Mr Sloan meandered home with that uneasy sense of something overlooked, forgotten, and only recollected what it was when his anxiously awaiting wife asked him if he had the mutton.

"Mutton!" he exclaimed with a sudden sinking of the heart. "What mutton?"

"Oh, John!" she said, "didn't you promise me to be sure and get a gigot for to-morrow? You know that it's the holiday, and all the shops'll be shut. What am I to do for dinner?"

"As sure as death I clean forgot it, talkin' with a chap aboot the stars," said Mr Sloan, contritely, as she helped him to take off his coat.

She put a hand into its pockets and produced a pair of reindeer gloves and a box of chocolates. "What in all the world is this?" she asked him, and he stared, himself, confounded.

"I don't have ony mind o' buying them," said he; "but that's a' right: I likely meant them for a peace offerin'."

"You're just a dear!" she cried, delightedly; "although you did forget the mutton." And she put the gloves on, finding them a perfect size.

There was a ringing at the door.

"I'm very sorry to disturb you at this hour," said Mr Swan, "but there's been a slight mistake. I have a coat the very neighbour of your husband's, and we got them mixed between us at the hotel. This, I think, is his; I wouldn't trouble you, so late, but I have to leave by the early boat."

"Oh!" she said, despairingly, "I might have known!" and started pulling off the gloves. "Then these are yours, and the box of chocolates?" The tears were in her eyes.

"No," said Jimmy firmly. "There was nothing in my pockets, Mrs Sloan: your husband must have bought them," and got his coat restored to him by a delighted wife.

"Who is he that?" she asked, when he was gone.

"Old Swan," said Mr Sloan, half sleeping.

"What is he?" she asked. "I liked the look of him."

"Travels for stars," said Mr Sloan, vaguely; "Bags full of joy! Old Jimmy Swan! He's drunk!"

## 2. *On the Road*

JIMMY WALKED briskly up No. 3 Platform, glanced in at the door of the luggage-van and counted his cases, gave two-pence to the boy who had carried round his rug and hand-bag, passed off the latest pantomime wheeze on the guard, whom he addressed as 'Alick', and sank into his seat in the corner of the smoker just as the train, with a jolt, awoke to the necessity of doing something for its living. It was barely across the river when someone had produced a pack of cards, and Jimmy's rug was stretched between the knees of half a dozen men who played at Nap.[1]

"Come up to Brady's!" said Jimmy time and again, as he slammed an ace down in the centre of the rug and scooped in another shilling's-worth of coppers. On three occasions he went double Nap and got it.

"You've got all the luck the day, Mr Swan," said one of the players, an ambassador in the interest of Dray Gunn's biscuits,[2] who looked anxiously out at every stoppage of the train.

"Wrong, my son," said Jimmy. "Cards are like commercial travelling — one-fourth luck, half pluck, and the balance don't-give-a-damness."

"Bluff, you mean," suggested Dray Gunn.

"Bluff's no use unless you have the stuff," said Jimmy, shuffling. "That's the Golden Text for to-day in cards or commercial travelling — I don't care to mention it, Maguire, but what about that twopence? — Thanks."

"Where's this we're at?" asked the biscuit man at another station. "Stewarton. By Jinks! I should get out at Stewarton,[3] but I'll take it on the way coming back. I'm not going to break up the company."

There was a young fellow in a corner seat who didn't play, but sat embattlemented round by a pile of magazines having snappy names, like *System, Success*, and the *World's Work*. He read them with the fervour of a budding sawbones studying for his First Professional. Sometimes he made notes on the back leaves of a traveller's order-book. Once he ate an apple, having pared it carefully first with an ivory paper-cutter, and Jimmy looked at him with paternal pity. It made him sad to see a fellow-creature recklessly spoil his appetite for dinner with such childish things as apples.

"Now that's a thing I never could do since I was a boy," said Jimmy — "eat apples in the middle of the day. It's a habit that grows on you till you become its slave. I don't say anything against the proper debauch of apples after business hours now and then — say at a Hallowe'en; but get into the habit of nibbling, nibbling, nibbling away at apples at all hours of the day, and before you know where you are your relatives begin to say there really ought to be Some Place of Confinement for unfortunate people with such a weakness."

"It's much more natural to eat apples than half-raw beef-steaks," said the stranger.

"It's much more natural being dead than living," retorted Jimmy, cheerfully; "for there's many more doing it, but hang it! look at the fun there is in being quite alive! I'm not blaming you, old man; I have some bad habits myself, but they're all in the interest of the firm. When I retire from business I'm going to take a house beside a water-fall."

"Man is really not a carnivorous animal," said the apple-eater; "He's frugiverous."

"I don't say that he's quite so bad as all that," said Jimmy, putting up the cards and handing them to their owner; "but he's a serious problem any way you look at him."

The young fellow got out at the same station as Jimmy, who was three-and-sixpence up on the forenoon's gambling, and as cheerful as if he had won a horse and trap in a sixpenny raffle.

"On the road?" asked Jimmy, mildly, as the porters trundled out cases for both of them from the van.

"Macdougall & Grant,"[4] said the other, handing him his card, and with the tone assumed by a visitor to Hamburg who says he is in the British Navy.

"A jolly good house!" said Jimmy, genially, though it was a formidable rival of his own. "Good luck to you! I'm Campbell & Macdonald;[5] name of Swan. So you're successor to old Kilpatrick? Good old Kil! He and I began together on the road in the Seventies. Had it all our own way in these days. And a good man, too! Kil and I would come out of any town you like to name in Ayrshire, neck and neck, and we had the whole North journey in the hollow of our hands. But Kil had to pay pretty sweet for it — Kidneys, they tell me. Wonder how's his widow."

"That sort of way of making business is done," said the young man, replete with all the philosophy of *System* and *Success*. "A man, to make his own way on the road now, has got to have some knowledge of psychology."

"Oh, blazes!" said Jimmy, as they walked to the same hotel together. "What's that? Don't tell me it's nuts, or lentil soup, or anything like that. Or do you mean bumps?"

"It's the knowledge of human nature,"said the young fellow, fervently. "You've got to study your customer. Don't waste his time. Come to the point. Tickle him with some novel lines. A customer is like a trout; you mustn't throw the fly in with a splash. You must give him the idea that it's there by pure accident, and that if he doesn't hurry up and grab it someone else will have it before him. Once he takes it, you must play him gently; no jerk, no tug; and when you have his order in your basket, get out as quick as possible before he has time to meditate and make it a couple of dozen assorted instead of the level gross. The thing is to watch your customer's eye."

Jimmy chuckled — one of those deep, rich, liquid chuckles that add twenty per cent to his value for his salary. Across the flush of his countenance went a hundred wrinkled lines — the furrows of fun, irony, care, calculation, years, weather, and a little droop at the corners of the mouth begot of that sentiment known as tenderness which may be the greatest of commercial assets. His deep eyes twinkled.

"Man, Watson," he remarked, falling into the vernacular he has always made great play with in the villages; "Man, Watson! I fear you're far gone on aipples! A chap canna go about all day munchin' here and there all by himsel' at aipples without doin' himsel' harm. If old Kil heard ye, he would turn in his grave. Ye'll no' get mony fish in your basket that way, either in Galloway or Ayr. Do ye think your customers are a' born idiots? Take my advice,

Mr Watson; I'm auld enough to be your faither: stop your
solitary aipple habit and burn a' your Yankee magazines.
There's only one way to catch and keep a customer — have
an honest liking for him as a human bein' just as clever in
his own way as yoursel', and see that your stuff's as good as
your warranty."

They dined together at the Buck's Head, where Jimmy
was *persona grata*. It couldn't very well be otherwise with a
guest who had been coming for twenty years; who had a
new cure for the rheumatism of Willie the Boots ("mix the
two and take a half-a-teaspoonful every morning in a little
tepid water, Willie. None of your hunker-slidin', now:
don't put ony spirits into the water"); who was deeply
interested in the landlady's Orpington hens, and had heard
in Glasgow a week ago with joy of her being a grand-
mother; who called the landlord Bob, and had a rattling
good cigar for him; and who asked the tablemaid when it
was coming off with her and John Mackenzie. Jimmy, to
the superficial vision, might seem an ordinary being sur-
rounded by a rather shabby suit of Harris tweed, but as a
matter of fact he bore, for twenty yards all round him, an
aura, a personal atmosphere which took the chill from the
coldest rooms, and someway gladdened every creature
coming within its bounds.

He asked young Watson to join him in a drink; not that
he wanted one himself, but just because it is a symbol of
liberty, equality, and fraternity. And because he was
Jimmy. But Watson wouldn't; he alone was impervious to
the influence of auras.

"Good lad!" said Jimmy heartily. "Then have a small
limejuice and soda. Nothing better for brightening up the
— what-d'ye-call-it? — psychologic eye."

A little later Jimmy went toddling round to Gardener's,
the biggest draper in the place, in more respects than one,
and found young Watson there before him, practising all
he knew of the psychological on Mr Gardener, who main-
tained a great aloofness behind a desk from which it looked
as if all the psychology in the world and a hundred steam-

derricks could not for a moment budge him.

"Here I'm again, Bylie!"[6] Jimmy cried in at the door. "How's the wife? But I observe you're engaged; I'll see you later. See and be good to my friend Mr Watson — one of the best, and a good first journey means a lot for a young chap."

The aura appeared immediately to influence Bailie Gardener; he ponderously raised himself from off his stool, and, with a perfunctory glance at drawers and shelves, discovered a few items in which his stock was short, though far from being so short as it might have been had Watson been the late Kilpatrick. The science of psychology otherwise had no more effect on him than a glass of buttermilk.

Half an hour later Jimmy came sailing in to Gardener's.

"They put some queer chaps on the road now, Mr Swan," said the Bailie. "I doot yon yin's no' the weigh o' auld Kilpatrick."

"It's aipples,"said Jimmy, roguishly. "Aipples, and low-browed underground smoking-rooms in Gleska, and black coffee in the forenoon, and Yankee magazines called *Success*. I'm sorry for the chap; a clever enough chap, mind ye, but spoiled wi' aipples. There's naething worse for wind. All the same, Bylie, we'll give the lad a chance; he'll learn. There wasna a greater idiot than mysel' when I first set out for C & M... I have a clinkin' story for ye for your next night's lodge harmony."[7]

Jimmy told the story as he walked behind the counter, pulled out drawers himself, and rapidly estimated how much of an order would bring the quantity of their contents to par. Bailie Gardener, sitting at the desk, complacently watched him turning over webs upon the shelving, running through the shirts, and totting up the blouses.

"Ye ken my stock better than mysel', I'm thinkin' sometimes, Mr Swan," said he, as Jimmy blandly booked what he reckoned should be the order.

"It's what ye call the psychologic eye," said Jimmy. "There's a whole lot o' books aboot it."

At high tea in the Buck's Head, Mr Watson seemed

unhappy; he had found the town a little unresponsive to the system of *Success.* and the other snappy magazines, and in the aura of Jimmy he confessed it. Psychology itself could not have suggested a policy more likely to engage the sympathy of Jimmy Swan.

"I know, old man!" said he. "Dour! I've been there myself. You'll find it'll be all right when they know you, if you treat them like men and not like bloomin' dominoes. Get it out of your head that you're out to sell and then to hook it; you're out to make friends for yourself and the firm. You can't make friends by any process of philosophy, though you may get casual customers."

"And how can I make friends?" asked Watson humbly.

"By being sure that you need them more than they need you," said Jimmy. "That's the start of it. Another way is to live, like me, to the age of five and fifty. And then your friends are apt to be far too many."


## 3. *The Fatal Clock*


DAN SCOULAR, the third man in the Mantles, was to be married on Hogmanay, and the warehouse expressed its consolation in the customary way by means of a smoker and testimonial — James Swan, Esq, in the chair. For nearly twenty years there has been no presentation to an employee of C & M at which James Swan, Esq, has not firmly rapped on the table with the chairman's mallet, looked round the company with a pawky smile of the utmost self-possession, and said, 'Gentlemen all!' preparatory to a speech which invested the occasion with almost national importance, and made the presentee determined that henceforth he should be worthy of the high encomiums passed upon his amiability, his genius, his industry, and general indispensability in the soft goods trade of Glasgow and the West of Scotland. Hundreds of brave and bright young gentlemen bound for matrimonial havens, or new drapery businesses of their own; for Leeds,

Bradford, London, Canada, or New South Wales, have gone out of Mancell's Restaurant[1] with Gladstone bags, gold watches, writing desks, silver salvers, eight-day clocks, or gorgeously illuminated addresses, whose intrinsic values were merely trivial as compared with that superimposed on them by the eloquence of Jimmy Swan. They might lose the illuminated addresses or salvers before they got home, but the memory of his speech was always a fragrant possession. For Dan Scoular's presentation, however, Mr Swan took up an unexpected attitude; he would not consent to preside as usual, unless the testimonial took some other form than a marble timepiece, and Scoular's preference was fondly set, as he told the committee, on this essential domestic feature.

"Mr Swan's determined on something else," he was told.

"What does he think it should be?" asked Scoular. "I'm sure there's nothing wrong wi' a good-goin' clock."

"He doesn't care what it is, but he bars a timepiece, and if we want him in the chair we'll have to meet his wishes."

"All right!"said Scoular. "Make it a case o' cutlery. It wouldn't be a testimonial at all unless we had him in the chair."

So a case of cutlery it was, and Mr Swan agreeably presided. When the moment came for the presentation rites, the cutlery case in tissue paper was suddenly produced in due and ancient form, as if by sleight-of-hand, from underneath the table, and Mr Scoular assumed the appropriate aspect of modest protestation and astonishment. As he said in his reply, he had not for a moment expected his friends to do anything so handsome.

Mr Swan sent the cutlery on a tour of the room that the subscribers might have the pleasure of reading the inscription on the case, and took the opportunity of expressing his gratification that the committee had selected this particular form of gift.

"For a young man startin' a house of his own," he said, "there are few things more appropriate than a case o' cutlery.

You have only got to lock it up and lose the key, and all risk of early bankruptcy due to the good-wife's social ambitions is averted. If I thought for a moment that the future Mrs Scoular was likely to use all that Sheffield steel and electroplate right off, I would advise Dan to swap it at the earliest opportunity for a sewin'-machine. But what she's sure to do, bein' a wise-like girl, as all of you know, since she has been five years in the silk department, is to place it carefully on the chiffonier,[2] with a biscuit-barrel on the top of it, till Dan becomes a partner. Meanwhile — except perhaps at a christenin' — she'll use the cutlery that's kept in the kitchen drawer. From scenes like these, gentlemen, auld Scotia's grandeur springs!"

"What about the clock?" cried some one in the background, and Jimmy twinkled.

"I was just comin' to the clock," he retorted, dropping into the vernacular his warmer moods demanded.

"Let me hasten to say, Mr Scoular, in case that remark has roused fond anticipations that are bound to be shattered, that there's naething mair for ye. There's no clock. And ye may thank me for there bein' no clock; if some o' the committee had their way o't, it's no' a dacent case o' cutlery ye would hae been gaun hame wi' on the Subway[3] the nicht, but a ton or twa o' the monumental sculptor's art on a lorry.

"Gentlemen," he proceeded, "I've seen far ower mony o' the stately tenement homes o' Scotland brought to ruin under the weddin' gift o' a massive marble timepiece, sometimes complicated wi' a couple o' objects reputed to be made o' bronze, and generously alluded to as 'ornaments'. It's a mean advantage to tak' o' ony young woman goin' to stay wi' a total stranger. For, remember, she has got to live wi' that timepiece a' day, and a' her days. Her man goes out to his work in the mornin' and comes back at night after a busy and cheerful day at the counter, and he never thinks o' her bein' shut up a' the time wi' an Italian monument that is for ever recallin' to her the shortness o' life and the solemnity o' the Necropolis.[4] There's no escape from it for her, poor soul! She canna lift it aff the mantelpiece and put it under a bed; it's as permanent in its place as a gasalier.

"The increasin' tyranny o' the marble timepiece has been obvious to some o' us for many years, but it is only within the last twa or three years I got a lesson in what it may lead to that has made me determined to discourage the marble clock as a presentation gift at ony function I may have the honour to be connected wi'.

"A customer o' mine in Mauchline went and got married three years ago. He was in the UF choir[5] and in the Rechabites[6] — a thing that micht happen to onybody — and the choir and the Rechabites agreed on a conjoint testimonial. They gathered £12. 10s., and when they broke the news to him that he was in for a presentation, he said he would have a marble clock, and would like to get pickin' one for himsel' in Gleska.

"Up he came to Gleska, which is the peculiar home and haunt o' the marble clock in the most deleterious forms, and drags me awa' from the warehouse to help him at the buyin'. I did my best to put him aff the notion by tellin' him o' happy homes I had seen broken up through the habit o' having aye a tombstone in the parlour; and I strongly urged a chiffonier and bookcase, or sewin'-machine, or a bedroom suite o' furniture. But no! Mac-Leerie had set his he'rt on a polished black sarcophagus, and would have me, richt or wrang, to a shop where they sell them in broad daylicht without the police interferin'. From scenes like these!

"I never thought there were sae mony ways o' bein' solemnly and distressingly ingenious in the cuttin' up o' black marble! The miscreants that do that kind o' work appear to have attempted everything! It was a pretty big shop, and it was full o' black monumental tombs that were made to look like Grecian temples, Roman altars, Rothesay villas, lighthouses, front elevations for Picture Palaces, tea-urns — ony mortal thing but clocks! Yonder they were, tickin' awa' like onything, and we walked up and down between the plots o' them, quite low-spirited, the same as it was a cemetery.

"MacLeerie had but the one idea about a clock — that it should be big, and black, and heavy. He picked the very biggest he could get for the money, and I tell you it was a whupper! It was three feet long and two feet high if it was an inch; had the weight of a fireproof safe, and was guaranteed a genuine reproduction o' the Madeleine Church in Paris. MacLeerie said he liked, particularly, the Madeleine touch.

"I protested to the last. I implored him, if he must have a clock, to take a small inlaid mahogany one wi' a sonsy, honest face, and buy a bangle for the mistress with the balance o' the money, but he was on for the mausoleum, and he got it! From scenes like these!

"The first time I was back in Mauchline after his marriage, he took me up to his house, and showed me the Madeleine in poseetion. I couldna have believed that ony earthly mantelpiece would stand the strain, but he showed me how it was done wi' brackets o' angle-iron.

"'How in the world did ye get it up the stairs?' I asked, and he explained that it was hoisted through the window wi' a block-and-tackle.

"That clock was in supreme possession o' the parlour! It brooked no rivals! It dwarfed the piano, the what-not, the saddle-bag suite, and the ancestral portraits. It took your eye away from the carpet, I was twenty minutes in the room before I noticed the tantalus spirit-stand. A more commandin' article o' British furniture I never saw than George MacLeerie's clock!

"But it wasna goin'!

"It hadna gone since it was erected! You see the pendulum could only be started from the back, or by givin' the whole edifice a shake, and gettin' into the back or givin' it a shake was out o' the question; ye might as well try to shift or shake the Pyramids o' Egypt.

"I ate brides-cake and drank the health o' the couple in front o' that amazin' clock, and I declare it was like layin' the memorial-stone o' a new Post Office! From scenes like these!

"Well, gentlemen, what was the natural and inevitable outcome o' MacLeerie's vanity? For a while it looked as if the couple was gettin' on quite satisfactory. By and by I found MacLeerie a little dreich in settlin' his bills, and heard that his wife was launchin' oot in the social line wi' regular days-at-home, progressive whist, and a vacuum-cleaner.[7] She was celebrated, ye understand, for having the biggest, heaviest, marble clock in Ayrshire, and she felt she had to live up to this distinction.

"She found, in a while, that her parlour furniture didna properly match the grand old Madeleine, and she had to get in a lot o' new things on the instalment system, includin' a pianolo and a fine new gramophone. The other ladies in the terrace would drop in on an efternoon and sit in front of the Madeleine listenin' to the music and thinkin' they were in Paris, and because the clock never went, they never knew the richt time, so that George's tea was seldom ready when he cam' hame. At last he didna come hame for his tea at a', but took onything that was handy at a public-house behind his shop; he couldna bear the sight o' his mausoleum. When grocers' accounts and the like o' that came to the hoose, Mrs MacLeerie aye stuck them behind the Madeleine for safety; and of course they never could be got oot again.

"The lang and the short o' it was that she, puir body, died one day in an effort to get below the clock and dust the mantelpiece, and her man, between her loss and his sequestration,[8] was so put aboot that he only survived a few weeks after her.

"It was only then the marble clock was put to its appro-priate purpose; the works were taken out of it; and it was re-erected on her final resting-place, where it mak's the brawest marble mausoleum in Mauchline. From scenes like these, gentlemen, auld Scotia's grandeur springs."

## 4. *A Spree*

HAVING FINISHED high tea at the George Hotel, Jimmy
Swan, a little wearied after a cross-country journey of five-
and-twenty miles in a badly-sprung waggonette,[1] sought
out his usual bedroom, and searched his bag for slippers.

They weren't there!

The ready-flyped[2] extra socks were there; the shirts with
the studs in them; the Cardigan waistcoat; the chest-
protector he had never used in all his life; the little 'house-
wife' or bachelor's companion, with needles, thread, and
buttons in it; the sticking-plaster; the bottle of fruit saline;
the pocket Bible and the Poems of Burns; but not a hint of
carpet slippers.

"I doubt Bella's gettin' a bit auld, like mysel'," he
meditated. "It's the first time she forgot my slippers since
we married. I'll hae to be awfu' angry wi' her when I get
hame — if I can keep mind o't."

He went down to the Commercial Room and rang the
bell for the Boots.

"Have ye a pair o' slippers, Willie?" he inquired.

"There's no' such an article in the hoose, Mr Swan,"
said the Boots, "unless I got ye the lend o' the boss'."

"Oh, don't bother!" said the traveller. "I'll can dae
withoot."

"We used to hae a couple o' dozen pair for the use o'
you commercial gentlemen," said Willie, "but nooadays
naebody asks for them; I suppose it's this new sanitary and
high-jinkin' education."

"The innkeepers made a great mistake when they
stopped providin' slippers," said Mr Swan. "There was
naething better for keepin' a customer in the hoose and no'
stravaigin'[3] roon the toon wastin' his money in other
premises. If ever I start an inn, I'll hae a pair o' slippers, a
rockin'-chair, and a copious free supply o' cake and
speldrins[4] for every customer. What's the result o' me no'
ha'ein' slippers? I'm just goin' awa' ootbye for a walk to

mysel', and there's no sayin' where I may forgaither wi' a
frien' or twa. No man's hame for the nicht until he has aff
his boots."

He lit his pipe, and walked through the little town at the
hour when the cows, that had been milked for the evening,
were released from their byres and driven back to their
common pasture. The Free Church bell was ringing for the
Thursday prayer-meeting. The shops were shuttered. An
odour of burning oak from the bakehouse, commingled with
the curious redolence from the hot oven-sole, impregnated
the atmosphere until he got so far as the smithy, where a
little earlier sheep's heads had apparently been singeing.
From what had once been the UP chapel,[5] and was now a
hall for the parish kirk, came the sound of choral voices.

Jimmy stood in front of the hall and listened. The
combined Established and UF choirs were practising for
the Ancient Shepherds'[6] annual church parade, and at the
moment singing Sullivan's 'Carrow'—

> My God, I thank Thee, who has made
>     The earth so bright,
> So full of splendour and of joy,
>     Beauty and light;
> So many glorious things are here,
>     Noble and right.

Outside, on the pavement, he put in a restrained, but
rich, resonant and harmonious bass. A lifetime of encoun-
ter with bleak weather had not impaired his naturally
mellifluent organ, and he counted no artistic joy so exquisite as the hearing of his own voice giving depth and body
to the parts of a well-sung church tune. He knew all the
words and harmonies of hundreds of hymns and psalms;
they were ineradicable from his memory, which could
never retain the words or air of a pantomime song for more
than a week.

"That's Bob Fulton, my customer, puttin' them through
their facin's for the Sabbath," reflected Mr Swan. "Good
soprano, capital alto, bass no' sae bad, but tenor, as usual,

no' worth a docken. Ye'll no' get a dacent tenor in Scotland out o' Gleska; it must be something emollient and demulcent in Italian ice-cream."[7]

A moment later, in a cessation of the singing, he put his head diffidently in at the hall door.

"Come awa' in, Mr Swan!" cheerfully invited the choir conductor. "We'll be nane the waur o' an extra bass."

"Oh, ye are daein' splendid, Mr Fulton!" said Jimmy, joining the musicians, with many of whom he was well acquainted. "Good attack; fine balance; tempo tip-top! Wi' an organ ye would just be as good as oor ain Cathedral."

But to his vexation, the practice was at an end. And he had just administered a peppermint lozenge to himself before entering, to get the proper atmosphere, and tone up the larynx!

"Hang it a'!" he said, "the night's but young yet, and I was fair in the key for a spree o' Psalmody."

"The minister's for naething but the newer hymns on Sunday — except the Old Hundred[8] to begin wi'," said Mr Fulton, and the commercial traveller made a grimace.

"New hymns!" said he. "New fiddlesticks! He'll be takin' to Anthems next, and a solo soprano cocked up in the gallery cravin' the Wings o' a Dove wi' her mind on a new pair o' wings for her bonnet. There hasna been half a dozen new hymn tunes made in my time I would tolerate at my funeral; there's only 'Peace, Perfect Peace!' 'St Margaret,' 'Lead, Kindly Light,' 'St Agnes,' 'Pax Dei,' and 'Carrow' — there's no' much more in their novelties to boast o'. I wouldna gie St George's, Edinburgh, for a' the rag-time stuff in Sankey."[9]

"Let us have a try at St George's," said the conductor; "No. 141 in Carnie's Psalter — 'Ye Gates Lift Up'." And the choir, to show Mr Swan the traveller what it was equal to, proceeded to sing with astonishing vigour and address. The summer shades in zephyrs and in hosiery; new stripe and twill designs; the Mona Lisa (specialty of C & M), the slump in Bulloch's order, and the rumour of sequestration for Macbain might never have been in the mind of Jimmy

Swan; he sang his bass like a soul transported high above the gross affairs of earth, and emulous of the cherubim. In the second part, where the voices of the males asked Who of Glory, no other bass infused the phrase with so emotional a sense of wonder, inquiry, and reverence; he might have been the warder Peter.

"Excellent!" he exclaimed, when they were finished. "I liked particularly the lah-soh-fah-me o' the tenors; it's the only bit we can aye depend on tenors gettin' a proper grip o', but a' your tenor, Mr Fulton, 's capital — what there is of it. If I might suggest another Psalm, it would be the Old 124th — 'Now Israel may say and that truly.'"

And the Old 124th it was. The inspiring bass of the visitor was enjoyed as much by the choir as by himself, and when he took his upper Bs with a clarity no less assured than the sonorousness of his lower Gs, there was an ecstasy in Jimmy's soul he would not barter for a fortune. He got his choice of an hour of Psalmody — Selma and Kilmarnock, Coleshill and Torwood, and Dundee, 'Oh, Send Thy Light Forth' and 'By Babel's Streams'; and Robin Brant, the joiner, leading bass, was put upon his metal. Himself a man in his prime, of six feet three, he was determined no grey-headed traveller from Glasgow, rather small in stature and slightly paunchy, should beat a voice that had been brought to its perfection by daily warblings, pitched in tone to the constant bizz of a circular saw. But Jimmy Swan was envious or emulous of no one, utterly delivered over to the art of harmony and the meaning of the lines. It would there and then have seemed but reasonable to him that the portion of the blest should be to sing eternal Psalms. The weariness of his journey was dispelled; sharing a Psalm-book with another chorister, he rarely needed to glance upon its pages; he was doing what had been familiar and inspiring for him to do ever since the day the crackle left his adolescent voice, and he found he was a singer.

The rosy face was lit with animation; the shrewd grey head just faintly moved in time to the wave of Fulton's pitchfork; when at 'Invocation' he said, "my harp, my harp, my harp I will employ," there was an absolutely luscious 'dying fall' in the opening notes for tenor and bass which gave the flexibility and colour of his voice magnificent exposition, and he knew it, for he glanced across at Fulton with the mute inquiry in his eye — "Did ye hear me that time?"

"Ye're no' oot o' practice onyway, Mr Swan!" said Fulton. "Where in a' the world do ye keep it up?"

"Maistly on slow trains, when I ha'e a carriage to mysel'," said Jimmy. "Ye have no conception o' my compass on the N.B. Railway oot aboot Slamannan.[10] But to tell the truth, I'm no' much use at solos; I think I'm at my best when I swell the volume."

He went home to his inn with a pleasing sense of having spent a profitable evening. He had not only helped the harmony, but from a copious lore about psalm-tunes and their history he had entertained the choir to an instructive, though unpremeditated lecturette; and pledged himself to Mr Fulton to give the same at greater length with the choir as illustrators at a public gathering when he next came round.

At the door of the George the innkeeper was standing speaking to Miss Bryce, the mantua-maker, one of Jimmy's customers.

"There you are, Mr Swan," he said, "I've been asking high and low for you; I found you a pair of slippers."

"I've been employing my harp," said Mr Swan, serenely blissful, "and I've had a glorious night o't, Robert.

So many glorious things are here,
    Joyous and bright!

"Man! it's a blessin' we're no' born dummies! Good evening, Miss Bryce; I'm just lookin' forward to seein' ye in the mornin'."

"I hear from Mrs Clark you're going to favour us some day with a lecture on Psalmody. I hope ye'll tell us some o' your funny stories!" said the mantua-maker, who had the greatest admiration for his gifts as a raconteur, and the traveller looked ruefully at his host.

"She's a worthy body, Robert, but she doesna understand the grandeur o' solemnity, and the joy o' sacred song
— if ye happen to be bass," said Jimmy.

# 5. *His "Bête Noir"*

ALWAYS, WHEN Jimmy Swan is doing Birrelton, he puts off
his visit to Joseph Jago's shop till the very last. The fact that
there is a Joseph Jago mars, in some respects, the perfect
bliss of his western journey, for of all his customers for a
quarter of a century, Mr Jago is the only one to whose
intelligence his peculiar humour has not penetrated. It is
not because Mr Jago is old, for there are nonagenarians on
the western journey who, for Jimmy Swan, are far more
interesting than youngsters. Nor is it because Mr Jago is a
dry old stick; Jimmy Swan makes a specialty of dry old
sticks, and loves to hear them crackling when he puts, as it
were, a match to them — the latest wheeze from the
Merchants' Club, or a joke from *Punch*, which does not
circulate to any great extent in towns like Birrelton. To
waste no unnecessary words on him, Mr Jago is old, and
dull, and dismal, and deaf. Any one of these disabilities
would seem a trifle to Jimmy Swan, but all of them combined in a single individual is more than even he can
swallow.

Most distressing of all is Mr Jago's rooted conviction
that C & M's traveller is a wicked man of the world. He
disapproves the knowing rake of Jimmy's business hat, his
own idea of a tile being something much more solemn,
straighter in its lines, and worn strictly perpendicular, only
on Sundays and at funerals. Jimmy's patterned waistcoats,
too, inspire distrust; for some unfathomable reason, fancy
waistcoats are associated in Mr Jago's mind with horse-
racing. And, finally, there is that unquenchable twinkle in
Jimmy's eye. That twinkle, for Mr Jago, betokens many
things — frivolity, foolish preoccupation with the things of
time, theatres, public-houses, catch-the-ten, novelles,

curling clubs, and Masons' meetings. When Jimmy Swan comes into Jago's shop, the owner always looks at him askance and troubled, feeling as he felt in 1876, when he was last away from Birrelton, and saw the frightful saturnalia of a Carters' Trip in Glasgow. It cannot be denied that Mr Swan is a first-rate traveller, and in that rôle indispensable to a country draper bound to keep abreast with the city's silly changes of fashions, but Mr Jago would have liked a man more grave; he cannot rid himself of the belief that Jimmy laughs at him, and sometimes tries to pull his leg.

Jimmy, having swept up all the other soft-goods orders of the town, went into Joseph Jago's shop the other day with a stifled sigh, prepared for a depressing hour and the usual misunderstandings.

Old Jago gave him a flaccid hand as cold and unresponsive as a flounder, and groaned some unintelligible salutation with a hanging lip and a rheumy glance of disapproval on the tilted hat.

"I would have been round sooner, but I was having a bite at the inn," said Jimmy cheerfully.

"Better without it! better without it!" said old Jago, shaking his head. "It's a perfect ruination, morally and physically."

"Which do ye think the more deleterious?" asked Jimmy smiling; "the tea or the ham and eggs?"

"Oh, I thocht ye said drink," said Jago, taken aback.

"Not at all!" said Jimmy. "Just a solemn, single-handed affair o' stoking boilers. That's no' cloves ye smell; it's the camphor balls my wife persists in usin' to keep aff the moths. If you were a modern Gleska warehouse,[1] Mr Jago, I wouldna need to go to the inn for tea; I could have it in your room de luxe."

"My what?" said Mr Jago, with a hand behind his ear.

"Room de luxe," said Jimmy patiently. "'De luxe' is French for a penny extra on the cup and a d'oyley naipken. All the big Gleska warehouses now, ye ken, have tea-rooms in them. The latest tip-top style o' decoration — Louis the

Quatorze furniture and Adams friezes on the walls, Festoons ..."

"Balloons," said Mr Jago, with a crafty look of incredulity.

"Ay!" said Jimmy, to save the time of explanation. "A band plays even-on behind a couple o' aspidestra palms, and ye can hear them quite plain daein' Maritana[2] or the Count of Luxembourg[3] quadrilles just the same as if it was in the West-End Park at the Exhibition."[4]

"It's droll I never heard of it!" said Mr Jago ironically.

"It's right, I'm tellin' ye," said Jimmy. "It's not only tea and buns they give you; if ye want a fish and chips or a luncheon *table d'hote* at eighteenpence, it's there."

"I suppose ye'll have a place like that in C & M's now?" said Mr Jago, marvelling at the traveller's imagination.

"Not at all!" said Jimmy. "We havenae any o' these facilities in the wholesale houses, and we just step out and round the corner wi' a customer the way we did in '76 when ye were there."

"Ye're a terrible man, Mr Swan!" said Mr Jago, shaking his head. "I think ye'll never be wise."

"I hope not," said Jimmy affably. "It doesna dae to be ower wise in this business."

Jimmy booked his orders as expeditiously as possible, but yearned to inform this obviously mistrustful mind of what it missed by vegetating in a shop in Birrelton. He got an unexpected opportunity. Old Jago turned again to the subject of Glasgow warehouse restaurants just to see how far the traveller's imagination would carry him.

"I suppose," said he, "they'll have the licence, Mr Swan? Ye'll can get a dram?"

"No fears o' ye!" said Jimmy. "They havena got that length yet. But there's no sayin' they're aye gettin' on. Some o' them have rooms where ye can get writin', and restrooms."

"What dae they charge for the best rooms?" asked Mr Jago.

"There's no charge at all; ye just go into them and sit down, and tak' your crotchet wi' ye if ye like. There's naething more exhaustin' to the female frame than walkin' for hours up and down a warehouse looking for the hairpin department, or for some particular pattern o' taffeta not yet invented, worth a half-a-crown a yard but sold at eighteen pence."

"Man, ye're a great wag, Mr Swan," said old Jago with a cynical dry cough. "I wonder ye're no' frighted! I suppose the customers'll come sailin' in in their balloons?"

"Balloons?" said Jimmy, amazed to find Mr Jago attempting a joke.

"Yes, ye said there were balloons."

"I never mentioned such a thing, Mr Jago," said the traveller, and Mr Jago groaned in tribulation for this errant soul.

"Ye did, indeed!" said he emphatically. "And may I ask if there's much advantage ta'en o' the fightin' rooms?"

Mr Swan put off his hat and wiped his forehead. His customer was decidedly more distressing than usual.

"It's no' the National Sportin' Club[5] I was talking about," he remarked, "nor the Suffrage Movement.[6] I was speakin' o' Gleska warehouses, Mr Jago. There's nane o' them hae fightin' rooms that I ken o'. When I think o't, it's maybe an overlook."

"Do you know, Mr Swan, I canna believe a single word ye tell me!" said the righteous draper, fixing a remonstrant gaze on the crimson dots on Jimmy's waistcoat. "Business is business, and it might occur to you that I'm no' so daft as to credit the shrewd drapery firms o' Gleska wi' fritterin' awa' their shop room, their time, tea, potato chips, and fancy luncheons, on customers comin' in aff the street for a bolt o' tape or a cut o' worsted. We're no' that far behind in Birrelton; just last week there was a lassie frae a cocoa firm in England three days in the Store presenting cups of boilin' cocoa and Abernaithy biscuits to all and sundry. I'm perfectly certain it was for naething but the advertisement. But that's a very different thing from settin' up a restaurant and givin' awa' fish teas and fancy dinners and — "

"I didn't say you got the tea and the dinners for nothing," bawled Jimmy Swan.

"Ye needna speak so loud; I'm no' so deaf as a' that," said Mr Jago. "And ye certainly declared there was no charge at all."

The traveller pocketed his order-book and packed his samples, incapable for a while of further disputation with this perverse and afflicted customer. But he was not done with him.

"It's a lang time since ye were in Gleska, Mr Jago," he remarked. "I'm no' surprised ye're dubious."

"I'm no' dubious at all; I'm just astonished at ye, Mr Swan," said Jago.

Jimmy chuckled. "And yet," said he, "it's naething to what ye'll see in some o' the shops in London. There ye'll can play a game o' cairds or billiards while your wife's at the bargain counter fightin' for her life; and the warehouse has a creche where the careful and devoted mother leaves her baby till she gets her pattern matched."

"Just that!" said Mr Jago dryly. "Keep at it, Mr Swan, while you're warm. Do they haud your dog for ye?"

"Upon my word they do!" said Jimmy. "They'll keep your dog or stable your horse for ye, or garage your motor-car. They would do ony mortal thing to keep you on the spot; I believe they would embalm ye if they thought your widow would come in at times to see ye."

"Oh, ye're an awfu' man!" said Joseph Jago. "Do ye no' think, Mr Swan, ye've come to a time o' life when ye should be settlin' doon to think soberly o' things? It's no' richt to be makin' a mock o' everything;" and his voice was full of a quaver of pious grief.

"Ach! to the mischief!" said the traveller in a discreet undertone, as he tightened a strap on a sample case. "I might as well try to talk to a skim-milk cheese!"

## 6. *From Fort William*

WHEN JIMMY Swan is travelling in the North, sufficiently remote from the Second City of the Empire to run any risk of being taken immediately at his word, he proffers his customers a Glasgow hospitality which would ruin C & M if it were exercised at their expense. But C & M have nothing to do with it; the only person who has cause for apprehension, if she knew the facts, is Mrs Swan. Her little house in Ibrox couldn't hold a fiftieth part of the people Jimmy invites to come and stay there. For the last week-end on which there was an International Football Match at Hampden,[1] he had five-and-thirty customers urgently engaged to come to Glasgow and sample the cosiest flat in Gower Street.[2] They were all to come from somewhere north of the Caledonian Canal; customers south of that got a genuine Mazeppa cigar.

Nemesis waits on such commercial strategists. Jimmy forgot, some weeks ago, that Fort William is on the wrong side of the Caledonian Canal, and instead of simply giving Peter Macaskill a Mazeppa cigar, he invited him to come to Glasgow soon and see the Kinemacolor[3] pictures.

"I would like fine!" said the draper eagerly, after hearing all about them, and the Gower Street flat, and Bella's fairy touch on pastry. "Would next week-end do?"

"Capital!" said Jimmy, beaming with delight, and taking out his diary. "I see there's a fine train at ten o'clock, and the fare's only 15s. 9d. return."

"Ay; that's the fare for ordinar'," said Mr Macaskill; "but there's a special week-end trip next Saturday at 9s. 6d. Depend on me bein' there."

"Good man!" said Jimmy heartily. "If you don't come, I'll be awfully disappointed. Mind and bring a waterproof, and leave your presentation watch at hame."

A week later, at the breakfast table, he got a wire from his customer: 'Arriving Queen Street 2.16.' He scrutinised it through his spectacles with mock dismay.

"What's the matter, Jimmy?" asked his wife anxiously. "Is Aunty Mary deid? Or anything wrong wi' James?"

"It's naething o' that sort at a'," he answered her. "It's the world that's gettin' ower wee. When I started on the road first, Fort William was aboot the length o' Malta; men were born, and grew up, and mairried, and were made deacons o' the kirk, and died in Fort William withoot ever clappin' eyes on a railway train.[4] Nooadays the great Scottish cigar belt is steadily pushin' north till a chap's hardly safe to hand oot onything but Mazeppas nearer hand than Ullapool and Lairg. The lang and the short o't is that Peter Macaskill's comin' this afternoon, and we'll have to put him up till Monday."

"Is he a good customer?" asked Mrs Swan, no way perturbed.

"The best," said her husband.

"Then I'll have to ha'e a hen!" said Mrs Swan emphatically, and Jimmy gently nipped her.

In England, I believe, it takes the form of a caress.

Mr Macaskill came with a reassuring hand-bag little bigger than a gynaecologist's, and under Jimmy's guidance steadily worked his way through all the picture-palaces within a radius of a mile from Sauchiehall Street. He had never seen the cinematograph before; it fulfilled every demand of a truly artistic soul hitherto starved upon pictures in the *People's Journal*[5] and monotonous scenic effects on Ben Nevis. The latest picture houses, where you could sit at a table earnestly drinking tea and eating penny sweet-cakes without the necessity for withdrawing your eyes for a single moment from the thrilling episodes of 'The Bandit's Daughter' specially appealed to him; he grudged every moment that they spent in the streets going from one show to another.

"He's like a new message-boy the first day in a sweetie shop," said Jimmy to his wife that night when their guest had gone to bed. "Another day o't would scunner him. I was never so tired mysel' o' cinemas in a' my days; I've seen as mony o' them, Bella, as'll dae me for a twelvemonth. I'll dream a' nicht o' horses gallopin' and tenements on fire. I almost wish the West Hielan' Railway wouldna pander to the rural districts wi gi'en them week-end tickets at rideeculous rates; the railway fares in Scotland's far too chape."

"Tuts! he's a nice cheery chap, Mr Macaskill," said Mrs Swan. "I'm awfu' glad to see him," and Jimmy gently nipped her.

"So am I," said he. "The only thing to worry me would be that he might be a bother to yoursel'." And again he nipped her, this time on the ear.

·On Sunday evening, still replete with hen, Mr Macaskill, whose salient characteristic was shrinking diffidence, became deeply and nervously engrossed in the contemplation of a penny timetable. Having cleared his throat noisily several times, he ventured the stammering remark that five in the morning was an early start.

"It depends on what ye're startin' for," said Mr Swan. "If ye're in a club, for instance, five o'clock in the mornin's no' a bit too early to go hame to supper."

"I was thinkin' o' the train to-morrow mornin' for Fort William," said the guest, embarrassed. "It leaves Queen Street Station at ten minutes to six. I'm vexed to think o' puttin' ye up for such an hour, Mrs Swan."

"Hoots!" said she, "there's surely a more wise-like train than that, Mr Macaskill?"

"Unless ye think the polis have a clue to your identity," said Jimmy. "Is the afternoon train no' good enough?"

"It would do me fine, but I'm an awful bother to ye," said Macaskill. "I'm takin' ye off your work."

"Not you!" said Jimmy, with genuine warmth. "It's a privilege. Stay till the 5.12 train in the afternoon, and see some more o' the picture-houses; there's dozens ye havena seen yet. Ye'll can easy find them yoursel' if ye follow the croods, and I'll meet ye at one o'clock for a bite o' lunch."

So Macaskill spent the forenoon writing home to his wife that he would be home to-morrow, and by four o'clock he had covered several quite fresh picture palaces and lunched with Mr Swan. At five minutes past four he looked at his watch, and stammered an allusion to the fact that there was a place called Fort William.

"There's no use o' ye goin' awa' there the day," said Jimmy, politely. "The shop would be shut before ye got hame, onyway; wait till to-morrow and go back in style."

Mr Macaskill gulped an unuttered explanation that no matter what day he went back he could not get from Glasgow to Fort William in time to find the shop open unless he started at 5.50 in the morning, and that night Mrs Swan had a splendid pie for supper.

"Ye're just a perfect wee wonder!" said Jimmy, and he nipped her.

On Tuesday, at breakfast, Mr Macaskill said, with something almost approaching firmness, that he must certainly make tracks for home in the afternoon.

"Dear me!" said Mrs Swan, "ye're surely awfu' tired o' us, goin' awa' already! I'm sure to-morrow would be time enough."

It shook him. He looked at the plump and rosy little partner of James Swan the traveller; marked the dimples and the genial smile of her, and felt that nothing he could do to please her must be left undone.

"Well," he said, "I maybe might could stay till tomorrow, but I must be there to open the shop on Wednesday mornin'."

"Good man!" said Jimmy Swan, effusively; "I was just hopin' ye would change your mind. Man! ye havena seen the half o' the picture-palaces!"

Mr Macaskill wrote a letter home to say he was unfortunately detained till Wednesday, and with now unerring instinct for the real good stuff in Glasgow, found several picture-palaces on the south side of the river, where he spent the best part of the day, though by this time most of the films were become familiar.

He lost his way, and got back to Gower Street at night a little tired, but adamant in his determination to leave by the early morning train, if Mrs Swan would waken him at half past four. That night there was for supper the finest brandered haddocks he had ever tasted.

"Look here, Bella!" said Jimmy Swan, when the guest had gone to bed; "is this a domestic house or sanatorium?"

"Don't be silly, Jimmy," said she. "I'm sure he's welcome; and him a valuable customer o' yours."

"But, my goodness!" said her husband, "if we keep him much langer awa' frae his shop he'll no' be a customer at all! It'll no' be there! Naething for me, after this, but the Mazeppa cigar, even, by heavens, if it was in Thurso!" But all the same he nipped her.

Of course, Mr Macaskill was not wakened in time for the early train; it was impossible, with all that brandered haddock. Mr Macaskill manfully concealed his chagrin at breakfast-time. He stammered and stuttered, and agreed that, after all, the afternoon train would suit him better. There are only two trains in the day from Queen Street to Fort William. He found he had overlooked some really creditable picture-palaces in the east end of the city, and renewed acquaintance with 'The Bandit's Daughter.'

That night, Mrs Swan had in a couple of friends who sang divinely, and some exquisite devilled kidneys. When their visitor talked of going on the morrow, she seemed to bridle up, and said she knew he was sorry he had come to Glasgow.

"Not at all!" he eagerly declared. "I've had a tip-top time! Ye've been awfu' good to me."

"Jimmy's oldest friend!" she said (it wasn't, strictly speaking, true), "you'll vex me greatly if ye dinna bide till Thursday."

"I should think so!" said Jimmy.

So Mr Macaskill waited till Thursday, when Jimmy casually suggested Friday as a better day for setting out to Fort William. Mrs Swan continued to have the most engaging suppers, and said that Friday was unlucky.

So Mr Macaskill did not leave till Saturday, having by that time discovered all the picture-palaces in the suburbs.

When Mr Macaskill got home to Fort William after a

week of absence, his wife was at the station in a condition of nervous prostration.

"What in all the world do ye mean by this carry on?" she asked him, tearfully. "I was just makin' up my mind I was a widow woman. Just three clean collars and one pocket-naipken wi' ye, and ye stayed a whole week! I'm black affronted!"

"As sure as anything I couldna get away a minute sooner!" said Macaskill, penitently. "Mr and Mrs Swan wouldna let me."

"Ye said ye would be back on Monday," said his wife.

"And every day since then ye wrote me saying ye would be sure to be tomorrow."

"And every time I wrote I meant it," said Macaskill. "But ye don't understand the Swans, Margaret; they're that hospitable; every move I made to go, they raised some opposition. I believe they would keep me a' my days in Ibrox if I didna summon up my nerve at last, and pick up my bag and make a bolt for it."

"And what in the name o' Providence did ye find to do for a week in Gleska?"

"Ye may well ask, Margaret!" said her contrite husband. "There's nothing yonder to be seen but picture-palaces. I went to them even-on, day after day, and I can tell you I was sick o' them! I would sit in them for hours on end plottin' what way I could get away home from Gleska without hurtin' the feelin's o' Mr and Mrs Swan. Nothing could exceed their kindness, but they might have considered the possibility that I had my shop waitin' on me in Fort William. I'm tellin' you, it's me that's the happy man to be home again, Margaret."

## 7. *Jimmy's Silver Wedding*

"Do you know what Wednesday week is?" asked Mrs Swan, with a surprising attempt at archness for a woman who had brought up a fairly large family.

"Wednesday week's a lot o' things, Bella," said Jimmy, brushing his hair in a pensive humour induced by the reflection that it was not getting any thicker on the top. "It's the day I have to get up and work, for one thing. It's the day I'm nearly goin' to lose the train. It's the day C & M's no' goin' to raise my salary. It's the day I'm no' goin' to get nearly as many orders as I think I deserve. It's the day I'm goin' to sell 1s. 4½d. Cotton Shantung at 1s., and muslin one-piece robes worth a guinea at 12s. 6d. It's the day I'm no' goin' to buy a motor-car or a steam yacht for ye. It's the day that's likely to be wet, for I'll be in Inverness. It's the day I'm goin' to wish to the Lord I had gone in for some other job than commercial travellin'. It's the day nobody's goin' to die and leave me anything. It's the day that's goin' to pass like any other day, and me a gey tired man at the end o't. Just the ordinary kind o' day, and when it's past it'll be bye!"

"Tuts!" said Mrs Swan, impatiently. "Do ye not mind what happened five-and-twenty years ago come Wednesday week?"

Mr Swan put on his coat reflectively. "Five-and-twenty years ago? Let me see, now. Was that the day I was teetotal. Or was I hame at exactly the hour I said for my tea?"

"Never in your life," said Mrs Swan, with emphasis. "But the 13th o' July's an important date you might well keep mind o'. It's the day that we were married. It's our silver wedding."

Mr Swan gasped, "Silver weddin'!" he exclaimed. "Man, I'm astonished at ye, Bella! Ye're a' wrang wi' your calculations. It's no' a dozen years since we were married; I mind fine, for I was there!"

"And where did a' the weans come from, James Swan?" asked his wife.

"Oh, well! if you put it that way!" said Jimmy. "Well, say fifteen years."

"John's twenty-one, and if Annie had been spared she'd have been twenty-three on Saturday."

"Silver weddin'! My jove, Bella, but that's a start! I aye thocht silver weddin's was for auld totterin' bodies wi' wan leg in the grave and the other on the road to the poorhouse. And look at us!" He surveyed himself in the looking-glass. "A fine, upstandin', fresh-complexioned, athletic young fellow, lacin' his ain boots every day he's awa' frae hame. And there's yoursel' — Bella Maclean or Swan; first in the Grand March, wearin' sky-blue dress with polka dots; the real and only belle of the ball; good for Wilton Drive![1] By jings, Bella, do ye mind the time I advertised ye? And there ye are yet, getting chubby a wee, but what an eye! And what a step runnin' up the stair! They're no' turnin' oot the same stuff nowadays at all. If only you could play the piano!"

Mr Swan did not go to Inverness on Wednesday week. Instead he took a silver wedding honeymoon holiday with his wife, and they went to Kirkfinn, chosen first because Mrs Swan had never been there, and second because there was never enough trade in the two or three drapers' shops of that sleepy village to tempt the commercial traveller to take his samples with him and combine sordid business with the poetic joys of a silver wedding celebration.

"Your cases 'll be in the van, Mr Swan?" said Charlie, the Black Bull boots, at the station.

"Not this time, Cherlie," said Jimmy. "Here's a bag; that's all. This is a special run; I'm here with a sample wife — ah! ye needna glower, ye rascal; it's ma ain. Ye'll no forget the extra pair o' boots in the mornin', and ye needna knock me up till nearly nine; nae hurl to Kirkmichael for me to-morrow."

"And this is Kirkfinn,"[2] said Mrs Swan. "It's no that big, and still many a pair o' sox you lost in it."

"It's no' the size that coonts wi' toons on the northern circuit," said her husband, cheerfully; "It's the genial atmosphere, and there's whiles when Kirkfinn is awfu' hard on sox."

She was surprised that everybody seemed to know him as they went along the street.

"Of course they do!" said he. "What would hinder them? I've been comin' here since the year o' the Tay Bridge storm,[3] and they look on me as a kind o' institution like Ord-Pinder's Circus. Ord-Pinder's clown and me's celebrities."

"It must be an awfu' dreich place in the winter," said Mrs Swan, though gratified by the public interest manifest in the lady accompanying a visitor who for more than a quarter of a century had seemed wedded only to a barrowload of sample-cases.

"Dreich!" he exclaimed, derisively. "Nae fears o't! When things get slack they start a cookery-cless or a sale o' work for a new flag for the Rechabites. There's nae dreichness about Kirkfinn, I'm tellin' ye!"

"At any rate, it must be a healthy place; everybody looks well up in years," said Mrs Swan. "They'll no' take many troubles in a bracin' place like this."

"Troubles!" retorted Jimmy. "They take every trouble that's goin' except the tattie disease, and whiles I think they don't miss even that. But that's because they're in the Rechabite Tent, and get the benefit."

"If they're all in the Rechabites," said Mrs Swan, "it must be a very sober place."

"A Tent's no' a tenement hoose," said Jimmy; "It's easier to get oot and in to."

Though he protested business was the very last thing he would permit to intrude upon their honeymoon, their dinner at the Black Bull Inn was scarcely over when the habits of thirty years possessed him, and the first place he must take his wife was to one of his customers. They started out ostensibly to walk beside the river, but for half an hour they never got farther than Abraham Buntain's shop.

"Here I am again, Mr Buntain," said Jimmy, bursting in on the drapery counter. "You wouldna get the usual card notifyin' ye o' my comin', but it's all right. A special line in quiet grey summer-weight fancy tweeds, for immediate holiday wear," and he brought his wife forward with an arm about her waist.

"None of your nonsense, Jimmy," said Mrs Swan, blushing becomingly.

"If the wearer goes with the tweeds," said Abraham Buntain, gallantly, "you can put me down for an immediate delivery. Glad to see you in Kirkfinn, Mrs Swan. We all know Mr Swan in Kirkfinn, but it's the first time he has given us the chance to see who turns him out so creditably."

"Well, there she is," said Mr Swan in his professional manner. "Unique. Chaste pattern. None of your French models; British throughout. Durable. Unshrinkable — quite the contrary. A little dearer to begin with than flashier-looking stuff, but pays itself a thousandfold in the long run. The colours don't run."

"You're making them run pretty badly all the same," said Mrs Swan, with a smile, and blushing more than ever.

"I must say I like the style," said Mr Buntain, entering into the spirit of the thing.

"I should think you do!" said Jimmy, buoyantly. "With any eyes in your head. It's a style that caught my fancy five-and-twenty years ago, and I've never tired of it. This season it's the tip-top of fashion — one of those Victorian revivals, you understand; nothing like the old patterns! Sometimes my eye's been caught — when I was younger, I mean — by a bit of Marquisite fancy voile or French foulard, but, bless your heart! there's no wear in them, and no warmth. I don't conceal from you, Mr Buntain, that I consider mysel' pretty lucky."

Mr Buntain was prepared to make the silver wedding Jaunt to Kirkfinn a satisfactory commercial proposition by giving a handsome order there and then for autumn lines, but Jimmy resolutely refused to book it now. "I'm not with C & M this week," he declared; "I'm with Mrs Swan, and we're on our honeymoon — and oh, by the way, I want to buy her a costume-length of your homespun tweed." And he did it, too, at strictly local retail prices, refusing to avail himself of any trade discount.

"Before we go along the river, Bella," said Mr Swan

when they came out of Buntain's, "I want to run in and say how-d'ye-do to Miss Cleghorn. Here's her shop — a good old customer of mine."

"Good gracious!" said Miss Cleghorn. "Your silver wedding! I would never have thought it, Mr Swan, and I'm sure I wouldn't think it of you, Mrs Swan."

"She doesn't look a bit chafed, does she, Miss Cleghorn?" asked Jimmy.

"She looks a good deal too good for you," replied the roguish shopkeeper.

"Don't spoil her by giving that away," said Jimmy. "It's the truth, but I've aye kept dark about it."

"Five-and-twenty years is a long time," pensively said Miss Cleghorn, who had lived that period at least in a state of virgin expectancy, and at times was apt to become impatient with the deliberation of the local matrimonial market. "Did ye never tire of him?"

"I tired of him the very first week I married him," laughed Mrs Swan, "and I think he tired of me in less."

"I did," said Jimmy, frankly. "And now I'm sure I wouldn't tire of her in fifty years. H'm! Inscrutable are the ways o' nature! I want to buy her one o' these Vienna sun-or-shower umbrellas we sent down to you last month, Miss Cleghorn."

"You're the happy pair!" said Miss Cleghorn, when this second wedding gift had been presented. She, too, had an autumn order for C & M in readiness, but the traveller would have none of it this visit, saying he had not his order-book.

As they were leaving the shop she laughingly cried them back. "I wonder," said she, "if Mr Swan wouldn't book me an order for a husband?"

"What kind?" said Jimmy, whipping out the orderbook whose possession he had just a moment before denied.

"Just one like yourself," replied Miss Cleghorn gaily, and still half meaning it. "I fancy I could not do better."

"Very good!" said Jimmy, gravely, and he wrote down: "Husband; middle-aged, but feeling fine; not righteous overmuch, a fair to middling quality. Must sing bass, and be a good deal away from home."

"I'll get him for you!" he declared as he pocketed the book.

# 8. *A Matrimonial Order*

MISS CLEGHORN was a jocular body, or conscious that she had reached the desperate stage of spinsterdom, or was, more probably, both, for a month having elapsed without James Swan implementing her order for a husband, she sent him a postcard with the expressive intimation, "Special order not yet invoiced." Jimmy took it home to his wife for her opinion as to whether his Kirkfinn correspondent was really in the market or only taking a rise out of him.

"I booked the order right enough," said he, "but I thought she was in fun."

"A maiden lady of Miss Cleghorn's age is never in fun about a thing like that, though she may think herself she is," said Mrs Swan. "Yon Kirkfinn's a very lonely place, nothing but the birds whistling, and even they get tired of it. You better hurry up and send the body what she wants before the season's over."

"It's no' in our line at all," said Jimmy; "She ought to apply to a Matrimonial Agency. They would send her down some samples or a likely fellow on appro."

"Ye were the sample yoursel', James," his wife retorted, "and she told ye she wanted something as near the pattern as possible."

"Bless your heart! I canna guarantee an absolute duplicate. There's no' mony o' my kind left, or we're aye picked up as soon as we're in the window. I have no idea where to look for the article she wants. All the bachelor chaps I ken are a bit shop-soiled and oot o' fashion."

"Ye were a bit shop-soiled yoursel', James Swan, when I got ye," said his wife. "But whit's a little Glasgow smoke? Ye were guaranteed to wash. Except that ye're a trifle frayed aboot the edges and wearin' thin on the top, ye're no discredit to your wife and family."

"She may be in fun," said Mr Swan, sitting down to tea, "but the honest truth is that Miss Cleghorn would be nane the waur o' a man. Yon shop o' hers would double its trade in a twelve-month if there was a man in it to give the genuine Gleska touch. Did ye ever see such windows? Tea-cosies and combinations, delaines[1] and Turkey reds,[2] sand-shoes and sun-bonnets; and every noo and then a bill to notify the public o' Kirkfinn that somebody's lost an umbrella. To the mischief wi' their lost umbrellas! It's no' her business to be advertisin' for lost umbrellas; let them come to her and buy a new yin! It's my opinion that when a case o' goods from C & M comes to Miss Cleghorn she just coups[3] as much as she can o't into her windows, wi' her eyes shut, and puts what's left in some cunning place below the counter where she canna find it again. The art o' shop-dressin', Bella, is for men. Miss Cleghorn, they tell me, is a tipper at trimmin' hats, the thing she was brought up to, but she has no more notion o' a well-trimmed shop than she has o' operatic music."

"I saw that," said Mrs Swan.

"Then she wants nerve — "

"Considering everything, I wouldn't say that was where she was deficient," said Mrs Swan.

"I mean business nerve. She's timid; wi' the 'dozen assorted' type o' mind. If I sent her a gross o' anything — and she could easy sell it — she would take a fit. So she can never buy so cheap as Abraham Buntain can. Her selection is fair ridiculous; if I didn't keep her right she would still be tryin' to tempt Kirkfinn wi' tartan blouses and silk mitts. But where she fails most lamentably is in credit to the wrong customers. Any kind o' fairy story 'll get roond Miss Cleghorn, and her ledger's mostly a' bad debts. 'Perhaps they havna got it, puir things!' she says. Maybe no', but they've got her! And still she makes no' badly aff her business."

"Enough to keep a man?" asked Mrs Swan.

"I'm tellin' ye the right sort o' man would double it. What that shop wants is b-i-f-f — biff!"

"What the shop seems to want, and what would suit Miss Cleghorn otherwise, I think," said Mrs Swan, "is Will Allan o' the Mantles."

Her husband stared at her with admiration.

"Ye're a most astonishin' woman, Bella!" said he.

"I never thought o' Allan, and he's the very man. What made ye think o' him?"

"Oh, he comes from her quarter o' the country, and he's like hersel' — ye mind he had a disappointment in his youth."

"Had she?" asked Mr Swan, amazed at his partner's knowledge.

"Of course she had!" said Mrs Swan, emphatically. "Can ye think o' any other reason for a wyse-like woman like yon lookin' after a shop in Kirkfinn? Forbye, she told me — when I met her on the Sunday."

That very night a letter from Mrs Swan was sent inviting Miss Cleghorn to spend some days with her in Glasgow.

Mr Swan took the earliest opportunity of having a little private conversation with Mr William Allan of the Mantle Department, and asked him casually to supper for the following Friday night. "I'll likely have one or two friends from the country," said he offhand. "There's one at least — a lady friend o' Bella's who hasna been in Gleska since the time the Haverley Minstrels[4] were in Hengler's Circus."[5]

"Lucky girl!" said Mr Allan, cynically. "There's been nothing really doing in Glasgow since about that time. I mind of taking a lady friend to see the Haverleys." It seemed a pious and moving recollection.

"Was her name, by any chance, Dunlop?" asked Mr Swan, with romantic interest.

"I don't know what it is now," said Mr Allan, pensively; "but it was certainly not Dunlop at that time. Painful subject, Jimmy; your wife knows all about it."

"She's gey close, the wife," said Mr Swan, craftily. "Anyway, this is a Miss Dunlop. Keeps a shop. No' far off fifty — "

"Prime o' life!" muttered Will Allan of the Mantles, with sober conviction; it was about his own age.

" — Plump. Fair-complexioned. As cheery as another chap's weddin'! It's a wonder to me, Will, that sort o' woman doesna marry, hersel'. Ye know Kirkfinn?"

"Fine!" said Mr Allan, emphatically. "I served my time there, but I haven't been near the place for twenty years. Painful subject, Jimmy; your wife knows all about it."

"It's no great catch havin' a bit shop wi' a lot o' bad debts in Kirkfinn. It's the sort o' place where the most attractive kind of girl might sit on a sofa till it was a' sagged down waitin' for a lad to sit beside her, and die o' auld age before the springs recovered their elasticity. It's the sort of place where it's aye so long to the Cattle Show, or so long after it. When I'm in Kirkfinn, the Boots at the Inn has to pry open my door wi' an iron pinch to waken me — sound sleep's the one thing that Kirkfinn is famous for. That and hens! Ye canna venture to walk through Kirkfinn without skliffin' your feet in case ye come on eggs."

"I aye liked poultry," confessed Mr William Allan. "And there's nothing wrong with Kirkfinn; I sometimes wish I had never left it."

Miss Cleghorn promptly accepted the Glasgow invitation, with a quite unconvincing story of being seized for the first time in many years with a desire to see the autumn shows.

"Glad to say I've managed to fill that line for you," said Mr Swan, turning up his order-book. "'Middle-aged, but feeling fine; a fair to middling quality; not righteous overmuch; sings a kind of bass, and is a good deal away from home.' I can send it off to you at any time."

"None o' your nonsense, Jimmy!" said his wife.

"I wouldn't insist on his being much away from home," said Miss Cleghorn, quite in the spirit of the thing. "You see it's pretty lonely in Kirkfinn. Is he on appro.?"

"Not in these goods, Miss Cleghorn," said Mr Swan. "They get so easily chafed. And we don't keep a big stock. You see the whole demand nowadays is for thin fancy stuff that gratifies the eye for a season at the most, but has no wearin' quality, no body. But I'm no' askin' ye to buy a pig in a poke; it's a Mr Johnson, and he's comin' here the night to supper."

Miss Cleghorn crimsoned. "Of course you understand I'm only joking, Mr Swan," she said, in nervous apprehension.

"So am I," said Mr Swan. "I'm the jokingest wee chap! Amn't I, Bella?"

When Mr and Mrs Swan retired to their bedroom that night, they sat down and laughed as heartily as consideration for the feelings of their guest next door would allow.

"My! didn't she get a start when she saw it was Will Allan?" said Mrs Swan.

"But did ye notice Will?" asked Jimmy, almost suffocated with suppressed amusement. "'I understood it was a Miss Dunlop,' says he, gaspin'. 'My mistake!' says I, 'the right name slipped my memory! Miss Cleghorn's up for autumn bargains; I had no idea that ye kent her.'

"And they quarrelled twenty years ago!" said Mrs Swan, tremulous with the thought of the still romantic possibilities of life. "She told me all about it in Kirkfinn."

"Have ye any idea what about?" her husband asked.

"She told me," replied Mrs Swan in a paroxysm of restrained merriment. "You could never guess! It was because he would insist on partin' his hair in the middle! She considered it looked frivolous. And now — oh, Jimmy, I'm sore with laughing! — now he hasn't enough to part one way or another any more than yourself!"

"Tuts!" said Jimmy, rubbing his head. "A trifle like that! No wonder they made it up again so easily! I'm sort of vexed for C & M; they look like losin' a first-rate man in the Mantles."

## 9. *A Great Night*

THERE ARE villages to which Jimmy Swan goes, burdened
with all his sample-cases, as conscientiously as if he were
visiting a metropolis, though it might appear that the
profits on the orders he secures will hardly pay for the post-
hiring. Among them is Birrelton,[1] which is so unimportant
that it isn't even given on the maps. When C & M's ambassador of commerce puts his cases down in front of the only
draper's shop in Birrelton, as he does twice a year, the whole
vehicular traffic of the Main (and only) Street is diverted
up the lane behind the smithy, and the populace realise
that the long-familiar range of tweeds, prints, winceys, voils,
and underskirts in Dawson's window will be completely
changed in a week or two in harmony with prevailing
modes in Glasgow, London, Paris. Though their husbands
don't suspect it, it is Jimmy Swan who dictates what the
Birrelton women wear — at all events, the fabric and the
pattern of it; Mr Dawson meekly leaves all the questions of
æsthetics to the traveller, who postponed the era of crêpe
de chine and ninon in Birrelton (it is said) for several years.

"About them foulards?" Mr Dawson asks with diffidence, lest their suggestion might appear presumptuous.

"Foulards are no' use for Birrelton; that's the stuff for
you!" says Jimmy; and so it is.

Jimmy 'takes in' Birrelton, not for any great profit in the
place itself, but because it is on the road to several other
important places. An hour of exposition and advice for Mr
Dawson; another hour to rest the horses and refresh
himself, and Jimmy is on the road again, in the heavily-
laden deep-sea wagonette himself and his cases call for.

Last week, however, a foundered horse broke down entirely under the stress of snowy weather, and the traveller
found himself for the first time in his life compelled to stay a
night in Birrelton. Its sleepiness lay heavy on his urban soul,
and early in the afternoon he suggested to Mr Dawson
that the village badly wanted cheering up in some way.

"It's aye a quiet time o' the year here," said Dawson apologetically. "And there's naething on till Friday week, when we hae a Parish Council meetin'."

"I'm no' goin' to wait for that," said Jimmy. "Could ye no' get up a concert in the aid o' something?"

"A concert!" exclaimed the draper. "There hasna been a concert here since Watty Sharp brought hame his gramophone."

"Has he got it yet?" asked Jimmy. "We could hae a tiptop concert, wi' a gramophone for the nucleus."

As a result of active and immediate steps on the part of Mr Dawson and the traveller, the village bellman announced a Grand Concert in the Schoolroom at eight o'clock that evening, James Swan, Esq., in the Chair. Collection in Silver in aid of Poor Coal Fund. The school was crowded.

"Ladies and gentlemen," said the Chairman, standing up at a table furnished with a gramophone, a jug of water, and a tumbler; "The town of Birrelton has long been celebrated for its local talent in the music line. A bush is about the very worst place on earth you could keep a talent under; the Bible says you should keep it on the house-tops. Look at Paderewski![2] Look at Madame Melba![3] But, passing on, I would ask your kind attention for a programme more than usually rich and varied in its items, a programme second to none, as I might say. Our object, I may say without the fear of contradiction, is a worthy one — to do a little for the Poor Coal Fund of Birrelton. The poor, as we know, we have always with us, and coals were never dearer.

I will now ask Mr Duncan Tod to favour us with 'Scotland Yet!'

The audience sat in petrified ecstasy while Mr Tod, the shoemaker, sang 'Scotland Yet!' in a high falsetto voice, impaired to a sad degree by difficulties of respiration and a nervousness which brought the perspiration to his brow, and compelled him constantly to dry the palms of his hands on a handkerchief whose more legitimate purpose was gently to wave in time with the refrain, in which the

audience joined with the encouragement and example of
Mr Swan. Mr Tod was apparently a sufferer from asthma;
at every bar there was a distinct interval in which, with
pursed lips, he noisily recovered all his wind, which had
apparently receded into the profoundest depths of his
anatomy; his efforts seemed to be attended with the utmost physical and mental agony.

"Thank heaven, that's bye!" he audibly remarked when
he was done, and resolutely refused to grant an encore, a
desire for which is manifested by a Birrelton audience by
whistling.

"We have a long programme," announced the Chairman, "and recalls must be strictly discouraged, but if time
permits we may have a chance later on to hear Mr Tod,
whose rendition of that fine old song shows us the stuff he
is made of. Now we will be favoured by Mr George Steele
of the Driepps — 'Aft, Aft Hae I Pondered,' or ' Memories
Dear.'

Mr Steele, wearing an extraordinary suit of checks,
which made him distinctly perceptible to the naked eye,
dragged himself reluctantly to his feet at the very rear of
the audience, came slowly forward, encouraged by excla-
mations of, "Good old Geordie!" by the younger members
of the company; cleared his throat loudly and carefully in a
manner that almost amounted to ostentation; fixed a bale-
ful glance upon a high and distant corner of the room, and
kept it immovably directed there while he sang:

Aft, aft, as I ponder on the days o' my childhood,
The days yince so happy — Oh come back again!
When I pu'd the wild brambles that grew in the
    greenwood,
And gied them awa' to my wee lovers then.

There were none of the studied and meretricious effects
secured by so-called voice production in Mr Steele's performance; his voice was the gift of nature, and suffused
with such deep pathetic feeling that he wept himself to
hear it. The tears, by the end of the second verse, were

streaming down his cheeks; in the middle of the third verse he broke down completely, overcome by his emotions, and abruptly sought his seat again with the remark, "As shair as daith, chaps, I canna come 'Memories Dear' the nicht."

"Go on, Geordie!" cried the audience, "'The Auld Quarry Knowe.'"

In the circumstances the Chairman's veto on recalls was suspended while Mr Steele, bashfully coming forward again, attempted to repress emotions which did credit to his heart in singing the ditty mentioned.

But it was too much for him: he stopped at daffing wi' his Jessie on the Auld Quarry Knowe, and bolted ignominiously for the door.

"There's nothing like the old melodies," said the Chairman, ambiguously, "and I'm sure we all owe a deep debt of gratitude to Mr Steele. But, passing on I have the pleasure to announce that the next item is of the comic gender — 'Tobermory,' by Mr William Gilkison. I would respectfully ask for strict silence at the back while we are listening to our good friend Mr Gilkison."

Mr Gilkison, with a look of ineffable sadness on his face, came forward, assumed a large red-topped Tam o' Shanter, and stared fixedly at a young lady in front, who blushed violently as she rose and took her seat at the piano, which had not hitherto been called into use. There was no music.

"It goes something like this," whispered the vocalist, and he hummed a few bars in her ear.

"What key?" she asked.

"Any key ye like," said he agreeably, "but I prefer the black yins."

After a few false starts, due to an absence of agreement between the singer and the accompanist, Mr Gilkison got fairly embarked on 'Tobermory' and the youthful males of the audience signified their high appreciation of its quality by beating time on the floor with their feet and joining in the chorus.

Not even James Swan, Esq., could oppose successfully

the vociferous demand for an encore, and Mr Gilkison, with modest diffidence, not too well assumed, stood where he was at the side of the piano and plunged into 'That's the reason why I wear the Kilt.'

"I rise to a pint of order," said an excited little gentleman at the end of the first verse, and the audience cheered.

"What is your point of order, sir?" asked Mr Swan, in the manner, self-possessed and firm, of the best Town Councils.

"Mr Gilkison's singin' a couple o' sangs I hae among the records for my grammyphone," said the interrupter. "Far better than he can dae them. By the man himsel' — Harry Lauder."[4]

"I am sure," said the Chairman suavely, "that the audience will be only too delighted to have an opportunity of judging whether Mr Gilkison or Mr Harry Lauder is the best exponent, as I might venture to say, of the songs in question. It will be an added pleasure, Mr Sharp, to hear the songs twice, once by the 'vox humana,' and once by — by the gramophone."

But Mr Sharp, considerably incensed that his repertoire should have been forestalled, withdrew from the room in dudgeon, fortunately, as it seemed, forgetting to take his gramophone with him, and Mr Gilkison was permitted to finish his song without any further interruption.

"We now pass on with the programme," said the Chairman, "and as a change we will have the well-known song, 'Imitations,' by Mr Peter Gourlay."

The audience laughed.

"Not a song!" whispered Mr Dawson, sitting beside the Chairman. "Imitations. Ventriloquial. Saws wud."

"I beg your pardon, ladies and gentlemen," said Mr Swan. "I find our friend Mr Gourlay's item is ventriloquial. Mr Gourlay will give imitations."

The artist came forward, singularly burdened with a draught-screen which he placed beside the table. Having secreted himself behind the screen, he produced sounds which were unmistakably suggestive of somebody sawing wood. From the same seclusion there followed what was understood to be an imitation of a joiner planing, and the audience cheered.

Mr Gourlay followed with an imitation, frankly in the open, without the aid of any draught-screen, of an infuriated wasp. He chased it over the table, up the wall, and round the back of his neck, and finally suggested its destruction by an abruptly terminated buzzing.

"I have heard all the best ventriloquial entertainers of the day," said Mr Swan, "but none of them had what I might boldly venture to call the realism of Mr Gourlay's great sawing and bumbee act. We will now pass on to the gramophone, the next item on our programme. Mr Sharp has unfortunately been called away by pressing engagements elsewhere, but perhaps there is someone present who understands the mechanism. It will form the second and concluding part of our evening's entertainment."

"Bob Crawford! Bob Crawford!" shouted the youths behind, and the young man alluded to, stuffing his cap in his trousers pocket, lurched diffidently forward, apparently with the reputation of being a skilled executant.

He selected a record, wound up the clockwork, looked anxiously about the table, and said, "Pins."

"Anything missing?" asked the Chairman.

"Pins," said Mr Crawford. "Ye canna play a grammyphone without the pins, and I think that Sharp's awa' wi' them."

It proved to be the case; the irate Sharp had successfully prevented any chance of Harry Lauder being placed in competition with Mr Gilkison, and, as nobody else would sing, the concert terminated with a speech, in which the Chairman said that the evening's entertainment had been of the most delightful character, far transcending the best that he had expected.

"Did ye hear what the collection in silver cam' to?" he asked Mr Dawson, as they wandered up to the little inn.

"Eight and six," said Mr Dawson. "No' sae bad for Birrelton!"

"Five shillin's for me, and the balance for the population," said Jimmy. "They have a better estimate o' whit a
Birrelton concert's worth than me."

## 10. *Rankine's Rookery*

THE TRAIN for Fort William stopped for a reputed five
minutes at Crianlarich,[1] and Jimmy Swan dropped off with
another Knight of the Road for some refreshment.

They entered a place in the station where the same was
indicated, and found themselves before a counter covered
with teacups and bell-shaped glasses, under which the
management seemed to be experimenting in the intensive
culture of the common Alpine or Edible Sandwich.

"They're thrivin' fine!" said Jimmy, peering through the
'cloches.' "Put them out in a bed wi' a nice warm southern
exposure as soon as the rain comes on, and they'll take a
prize at the autumn show."

"Tea?" said the lady behind the bar, already with a cup
below the tap of a steaming urn.

"No tea," said Jimmy firmly; "I had a cup on Sunday,
and it doesn't do to make it into a habit. Say two bottles of
lager beer, and — and a bunch of sandwiches."

"Licensed drinks in the refreshment room farther
along the platform," said the lady, turning to another
customer, and Jimmy and Mr Dawson went to the other
refreshment room with great celerity, as there was no time
to lose.

"Lovely weather," said Jimmy to the lady-attendant
there. "Two lagers and a brace of sandwiches."

"We have no eatables here," said the lady, preparing to
pull the corks. "You'll get sandwiches at the other refreshment room farther along the platform."

"Great Scot!" said Jimmy, "could you not combine
both shops and have one regular Refreshment Room, the
same as they have on the Continent? It might be wicked,
but it would be handy."

"This is not the Continent; it is Crianlarich," said the lady tartly, and Jimmy smiled.

"I knew there must be something to account for it," said he. "Drink up, Dawson; there's the whistle! After all, there's nothing worse than the eating habit. That's one up in temperance reform for Crianlarich."

Back in the compartment, Mr Dawson, who had been gloomily reading a newspaper all the way from Queen Street, descanted upon this idiocy of the refreshment department at Crianlarich as one more proof that Great Britain, so-called, was precipitously going to the dogs. He represented a modest brand of East Coast whisky (patent still), which percolated through the country quite incognito as Genuine Old Matured, and which he said himself, in strict confidence to friends, was so young and robust it couldn't be put up in bottles without cracking them.

"No wonder there's all this labour unrest," he said; "Every other day there's some new Act of Parliament that gets you on the neck. It's coming to't when you can't get a bun or a biscuit at a station bar unless you take a cup o' tea to it," a manner of stating the case not strictly fair to Crianlarich.

"Keep it up! " said a stranger, who had joined the train at Garelochhead. "Blame Lloyd George!"[2]

Mr Dawson cordially accepted the invitation, and said things about Mr Lloyd George which it would greatly vex that statesman's wife to hear. It then transpired that the stranger was a Comrade, who had his own views about the social and industrial chaos in the country, and a firm conviction that the most urgent reform demanded was the abolition of all landlords.

"Hear! hear!" said Jimmy Swan, and the Comrade beamed fraternally on him.

"Look at the land round here," the Comrade added with a sweep of the hand that comprehended the Moor of Rannoch, through which the train was now proceeding. "Nothing but deer! Nationalise it, and you'll see a healthy, prosperous, and contented population pouring back from the cities."

"I suppose you will," said Mr Swan agreeably. "When they start pouring they'll be well advised to bring waterproof top-boots with them and a good supply o' tinned meat, for the Moor o' Rannoch's not exactly the Carse o' Gowrie.[3] I doubt they'll no' pour much at first unless they're dragged wi' ropes."

"I thocht you were a Land Nationalist," said the Comrade.

"So I am," said Jimmy. "I'm tired o' bein' a landlord."

"I didn't know you were a landed gentleman, Mr Swan," said Dawson in surprise. "All I have myself, in that line, is a couple o' flower-pots and a lair in Sighthill Cemetery."

"I'm one of the bloated miscreants," said Jimmy. "I've been one for nearly fifteen years, but lyin' low in case I would be suspected. You don't catch me goin' round wi' a nickerbocker suit and a couple o' retriever dugs. Forbye, it's no exactly land I'm laird o'; it's stone and lime; at least it was stone and lime when I saw't the last time. If all the landlords were like me, the steamers bound for Canada would be crooded wi' them — third-class, and their beards shaved off for a disguise. ... Do ye ken Dundee?" he asked the Comrade.

"I've been there," said the Comrade, with the air of one who could say more, but refrained from motives of politeness. "I was there last autumn."

"You're a lucky man," said Jimmy. "I had to cut Dundee out o' my circuit more than a dozen years ago, and hand it over to my fellow-traveller, Maclintock. And Dundee was a place where I aye did splendid business.

"Fifteen years ago," proceeded Jimmy, "I had no more politics than a cow; at least if I had, my customers never discovered them."

"Sat on the fence?" suggested the Comrade nastily.

"Just that!" said Mr Swan. "There was so much glaur on both sides o' the fence I couldna' venture down withoot dirtyin' my boots. But I really didna give a rap for politics; I never could bring to them that personal animosity which political enthusiasm seems to demand. When it came to the elementals, I found that folk were much alike, whether Whig or Tory. But the Will o' an Uncle I had in Montrose, ca'd Geordie Rankine, that I hadna seen since I was a boy, put an end to this blissful frame of mind; he left me a land o' hooses[4] in Dundee, and I found I was a red-hot Tory.

"The day I got the lawyer's letter and a copy o' the Will, I gave a dozen chaps in the warehouse a slap-up supper round in the Royal Restaurant, and I tell you the Landed Interests got their hair damped that nicht. There wasna a sealskin jaiket in the wareroom too good for Bella; and I bought mysel' a meerschaum pipe wi' a shammy-leather waistcoat on't to keep it from bein' scratched. Next mornin' I was up wi' the very first train, that landed in Dundee before the milk, and I got a night-polisman to show me my estate. It was the best-known property in Dundee, as famous as the Tay Bridge,[5] the Baxter Park,[6] or the Bunnet Law,[7] he said, and I saw what he meant when he took me to the most dilapidated tenement in one o' the most appallin' slums I ever set eyes on.

"'Do folk pay rent to get livin' in a place like that?' says I, dumbfoundered at the look o' my bonny property.

"'No fears o' them!' says he. 'It taks' the puir sowls a' their time to pay their fines on a Monday mornin' at the police-coort. The Corporation condemned the place to be demolished a couple o' years ago, and jist when they were gaun to dae't themsel's at the landlord's cost he went awa' and died on them!'

"'And wha's the landlord noo?' I asked.

"'Some chap in Gleska,' says the polisman; 'I'll bet ye they'll nick him fast enough.'

"'Will they, faith?' says I to mysel', and I made tracks for the 7.49 a.m. for Gleska, wi' my collar turned up in case I might be identified afore I got to the station.

"When I got hame, the first thing my wife asked was if I had brought a picture postcard o' the property. I broke the news to her as gently as I could, and sent word to the lawyer in Dundee to sell the place for onything it would bring. He wrote me back that I might as well try to sell the Scourin'-burn[8] for a mineral water works. My Uncle Geordie had given up all hope o' sellin' the place in the early Seventies. A man that lived in the tenement was factor[9] for the property, and for his trouble was supposed to sit rent-free, but he considered he ought to get something extra, him bein' factor, seein' nane o' the tenants ever could be got to pay a penny, and in that way were as well aff as himsel', withoot haein' his responsibility.

"I wrote to the lawyer, then, that I refused to accept the property; he could give it awa' for naething if he liked. He replied that the property was mine by the law o' Scotland, whether I wanted it or no', and that naebody would tak' it in a gift. He also sent a bill o' charges and another for rates and taxes.

"I paid them, and then he wrote that the tenement must be demolished by the Corporation's orders, at a cost which he put at £150. I never answered him, and he wrote once or twice a week till I had to flit, leavin' no address. I tell you I was gey annoyed at my Uncle Geordie.

"For five years I heard no more about my property except when I was in Dundee on business, and then it seemed to be growin' more notorious every month. Luckily it was Uncle Geordie's name that stuck to it, and 'Rankine's Rookery' was never, by any chance, associated wi' the traveller for C & M. I used to go round and look at it; it was getting mair and mair disgraceful every time, and every now and then the subject o' 'Rankine's Rookery' would be up before the Council. It seemed there was some legal difficulty about haulin' it down without due notification to the owner, and the owner wasna to be found.

"'Who is he?' the Labour gang would ask, indignantly, and the Toon Clerk would reply that he was a man in Gleska, but exactly whereaboots was undiscoverable.

"Then the Labour chaps would harangue aboot the scoundrel battenin' on the rents o' the miserable wretches livin' in his property, nae doot knockin' about in his    motor-caur and smokin' ninepenny cigars. Me! I never battened on as much as a penny bap aff the property, and the only motor-caurs I travel in belang to the Gleska Corporation.

"The agitation aboot my tenement got so furious at last, a dozen years ago, that I got frichtened, and since then I've never gane near Dundee, in case I would be arrested. And that's the way I'm for nationalisin' property, and daein' awa' wi' landlords. Whether my property's standin' yet or no' I never venture to inquire; to indulge my curiosity on that score might cost me far mair than I bargained for."

"That all bears out my argument," said the Comrade. "The land must be for the people!"

## 11. *Dignity*

"THE SELLIN o' soap, butter, music, poetry, pictures, or soft goods, is just as great an art as making them," said Mr Swan, chipping the top off his second egg. "I was years ago in a factory where they made Balmoral bunnets. They had a big machine that just fair squirted oot Balmoral bunnets; the yarn went in at the one end by the ton, and the bunnets poured out at the other, a' complete, even to the toorie. I was spellbound lookin' at the thing, and the man that had the factory says to me, 'That's a great machine, Mr Swan. I see ye're lost in admiration.' 'That's just what I am!' says I; 'but it's no' at the machine; I think far more o' the men who can keep up wi't at the sellin'. Noo that keps are comin' in, it takes me a' my time to sell a dozen bunnets in a year.'"

"That's quite true," said a man on the road for jams and sweetmeats. "Every year commercial travelling grows harder. I sometimes think the men that have to sell soor draps and kali sookers[1] after we're away 'll need to have a college education."

Dunbar & Baxter's new young man, on his first journey, stirred his coffee, and listened with great respect — indeed with veneration — to these veterans of the road. What roused this feeling in him was the thought that they should have kept their jobs so long; his own beginning was so unpropitious. Yesterday had been a rotten day, and he had said to himself, "Another week like this, and it's back wi' you to the counter, Willy!" It was not a pleasant feeling for a chap who was doing his best. It was all the more unpleasant because there were features of his new job that greatly pleased him — the sense of freedom, space, and personal responsibility, so different from being in the shop; the travelling by trains and steamers; the sight of new places, the living in hotels — particularly the living in hotels. To a young fellow who at home in Glasgow lodged in Raeberry Street,[2] and had no interest in any food he got except the midday meal picked up at a restaurant, this living in hotels was thoroughly and completely quite all right. Deferential Boots and waiters; fish, ham-and-eggs and kidneys for one's breakfast (all together, mind you, and no stinting!) a regular banquet called a lunch, and a high tea quite as lavish as the breakfast! It would be a deuce of a dunt to tumble back from these high altitudes of luxury to the hopeless and prosaic levels of Raeberry Street!

He nervously crumbled a breakfast roll and cleared his throat, and meekly put a question.

"What would you say was the secret of success in our business Mr Swan?"

Jimmy flushed. He could have laughed but remembered that he had one time been young on the road himself and full of strange illusions, and being a gentleman he made his best pretence at answering a question to which in the nature of things there is no answer.

"The secret of success, Mr Spens," said he, "is to be born lucky."

"But you need more than luck," said the jam man hurriedly. "You need brains, and pluck, and foresight, and habits of industry, and — "

"And what's all that but bein' born lucky?" broke in Jimmy. "There's many a one gets on dashed well without them, too; but that's another kind o' luck."

"I'm not sure that I have either kind," said Spens, "but

I'll guarantee I do my best to sell Dunbar & Baxter's flour, and I'm finding it a gey dreich business. I begin to think that I'm a failure."

Jimmy puckered up his face, so red and weathered, like a winter apple; looked across the table at the lad with a twitching of his bushy eyebrows, and liked him for his unaffected innocence.

"Ye're all right, Mr Spens!" said he with peculiar gentleness. "The worst ill-luck I ken is to be born self-satisfied, and that's been spared ye."

"The great thing," said the jam man, "is dignity. Aye stand on your dignity, and make the customer respect you."

This time Jimmy laughed without compunction. "Man, Simpson," said he, "I'm astonished at ye. If ye had to depend upon your dignity ye wouldna sell a sweetie. Do you ken the way Scotch travellers are the best in the world? It's because they have nae dignity. A man wi' a sense o' dignity is like a man wi' a broken gallus; he's aye feared something's goin' to slip. The thing is to have your galluses[3] right, and then ye needna fash about your dignity. I'll tell you and Mr Spens a story. I used one time to think dignity was a great thing too; that it was a thing ye wore like a white waistcoat, and that the customer liked it. My George! I had as much dignity in these days as would do for half a dozen o' statesmen or a couple o' point polismen. When I started with C & M I scared away half my customers by wearing my dignity like an ice-bag on my chest, and talking London English. But I got a lesson, and the only virtue ever I had in this life was that I never needed to get the same lesson twice. For five years I was travelling every season to Auchentee,[4] a place whose only interest for me was that it had three drapers' shops in't. The drapers were all MacLellans; they were all related; they were a' in the same wee street. Auchentee's eight miles from the nearest railway station. For five years I drove up to Auchentee in a tip-top wagonette wi' my cases, and my hat cocked to the side the same as I was the Duke o' Sutherland.

I lavished a' my art on the MacLellans: I choked the syvor[5] in front o' their shops wi' my cases; I flourished sixpenny cigars, and talked through the top o' my head like a man from Sheffield.

"But there was naething doin'! I never booked an order! They were gettin' their stuff from Edinburgh; they had aye got their stuff from Edinburgh, and a' they kent aboot Gleska was that it was on the maps. Three auld snuffy deevils, I mind, they were — the MacLellans; and when I offered them bargains I would lose money on, they just took another pinch o' snuff and said they couldna think to change their house.

"One day I landed at the station, took my dinner at the inn, and ordered the wagonette for Auchentee. It was goin' to be my final visit; if the MacLellans failed me this time, they could go to bleezes. There was nae wagonette; it was awa' at a roup, and the only thing left on wheels was a cairt. I said to mysel', 'There's no' much daein' wi' dignity in Auchentee,' and I took the cairt. It was an awfu' day o' wind and rain, and I had a fine silk hat, a cashmere mornin' coat, and a blue-sprigged waistcoat on. There I was, sittin' in the cairt wi' my cases piled behind me, far mair like an undertaker than a traveller for C & M, and I tell you it was rainin' ! When I landed in the main street o' Auchentee, I created a sensation. My hat was into pulp; I was drookit to the skin; a' the dignity I had could be spread oot on a threepenny bit, and ye would see the printin' through it.

"The whole toon gathered oot, and laughed; I was the bonny spectacle, cocked up there on MacGillvray's cairt, and naebody laughed looder nor the MacLellans. It was the first time they had ever seen I was a human bein', subject to the immutable laws o' nature. Now, folk that get a hearty laugh at ye aye feel kindly to ye after. One o' the MacLellans took me in and dried my clothes; another o' them gave me my tea; the third one put me up for the night, for the inn of Auchentee was full o' county gentlemen. And, what's mair, I got a slashin' big order from a' the three. The moral is that dignity's no' worth a dump in travellin'."

Ten minutes later Jimmy was smoking in the hall with Simpson.

"That's a great lesson!" said Simpson seriously.

"Ay, it's a great lesson right enough," said Jimmy, cleaning out his pipe. "It's a good enough lesson for a young man startin', just to put him on the right lines, but it wouldna be ony use to you. Ye see, I didna finish the story for Spens; I didna want to spoil it."

"What way spoil it?" asked Simpson.

"Well, you see, the three MacLellans a' worked in one another's hands; they a' went into bankruptcy three months efter that, and a' we got o' their accounts was ninepence in the pound!"

## 12. *Universal Provider*

THERE ARE small paraffin-oil-lamp towns in many parts of the country for which Mr Swan is Fairy Godmother, Perpetual Grand Plenipotentiary, and Deputy Providence. Half of his time in Glasgow is taken up with the execution of countless petty commissions for his rural customers and their friends, the selection and purchase of goods quite out of his own drapery line. I met him recently in a music-warehouse critically inspecting pianos on which he gave a masterly one-finger exposition of 'We're a' noddin'.' "For a customer of mine in Aviemore," he told me. "He wants a genuine £16 extra-grand, high-strung, Chubb-check-action walnut one with the right kind of candlesticks on it. I think this is about the article for Aviemore," and he indicated one with gorgeous candlesticks and a singularly robust tone.

"Why don't they come and buy their own pianos?" I asked innocently.

"They think they would be swindled," said Jimmy, "and I daresay they're right. Besides, they don't know a thing about pianos, and they know that I've bought hundreds of pianos in the past five-and-twenty years. I never bought one for a customer yet that failed to give satisfaction. It's all in the touch" — he touched a sprightly bar of 'We're a' noddin'' — "and I could tell the right touch with my eyes shut."

"You must get some odd country commissions," I said, as we left the warehouse together when the transaction was completed. "I shouldn't care, myself, to buy pianos for other people."

"In my line," said Mr Swan, "I can't afford to be particular. I don't make a penny off the job directly, but it helps to keep a good customer on the books of C & M. A piano's a simple matter; I once had to buy a brass band for Larbert, and a dashed good brass band, too; you never heard a louder! A customer of mine was chairman of the committee, and he said he couldn't trust another man in Glasgow but myself to get the proper instruments. I got the dandiest set you ever set eyes on, and seven-and-a-half off for cash, that bought a tip-top banner, and they never expected the money they had would run to a banner."

It is impossible to enumerate the variety and extent of Mr Swan's private commissions for his country customers, who haven't the time to come to Glasgow or sufficient confidence in their own judgment to buy either a piano or a presentation silver albert and appendage for a young friend going away to Canada. He has taken the blushing orders of innumerable lads who felt the time had come for shaving, but were coy about purchasing their first razor in a local shop. There is no better judge of an engagement-ring in Scotland; and there is a piece of cardboard with a hole in it in his waistcoat pocket almost every time he returns to town from Perthshire. His knowledge of the cradle and perambulator trade is copious, and more than once he has executed telegraphic orders for a superior kind of oak coffin unprocurable in Mull.

"I never made a mistake but once in my life," he says, "and it cost me one of my very best Kirkcudbright customers. She was a widow woman getting up in years, and she had been reading somewhere or other that Society ladies kept their fine complexions by putting on cosmetics. One day after giving me a good order for autumn goods, she took me into the back of the shop and slipped five shillings in my hand. 'I want you to send me that amount of good cosmetic, Mr Swan,' she whispered; 'it's for a friend.' 'Right you are, Mrs Lamont,' says I, and made a note of it. The only place I ever saw cosmetic was in a barber's shop, so I went to one in Gordon Street and bought five shillings' worth, and sent it off to Mrs Lamont. She would never look at me again! You see it was what they call Hong Grease cosmetic for sticking out the moustache, and she distinctly had one. The best of it is that, so far as I can find out, there's not any other kind of cosmetic sold in the whole of Glasgow than the grease of the foresaid Hong."

The confidence of the agricultural districts in Mr Swan's good taste and commercial acumen is no greater than their faith in his ability to do any mortal thing for them that demands a knowledge of the world, and influence. When the drapers of the Western Journey want to start a son on a career in Glasgow, it is to Mr Swan they instinctively appeal for the requisite advice and aid. No boy is too hopelessly useless for Jimmy to find a job for in the city; the last decennial increase[1] in our population is mainly made up of immigrants to whom he is credited with giving their urban start in life.

"Send him up to me," says Jimmy airily, "and I'll bet you I'll push him on to somebody."

The method of procedure in these cases is simplicity itself. "I take the young chap out to stay with me for a week," he told me; "get his hair cut to begin with, and another kind of cap for him. Then I take him out and start him at one end of West George Street after breakfast and tell him to make his way to the other end, going up every stair *en route* and asking a job at every office till he gets one. He generally gets a job before the third day, just because he is a country-bred boy with a fine red face. Glasgow businessmen like to have an innocent country boy about the office; it makes them think of what they might, themselves, have been. And the best way to start a boy in life in Glasgow is to let him understand that starting, like staying, all depends upon himself."

The fact that Mr Swan has often bazaar tickets and invitations to artists' exhibitions for disposal gratis to customers in from the country creates the impression that he can get a friend in anywhere, at any time, for nothing. He has rarely encouraged this flattering illusion at the cost of a pair of stall tickets for the pantomime, but no customer or customer's friend has ever failed to get a ticket for a football match, for Mr Swan has apparently the mysterious power of tapping inexhaustible supplies of free tickets for football matches.

"But the nerve of some folk is unbelievable," he told me. "Not long ago a customer from the North wrote asking me to get him a pass by the Caledonian Railway to London."

"Did you manage it?" I asked.

"No," he answered, "I'm not exactly God. The best I could do for him was to give him an introduction to the guard and a list of places that he mustn't miss going to see in the Metropolis, so-called. I carefully explained to him that all the usual privileges in the way of free passes were suspended on account of the coal strike, so my reputation as The Universal Provider-to-the-North-for-Nought is not in the least impaired."

Another customer of Mr Swan's found the air of Glasgow so exhilarating as compared with that of Dingwall that he spent an evening in a police cell, and had to send for C & M's traveller to bail him out on the following morning. His peculiar dread was that the newspapers of the city would give a copious and sensational account of the unfortunate affair, which would be copied into the *Northern Star*,[2] and spoil the sober reputation of a lifetime. Mr Swan did not tell him that trivial indiscretions of this sort were never recorded in Glasgow newspapers.

"I'll fix it all right !" he said. "You can depend on me. I have only got to pass the word along to the editors that you're a friend of mine, and the thing is done."

There is a draper now in Dingwall who is convinced that
Mr James Swan has the British press in his pocket. But the
oddest commission Mr Swan ever got was to supply the
parish of Birrelton with a minister. It would have staggered
any other man, but Mr Swan set about its execution with
as much cheerfulness as if he had been asked to send on a
mouth harmonium.

Birrelton had spent some months of Sundays listening
to candidates for the vacant charge. Every one was better
than the other, and it was plainly impossible to get the
congregation into a definite attitude of mind which would
give the pulpit to any particular one. After many squab-
bling meetings the leading draper, who was ruling elder,
said he saw no hope of their ever agreeing upon a minister,
and proposed that Patronage[3] should be re-established to
the extent of asking the traveller for C & M to pick a
suitable clergyman in Glasgow.

"So I got the job," said Mr Swan. "It took me a couple
of weeks. I knew exactly the kind of chap they would need
in Birrelton — not too fancy, you understand, for fear
some other kirk would grab at him before the Birrelton
ladies' presentation Geneva gown[4] was right out of the
tissue paper, and still, on the other hand, not one so dull
that he would be likely to be left on their hands till he died
at the age of ninety. The minister they aye want in places
like Birrelton is a combination of the Apostle Paul,
General Roberts,[5] and the cinematograph which never
gives a word of offence to anybody, and that kind of
minister is not a glut on the market. I did the best I could.
I consulted all my acquaintances, and every man jack of
them had a first-rate minister he would recommend
heartily for the vacancy. It was always their own minister,
and their eagerness to see him doing well for himself by
shifting somewhere else was most significant.

"At last I found a young assistant something like the
thing I wanted, and put the Birrelton pulpit to him as a
business proposition. He jumped at it like a brave wee

man, and I wired to my customer: 'Esteemed order will be dispatched per passenger train on Monday.'

"He's a great success," said Mr Swan, tapping his pipe on his boot-toe. "Everybody's delighted with him. I got a letter from the session-clerk thanking me for putting such a fine minister their road, and asking me if I could recommend the best place to buy a silver tea and coffee service."

"You're a marvel, Mr Swan," I said.

"Not at all!" said Jimmy. "I'm only a business man. You can get any mortal thing you like in Glasgow if you have the business experience and the ready money."

## 13. *The Commercial Room*

His *confrère* Grant being temporarily off the Road on account of a prolonged attack of influenza, Jimmy Swan last week took up the Fifeshire journey for him, and put up one night at an hotel he had not visited for over a dozen years. In those dozen years some drastic changes had been made on the old Buck's Head.[1] It had been re-created, mainly in the interest of golfers and the automobile traffic. Its geography was now unfamiliar to Jimmy, who, at one time, could have found his way through every corner of it in the dark. He had now the choice of sixteen wash-hand basins, all in a row; a prominent announcement in the hall informed him that eleven bathrooms were at his august command; a beauteous languid creature, with an amazing rick of yellow hair, put down his name and handed him a circular ticket with the number of his room.

"I hope," said he, "it's a southern exposure, and has a fire-escape and a telephone in it?"

The fair being, with a wonderful pretence at talking into empty space, mentioned that the Buck's Head's bedrooms always gave satisfaction.

"Dinner, sir?" said a German voice at his shoulder, and turning round, Jimmy sighed. At that exact moment he had remembered how old Willie Boyd, for twenty years the

waiter and boots of the Buck's Head, as it used to be, was
wont to welcome him.

"No; tea," he answered curtly. "And ham and eggs;
with two boiled eggs to follow."

The Teutonic minion sped upon this mission; Jimmy
washed his hands in five of the sixteen basins, in order to
test the plumber work, and, still without having seen any
signs of a proprietor, walked into the old Commercial
Room.[2] It had lost the printed designation on the door,
and in some respects was fallen sadly from its old estate.
He had it wholly to himself.

By-and-bye the waiter came in to intimate that tea was
ready in the Coffee Room.

"Good!" said Jimmy. "But I want mine here. I suppose
this is still the Commercial Room?"

"No, sir," said the waiter; "it is the Chauffeurs' Room; a
Commercial Room we have not now got," and on that
Jimmy said a bad word. He looked again about the room;
there was the old familiar grate with a glowing fire in it; the
sideboard and the chairs were as they used to be; there was
no change in the steel engravings on the wall. A host of
memories beset him.

"I don't care what it is," he said at last; "Bring my tea in
here. I suppose the Buck's Head has some sort of a landlord still; don't trouble to waken him, for I haven't got my
motor-car wi' me this journey. I take it you haven't such a
thing as a pair of commercial slippers? ... No; of course
not! It doesn't matter; I aye carry my own, and I used to
put the house ones on just to please old Willie Boyd.[3] Did
ye ever hear of Willie Boyd, the Original Human Waiter?"

"Yes, sir," said the German. "He died."

Jimmy's face fell. "If I were you, Fritz, I wouldn't put it
so blunt as that," he said. "News like that should be
broken gently; the man had a thousand friends, God bless
him! ... 'You must tak' another herrin', Mr Swan'; 'I
wouldna risk the silverside the day, Mr Swan'; 'Still the
rheumatics, gentlemen, but no' complainin'; 'A' to your
beds, now, like gude boys!' ... Aye, aye, and Willie's gone!

No wonder I didna recognise the old Buck's Head!"

He took a solemn meal, and was ruminating wistfully at the fire when the landlord plunged into the room with tardy greetings. "Man, Mr Swan," said he, "the silly folk in front there hadn't the least suspicion who ye were, and never sent to the stable for me! I've been buyin' horse. And what in a' creation are ye daein' here in the Chauffeurs' Room ? — I'm black affronted!"

"The room's fine, Mr Lorimer," said Jimmy Swan. "Forbye, I clean forgot to bring my evenin' dress wi' me. And it's still yoursel', John Lorimer! I'm glad to see ye; I thought there was naething left o' the auld Buck's Head but this grate and sideboard, and a wheen chairs. I hear that Willie's gone."

"Three years ago," said the landlord, sitting down; "He was gey frail at the hinder end."

"Was he? Dear auld Willie! Slept in himsel' at last; I'll warrant ye it never happened once in twenty years wi' a customer that Willie had to waken for the early mornin' train! ... Ye've made a wonderful change on the house since I was here last, Mr Lorimer; but sittin' here my lone at my tea, I was feelin' eerie."

"Tuts, man! ye should have gone to the Coffee Room," said the landlord. "It's perfectly ridiculous!"

"No," said Mr Swan; "I never could turn my back on the auld Buck's Head Commercial Room; do ye know it's the first I ever set foot in?"

"I mind!" said Mr Lorimer, chuckling. "You were a little jimper[4] at the waist then. You're gettin' fat, like mysel', Mr Swan."

"That's not fat," said Jimmy, soberly; "it's philosophy. ... I mind on that occasion I asked a customer, old David Graham, to come round to the Buck's Head at night to see me, and it was wi' a gey red face I did it, I can tell ye, for he micht hae been my father. He came in at night, and in a little I asked him what he would ha'e. 'I drink naething but champagne,' says David Graham; 'I'll ha'e a bottle.' My he'rt sunk into my heels; the price o' a bottle o' champagne was mair than I would mak' o' profit on the journey! But the deed was done; I couldna back oot, and I rang the bell for Willie. 'A bottle o' good champagne and a bottle o' beer,' I said to him; he never blinked an e'e, though I was but a boy, and oot he goes and comes in wi' twa bottles o' beer.

"'I said champagne for one o' them,' says I, quite manly; and David Graham — peace be wi' him! a worthy man! — laughed in a quiet way, and says, 'Willie kens my auld trick wi' the young traiveller too weel to bring ony champagne in here. Na, na, laddie; beer's better for us, and I doubt it'll be mony a day before ye'll be able to afford a bottle o' Pomeroy for a country customer!'

"I'm sorry ye've given up the auld Commercial Room," proceeded Jimmy. "I look upon it in a kind o' way as consecrated. Auld times! auld men!"

"We had to move wi' the times, Mr Swan," said the landlord; "I had to make a place for the chauffeurs some-where, and our commercial trade is not what it used to be."

"I daresay no'," said Jimmy. "Neither is commercial traivellin'. Do ye mind o' Cunningham and Stewart, Kerr, MacKay, J. P. Paterson, and MacLennan? Where's the like o' them the day? Kings o' the Road! By George! I've seen a polisman up in Brora touch his cap when a barrow passed wi' auld MacLennan's cases."

"Faith, aye! This room has seen some cheery com-pany!" said Mr Lorimer.

"The first Sunday I took my dinner in't, I felt as if I was in the House o' Commons. Everything was done by ritual; J. P. Paterson in the chair. I was formally introduced as if it was the twenty-ninth degree in Masonry; Paterson made a canty[5] speech, and wished me well on behalf o' the company, and they drank my health. And there was the usual bottle o' wine — I was jolly glad, I can tell ye; it was port, for port was the only wine at the time that hadna the taste o' ink to me. I've never seen a bottle o' port more ceremoniously disposed o' than the customary bottle on the Sunday in Commercial Rooms. It was an education in the *haute politesse!* At first it used actually to mak' me feel religious! And always 'Mr President, sir!' and 'By your leave, gentlemen!'"

"I havena sold a bottle o' port to a commercial in the past ten years, Mr Swan," said the landlord. "They've lost the taste for wines, I'm thinkin'."

"Not them! The only thing they've lost is the means o' payin' for them. There's no' mony pound-a-day men[6] left on the Road, Mr Lorimer. And onyway port, I take it, is no' what it used to be. Do ye know what I was thinkin' to mysel' sittin' here mopin' at the fire afore ye came in? It was that naething nooadays was quite so good as it used to be. The ham's gane aff, chops are no' so thick and sappy as they were before the Tay Bridge storm, and ye've a' lost the art o' branderin'[7] them. The cut off the joint is no' what it was, and finnen-haddies[8] are completely aff, and there's no' the auld taste to potatoes. … And — and Willie Boyd's awa' frae the Buck's Head Inn! And it hasna' a Commercial Room ony longer!"

"The port's as good as ever it was," said Mr Lorimer with a twinkle.

"Take me in a bottle, then," said Jimmy Swan, "and join me in a sentimental glass to the auld Commercial Room, the memory o' honest Willie, an' the auld Knights o' the Road!"

## 14. *The Changed Man*

JAMES SWAN had a friend, a traveller in the line of Fancy Goods, who came originally — of all places in the world for a seller of photo-frames and jumping-jacks — from the Isle of Skye. His Christian name was Donald; Jimmy always called him 'Donald-of-the Isles — the fusel-iles,'[1] and that, alas! did no injustice to his salient weakness, which was a preference for mountain dew at its very freshest, before the warmth of the still was out of it. He took it in considerable quantities for years, with no apparent ill effect upon a constitution which seemed to be impervious to the erosive influence of moisture, like the Coolin hills or the Quiraing. The parlour what-nots of countless happy homes in the West of Scotland were laden with celluloid jewel-boxes, antimony silver ash-trays, fantastic cats with nodding heads, and Goss-ware,[2] presents from Dunoon, or Campbeltown, or whatever the case might be, which owed their prevalence in country shops almost wholly to the persuasive eloquence of Donald. He had a way of showing jumping-jacks and expounding the moral value of Teddy Bears[3] that was positively irresistible anywhere ten miles out of Glasgow his exposition of a doll that would say 'Mama,' and horizontally shut its eyes was acknowledged to be unique. In Donald's hands it assumed the dignity of an epoch-making laboratory experiment by the late Lord Kelvin.[4]

For Fancy Goods Jimmy Swan had the most extraordinary contempt. He looked (and not unreasonably) upon Fancy Goods as the proof that fancy itself, the cheapest and loveliest of all adornments, was, like porridge, almost obsolete in Scotland, and he never referred to Donald's stock of samples but as 'dolls'. "Anything fresh in the doll line, Donald?" he would say. "Are shammy-leather legs goin' to hold their own this season?" Or, "I see from the Board of Trade returns there's a slump in mouth-harmoniums; I doubt you are losing ground, Donald."

But all the same they were the warmest of friends. It has recently been discovered by Professor Spiltzbaum[5] of Heidelberg that the specific organism of alcoholism is a very minute motile coco-bacillus measuring from 1 to 2 micro-millimetres in length, with terminal spiral flagella. In the body of its host, the unfortunate victim of the alcoholic disease, this anærobe has a curious tickling effect. It tickles the sense of confidence, laughter, toleration, and human kindness, and is the inveterate foe of those pink hæmatozoa which are now identified in bacteriological research as the cause of self-righteousness. Thus we have explained the remarkable fact that unfortunate victims of alcohol, like Donald, are often so much more jolly to meet than fine healthy fellows without a single coco-bacillus about them.

Donald was a good traveller, and could sell a gross of mechanical mice with broken springs in the time another traveller would be shutting up his umbrella and fumbling for his pencil. He was generous, tolerant, amusing, fearless, frank, and simple as a child when the coco-bacillus tickled with its spiral flagella; he could be the most charming of companions, and most loyal of friends.

"I like Donald," Jimmy Swan would say. "I suppose it's because he's a bit o' an idiot like mysel', no' a'thegither given up to the main chance, nor always homeward bound. But I whiles wish he would settle doon and start the domestic and temperance virtues. I'm aye tellin' him that if he takes them up in the proper spirit they're almost as much fun as the other thing — forbye bein' money in your pocket."

Unfortunately the alcoholic bacillus in course of time by the assiduous application of its flagella in the tickling process wears them down to a stump, and deprived of its power to tickle to any great extent, it goes ramping round the whole intestinal system biting. An agonising thirst is created in the patient, only to be allayed by increased applications of mountain or other dew, with which, of course, are imbibed fresh colonies of the organism which take up the tickling, handicapped, however, by the increased difficulty of getting a dry spot to work on.

One day Donald came to his friend, Mr Swan, in a quiescent moment of the bacilli, looking very blue, and borrowed £10 upon the touching presentation of a story about a Sheriff-Court summons.

The occasion was too obviously providential to be neglected, and Jimmy talked to him like a teetotal lecturer. "All I needed to be John B. Gough[6] was a drunken past, my thumb-prints in the polis books, and a white dress muslin necktie," he said afterwards to his wife, describing the interview.

"Look here, Donald," he said; "not to put too fine a point on it, you're a d — d fool."

"It's the true word, Mr Swan!" admitted Donald, contritely.

"I'm the last man," said Jimmy, "to say a chap should begin in life by bein' a perfect model, for there's naething left for him to dae in the way o' self-improvement if he's perfect to begin wi', and the later part o' his life 'll be awfu' dreich. I started, mysel', wi' the full equipment o' a first-class idiot — worse than you, but for the last ten years I've got a wonderfu' lot o' pleesure and satisfaction tryin' to be better. I tell ye this — it's far more sport than keepin' a gairden!"

"The way ye are," continued Jimmy, "you're just a wasted man! Ye have a' the qualities o' a good yin except the will to use them. Men no' half your weight, nor wi' half your wits aboot them, are laughin' at ye; I'll no' say that they're takin' the prizes you should have, for that's a point that would appeal to neither me nor you, but they're laughin' at ye — no, no! I'll no' say that o' human nature; rather will I say they're sorry for ye. That should sting a Skyeman!"

"There's something in it, Mr Swan," said Donald.

"Of course there is!" said Jimmy. "A man at your age canna learn much more, but he can get a lot of fun in unlearnin'. But for heaven's sake, Donald! — always in the proper spirit! — not too certain o' yoursel', nor too self-satisfied, nor too bitter on the weaker brethren."

Donald went away, impressed, and became a changed man.

Everybody noticed it, first of all his firm, which experienced a lamentable and unaccountable decline in the demand for autograph albums with real leatherette covers, mechanical steam-engines (with broken springs), celluloid dromedary inch-tapes, and golliwogs, on the West Coast journey. Donald was blatantly and offensively teetotal; once generous, he was now as hard as nails; once full of fun and kindliness, he was now as dull as crape; once fearless, he was become as timid as a mouse; once disingenuous as a child, he was become as crafty and suspicious as a shilling lawyer. The coco-bacilli, realising the situation, uttered an agonised shriek, and turned on their backs and died. When he came to Jimmy Swan after a year to repay the borrowed money, Jimmy, who had not seen him much of late, looked at him with disappointed eyes.

"Do ye feel like a bottle o' cyder, Donald?" he asked him.

"Thank goodness, I'm beyond that sort o' thing! " said Donald. "Have ye a drop o' soda?"

Jimmy gave it to him, sadly.

"Thank ye for the money, Donald," said he; "It was good of ye to mind it. There's something aboot ye that puts me in mind o' the smell o' a wet leather school-bag. What way are ye gettin' on?"

"Oh, not so bad," said Donald, solemnly. "I have the approval of my conscience, though the firm is not quite satisfied."

"Just that! " said Jimmy, fingering the notes carelessly. "You're a muckle-improved man, but I'm feared I spoiled ye for a traiveller, and I ken I've lost ye for a friend. I told ye, man, to go about it in the proper spirit!"

## 15. *Vitalising the Gloomy Grants*

JIMMY SWAN, with his hands in his jacket pockets, his hat at just the tiniest angle, his chest thrown out, and his waist reduced by a conscious effort of the abdominal muscles — which things all betoken a determination never to grow old, walked along Shore Street humming 'Onward, Christian Soldiers'. He was, if you take me, feeling good. The sun shone on the sea-front like a benediction; enough and no more autumnal sting was in the air to give it bracing qualities; he had done a good day's business yesterday at Inverness; had slept like a babe, and breakfasted like a sailor; was freshly shaved to that degree that his cheek was like a lady's; he knew this journey's stuff was irresistible. It was going on in front of him — six weather-beaten cases in the wheel-barrow of Peter Melville, packed with sample lines to make the hair of any discerning draper fairly curl.

He felt as men feel who come with relief to long-beleaguered cities; there ought to have been a band before him playing 'Umpa-umpa-ump!' and a few assorted banners. That was why he hummed, providing for himself a private and appropriate kind of military pomp. Other commercial travellers might sneak ingloriously into these northern towns and go cringing through the shops with self-depreciatory airs, inviting insults and rebuffs instead of orders — not so Mr Swan, ambassador of C & M, Perpetual Grand Plenipotentiary and High Prince of the Soft Goods world, backed by a century's tradition, conscious of quality unassailable and prices strictly bed-rock, having due consideration for the quality.

In thirty years of the Road for C & M he had acquired a Psychic Touch with customers; not only did his stuff talk for itself — why, C & M's trade-mark on a web of Bolton sheeting was portentous as a statesman's speech! — but his manner magnetised, and he would insinuate a new line of zephyr prints into the conversation like one who was quoting a fine unhackneyed passage from Shakespeare. He did not seem so much to seek to sell you goods as to give you the inestimable privilege of taking part with the great firm of C & M in a grand disinterested campaign to make the people of Scotland wear the real right thing. No city superiority or condescension, mind you! no bluff or airs! Jimmy Swan had a shrewd appreciation of the psychological advantage of liking your man to start with; of being absolutely disingenuous, and confident of the character of your own stuff.

No wonder he marched into R. & T. Grant's humming 'Onward, Christian Soldiers' in his mellifluous bass, while Peter Melville out on the pavement took the straps from off the cases.

He was no sooner at the counter and shaking hands with

Robert than he realised, intuitively, that the morning's sunshine and its bracing airs had no effect on the spirits of that struggling drapery concern. The shop looked more disheartened than it ever did before — more haphazard of arrangement, more dingy, more out-of-date. Robert's eye (the straight one) had the unmistakable lack-lustre of frustration and defeat. Thomas, the elder, totting up the greasy ledger in a corner, stopped in the middle of a column and came forward smiling automatically as to a customer, but lapsing instantly into a mask of gloom, his voice subdued to a funereal melancholy. The brothers were barely middle-aged in years, but for long they had indulged a singular illusion that solidity and success in commerce were only for men who looked mature, and they had always carefully cultivated an appearance of being twenty years older than they really were. Gladstone collars, made-up padded neck-ties, morning coats of the period of the Tay Bridge storm, and — whiskers! And when I say whiskers, I mean actual mid-Victorian side-wings, not mutton-chops, but fluffy cheek appendages, the dire absurdity of which not even a doting mother could condone.

"How's business?" asked Mr Swan, with the cheerful air of one who is confident of learning that business was never better.

"Bad!" said Robert Grant, laconically. "I don't think you need to open up your cases, Mr Swan, this trip."

The countenance of the traveller fell for a moment; then he said airily, "Tuts! it's only temporary. Everything's on the upward trend; ye're maybe just a season later here in the North to feel it, but it's working up the Highland Line, and I make out that in less than a week the Boom will be the length o' Kingussie or Aviemore."

Robert Grant shook his head till his whiskers almost made a draught. "It's too late of comin' for us, Mr Swan," he said lugubriously. "Tom and me's tired o't. We're done! What trade we ever had is goin' back. It was never a fat thing at the best, but now it's driftin' over to the Store[1]

across the street; ye see they've started a drapery department."

"Let them start it!" said Mr Swan, contemptuously.
"I'm sure ye ken the slogan o' the Grants — 'Stand fast,
Craigellachie !' The new department at the Store should
be a tonic to ye; send ye brisker about your business than
ever ye were before; I never do so well myself as when I'm
faced wi' solid opposition."

But the Grant brothers wagged their preposterous
whiskers, and sunk their chins lower in their obsolete
Gladstone collars, and assured their visitor that affairs
were hopeless. Thank God they could still pay twenty
shillings in the pound and have a little over, but there
seemed to be nothing now for it but Canada. Everybody
was going to Canada.

"What'll ye dae there?" asked Mr Swan, bluntly. They
would look around them for a while, and no doubt hit on
something, they remarked, and Robert's defective and
erratic eye went flashing round the shop in a manner which
suggested that at looking around in Canada he would be a
perfect marvel.

James Swan walked to the door and looked at his open
cases; threw out his chest and took a deep breath of the
stimulating sea-born air, then turned back to the counter,
and addressed the disconsolate brothers.

"Do ye ken what's the matter wi' this business and wi'
you?" he asked. "It's whiskers! Nothing else but whiskers!
For the love of Peter, shave yoursel's clean like me, or start
a moustache, or a Captain Kettle[2] beard wi' a peak to't,
and be upsides wi' modern civilisation. Gie your cheeks a
chance; take aff these side-galleries and look like the year
o' grace 1912, no' the start o' the Franco-Prussian war."[3]

The brothers, too well acquainted with their visitor to
resent this personality, smiled ruefully. "I see from the
papers," said Robert, "that side whiskers are comin' into
vogue again. Tom and me's just a little ahead o' the times;
we'll soon be in the height o' fashion."

"The height o' nonsense!" cried Jimmy Swan. "There's

no wise-like folk gaun back to whiskers ony mair than to the crinoline or the chignong. In either case the women wouldna stand it, and it's them that rule the fashions. Man, it's no' an age for whiskers; ye need a face on ye as clean as the bow o' a cutter yacht to sail into the winds o' commerce nooadays, and there's the pair o' ye beatin' to the marks wi' spinnakers. There's naebody wears whiskers now but undertakers and men on the Stock Exchange that havena ony dochters to cod them into common sense. If any employee o' C & M's came into the warehouse wi' a whisker on, the partners in the business would tak fits, and the rest o' us would bray at him like cuddies. If the police o' Gleska saw a man your age wi' whiskers they would track him up a lane at night and hammer him wi' their batons. The way ye are, ye're an affront to me; ye're no' a day aulder than mysel', and yet ye might be onybody's faithers. The first thing they would dae to ye in Canada would be to lay ye on a block and clip ye — "

He broke off with a chuckle which disarmed annoyance; there were no customers of C & M for whom he had a greater respect — if only they would shave themselves; and he knew they knew it.

"Ah, if it was only a question o' whiskers!" said Thomas, sadly.

"It's ALL a question o' whiskers!" vehemently retorted Jimmy Swan. "There's naething criminal or immoral about whiskers, but in a drapery concern they're a Symbol. Your fine half-Dundrearies are an indication o' your state o' mind. The world is a' for youth — which I take to be onything under sixty, and there's the pair o' ye advertisin' that ye're nearly centenarians. It's no' on your face only that there's whiskers; they're in your philosophy and on your business. Twa men your age, wi' health, and twenty shillin's in the pound, and an auld-established business, should be oot in the mornin's whistlin' like mavises[4] and gambollin' round the shop like boys."

"I doubt we're not the gambollin' kind," said Robert humbly, for the first time in his life painfully conscious of his whiskers. "But nobody can say we haven't paid strict attention to business. ... And walked in the fear of God," he added as an afterthought.

"That's it!" said Jimmy Swan. "More whiskers! It would suit ye better to walk in his glory and sing the 27th Psalm.[5] It's no' in the fear and admonition o' the Lord ye're walkin', but in mortal terror o' the Store. Bonny-like Grants ye are? Wi' a motto like 'Stand Fast!' that ought to stir ye up and stiffen ye like a trumpet! Man, the very sound o't dirls like the tune Dunfermline!"

"There's something in it!" said Thomas tremulously. "Perhaps we were a little too timid about the Store, Robert?"

"Ye couldna help it wi' thae whiskers!" said Jimmy Swan. "There's nothing worse for the nerve than fluff. Shave off your whiskers and I'll guarantee that between us we'll make the Store look silly. I never saw the sense o' Stores; they don't get their stuff from C & M."

"Could ye suggest anything, Mr Swan?" asked Robert, also infected by this fearless spirit; "anything to, as it were, buck us up in the business?"

"Man, amn't I tellin' ye? — Whiskers! whiskers! whiskers! Get them aff! Be as young as I am — twenty-six; I only begin to count from the day I married. It's a' nonsense about bein' douce and demure, and auld-lookin' — at least, in the drapery trade; it may suit a' right wi' undertakers. Take the whiskers aff your shop, and aff your stock, and aff the dressin' o' your windows!"

"There's maybe something in what you say," admitted Robert, "but there seem to be such chances out in Canada!"

"Of course there are!" said Jimmy Swan. "Wherever there's clean cheeks, there's chances, and every man in Canada has a safety razor. But, bless your heart, man! Canada's no' the only place! If half the folk that went to Canada had only stayed at home and shaved themsel's, and took the side-wings aff their business, and the fluff frae their way o' lookin' at things, there would be nae necessity to emigrate. Are ye stupid enough to think this country's done because the Store has added drapery? It's a sign that it's only startin', and that better men are wanted. Good luck to them in Canada! but let you and me stay here and shave oursel's."

The brothers Grant looked at each other. "I think, after all," said Thomas, "you might show us some of your winter lines."

"Certainly," said Jimmy Swan with the utmost alacrity, and, humming 'Onward, Christian Soldiers', went outside to fetch his samples.

# 16.  *Blate Rachel*

JIMMY SWAN, with a superb carnation in his coat-lapel, was leaning on the counter of the widow Thorpe, recounting all the splendours of a wedding he had been a guest at on the previous day, when he observed a tear was in the widow's eye. He promptly changed the subject, and went back to the claims of Union Shantung for good hard wear and smart appearance.

"You never can tell," he thought, "when a widow woman's too far on in years to be sentimental; the puir old body's envious." But he misunderstood.

"Everybody has luck but me," she said to him, indifferent, for the moment, to his Shantung samples; "There's my lassie Rachel, and there's no' man looks near her."

"Toots!" said Jimmy blithely, "what's the matter wi' her? Is she skelly-e'ed?"

"There's naething wrang wi' her," replied the widow peevishly; "She got a better chance, to start wi', in her looks than ever I got, but she's blate.[1] Put her next a lad, and she's so shy she might be skelly[2] in both e'es and he wouldna get a chance to see it."

"Blate!" said Jimmy, with surprise. "That's a female disease I thought was oot o' fashion. Are ye sure it's no' her adenoids?"

The widow positively wept as she disclosed the troubles she had had with Rachel. She had given her a first-rate education, up as far as Chemistry and Elocution; she had lavished dress upon her to the point of gold watch-wristlets, petticoats of silk and patent American pumps; she had taken her to hydros.[3] "But there she is!" bewailed the mother; "goin' on eight-and-twenty, and I'll swear she never had a box o' chocolates I didna buy for her mysel'! It's rale disheartenin', Mr Swan. I'd give a lot to see her settled down. But there! — ye'll think I'm just a sly designin' woman."

The traveller smiled. "So far as I can see," he said, "the trouble is that ye're no' half sly enough nor much o' a dab at the designin', or otherwise, if Rachel's like the world, you should hae been a granny. I've never seen her."

"Come up the stair and ha'e a cup o' tea," said Mrs Thorpe; "I'm no' ashamed to let ye see her."

"I will!" said Jimmy with alacrity, and gave a little twitch to his superb carnation. If Rachel Thorpe was blate she showed no signs of it to him. He told her three quite funny stories, led the conversation on to operas, and sitting down to the piano vamped his own accompaniment (three good chords and a twiddly one) to 'Star of Eve', which, he explained, was a good deal finer when sung by a tenor who could really sing. Rachel, thus encouraged, gave a palpitating rendering of 'The Rosary', the widow looking all the time at Jimmy in expectant anguish as if he were an *entrepreneur* who was testing a soprano.

"Capital!" he murmured at the end of every verse. "Expression! Feeling! Temperament! Particularly that rallentando bit! For such a heavy song, she's simply wonderful!" He finally presented her with the carnation.

"Now, can you tell what's the matter wi' her?" asked the mother when she got him back into the shop. "Time's aye slippin' past, and a' the diffies[4] in the place are gettin' married, and Rachel's jist the way ye see her."

"A bonny, wise-like lass!" said he, with emphasis. "Perhaps it wasna fair to call her Rachel. Rachel, Ruth,

Rebecca — ony o' them's a handicap in this dull material age, Mrs Thorpe; ye want a snappy, cheery sort o' name to give a girl a chance. 'Rachel's solemn; it takes a lot o' pluck to put an arm about a Rachel. Ye should have ca'd her Jean. But she didna strike me as out o' the ordinar' shy; we got on together fine."

"Ah, yes," said Mrs Thorpe; "she got on a' right wi' you, for you're a married man, but if a lad comes to the house she hasna hardly got a word to say, and I've to do the talkin'."

"What do ye talk about to them?" asked Jimmy.

"Oh, anything at all," she answered, rather puzzled at the question. "Thank God, I never was at a loss for conversation! And Rachel, she sits fidgin'!"

"Yon's an interestin' photo album," said Jimmy, who had been personally conducted through it. "I suppose ye'll show them that?"

"Ye had to entertain them some way," said the widow sadly. "Expecially if your daughter is a dummy."

"H'm!" said Jimmy, and rubbed his chin. "It's hardly fair to Rachel! There's half a dozen photos o' her yonder that amount to a complete exposure o' her past. 'Rachel as a baby' — nice, and wee, and fat; 'Rachel at the period o' the fringe,' 'Rachel when she won the ping-pong prize' — wi' a bolero jacketee, accordion pleats, and a motor kep. Ye shouldna rake up her past like that in front o' any chap ye're wantin' to encourage. It mak's her look like the History o' Scotland in monthly parts."

"I never thought o' that!" said Mrs Thorpe.

"Besides, the album, as a whole, is obsolete as a social and domestic cheerer-up. It's done! Ye might as well attempt to rouse enthusiasm wi' a game o' dominoes or a spellin'-bee. Any young man that you show through yon album is bound to get a fright when he sees three generations o' the Thorpes and a' their ramifications down to sixty-second cousins. It reduces Rachel to a mere incident. He's apt to say to himsel', 'Great Scot! she's no unique at all: there have been hundreds o' her!' And it's so unlucky there's so mony o' them deid! Brief life is here our portion, as the hymn says, but we needna rub it in to Rachel's friends that even the Thorpes get old and disappear; they want to think of her as in eternal youth, forever gaily skippin' across the sands o' time in a hobble skirt and clocked silk stockin's."

"Ye're a droll man! " said Mrs Thorpe laughing.

"And then there's another thing," said Jimmy twinkling. "I'll wager ye're far too anxious to be nice to any young man ye see in Rachel's company. That's no the way to take the situation at all! My mother-in-law knew better than that when I was after Bella — that's the mistress. She forbade me to come near the house after her lassie, and used to look on me like dirt. She said the Swans were a' geese, and warned Bella to have naething to dae wi' me. Up till then Bella, wi' me, was just a lass for walkin' hame from the dancin' wi'; but when my pride was roused I up and married her! And the auld yin laughed!"

"That might do wi' others," said the widow, "but no wi' Rachel; she's so blate."

"Blate!" said Jimmy. "That'll be her salvation; there's far mair chance for a blate yin than the other kind. If she's really blate, and we had her down in Gleska she would be a novelty. Onything out o' the ordinar' takes in Gleska. Send her down for a week to Mrs Swan, to see the shops; there's nothing beats a change o' air for blateness."

"It's very kind of ye," said Mrs Thorpe. "She wouldna be the worse for't, maybe. But ye'll think I'm an awfu' designin' woman!"

"Good!" said Jimmy heartily. "Bella will be glad to see her. And as for the designin', Mrs Thorpe, God meant it."

## 17. *Rachel Comes to Town*

JAMES SWAN had mischievously described the girl from Banchory[1] to his wife as 'a spindly one wi' ruby hair, a voice like the start o' a gramophone, and clothes picked up in the dark at a jumble sale,' and when the visitor jumped out of a taxi-cab, which also bore a substantial trunk, a leather hat-box, a neat morocco dressing-case, and a bag of golf-clubs, from the railway station, Mrs Swan immediately realised that she had been badly done.

"I can't believe a word you say to me, sometimes, Jimmy!" she exclaimed with agitation, as the door bell rang.

There was nothing spindly about Rachel; her hair was a glorious golden; her voice was sweet and mellow as a mavis' song, and her dress alone was summed up in two seconds by Mrs Swan as costing anything over £6. 10s.

"And where's the blateness of her?" Jimmy was asked at the earliest opportunity. "I thought from your description that you couldn't drag a word from her except in the dummy alphabet."

Jimmy chuckled. "I only told ye what her mother said," he answered. "The case is desperate. She's goin' on eight and twenty — "

"Just a child!" said his wife from the point of view of forty.

"Everybody in Banchory's gettin' married but hersel'; take her round the town before we go to Kirn,[2] and give her wrinkles."

"The only kind of wrinkles I have nowadays are the sort a woman gets from being married," said Mrs Swan with a look at herself in the overmantel mirror.

But really Rachel Thorpe required no wrinkles. Jimmy was off the road for a week and busy at the warehouse; for three nights in succession, when he came home at tea-time, he found a vacant house and the fire out; a hitherto conscientious wife was being dragged around the town at the heels of the blate young thing from Banchory, and wasn't even ashamed of herself.

"I never go anywhere, James," she said; "You never take me over the door. I've seen more of Glasgow in the past three days with Rachel than I've done in twenty years with you."

The ladies together went to picture-palaces, tearooms, parks; they paraded Buchanan Street and Sauchiehall Street by the hour, fascinated by windows; they rode on the outside of tramway cars as far as cars would take them; one night they were not home till ten; Rachel had insisted on a music-hall.

"Oh, it's all right!" said Jimmy, meekly. "I'm vexed I never thought o' makin' ye a hot supper. I'll leave the door on the Chubb after this, and ye can jist slip in when ye like. There'll be something cold on the sideboard. But for goodness' sake don't start singin' and pullin' beer and make a row and wake me; mind, I'm gettin' up in years."

"You should come out with us," seriously suggested the girl from Banchory. "What's the sense of sitting in here moping all alone when you might be enjoying yourself? Mrs Swan and I are going to see 'Way Back in Darkeyland' tomorrow night. I've just been telling her I hear it's fine."

"No," said he, ironically; "I canna be bothered goin' anywhere unless I can get dancin'; I'm vexed it's no' the social season; you and Bella would like a ball."

On his wife had come the most extraordinary transformation. The fashion in which she put up her hair was preposterously antiquated, according to Rachel, who dressed it to look three times as thick as it was before, with glints of sunshine in its bronze that no one had hitherto suspected. Rachel also in an hour or two devised a hat for Mrs Swan, so chic and saucy that of itself it immediately knocked ten years off her age, and induced in the wearer a corresponding spirit of youthful gaiety. She took about a breadth from the width of her Sunday gown, reduced its length amazingly, bought the nattiest kind of shiny shoes, and displayed in the frankest manner a beautiful pair of shot-silk stockings. Her husband saw her one day jump on a car with Rachel, and they looked like a couple of soubrettes in 'The Girl in the Film'.

"Ye seem to have picked me up a' wrang, Bella," he said to his wife when they were alone that evening.

"The idea was that Rachel Thorpe was to have her shyness polished off wi' a week in Gleska, and maybe learn a tip or twa on the way to get a sweetheart. There's no' that mony sweethearts disengaged in Gleska that ye can look for one apiece. Besides, as lang as I hing on, it wouldna be respectable."

"Pooh!" said Bella, radiantly; "you want to see me going out a perfect fright. I never had a fling to myself since I was married, and now that Rachel's here I'm going to have it. Your idea of what is fit and proper in a married woman's fifty years behind the times. Rachel was quite astonished at the life I lead."

"And that's the girl her mither thinks is blate!" said Mr Swan, derisively.

The Swans had taken three weeks of a house at Kirn; they removed to the coast on Monday, and the girl from Banchory went with them. In two days she had taught Mrs Swan the game of golf, how to swing most effectively in a hammock, the two-step, 'Hitchy-Koo',[3] and diverse other pleasing ditties, the right deportment for a walking-stick, and the way to clear the bows of a steamer by ten yards in a rowing-boat so as to get the rocking of the waves and a good view of the captain dancing with rage on the bridge.

Jimmy came down from town one afternoon, and saw them waiting for him on the pier. At first he had looked at them with amiable and even approving interest, for he did not, at a distance, recognise them. They had white serge skirts, white shoes and stockings, knitted sports-coats of a vivid mustard colour, knitted caps conform thereto in hue, and walking-sticks. They were distinctly making gallant play at coquetry with two young gentlemen he did not know, and to whom he was introduced with some embarrassment on the part of all concerned.

"There's just one thing ye have overlooked," he told his wife, who had dropped behind with him while the blate girl from Banchory went up the pier between the two young gentlemen, putting down her feet with splendid artfulness so that nobody could help looking at them. Next to Mrs Swan's they were the neatest feet on the Cowal side of the coast that day.

"What do you mean? What did I overlook?" asked Mrs Swan, who seemed deliriously happy.

"The dug," said Jimmy, seriously. "Ye need a wee bit toy terrier under your oxter,[4] and instead o' the walking-stick I would hae a tennis-racket. If I may ask, where did ye pick up thae twa misguided gentlemen?"

"Oh, just on the quay," said Mrs Swan. "They're very nice. They came off a boat from Rothesay."

"Did they just wink at ye, or did you see them first and say, 'Ha, Berty!'?"

"Nothing so common!" said Mrs Swan, with dignity. "We pretended we didn't see them, but they would insist on speaking to Rachel."

"Just that!" said Jimmy. "I'm goin' to write to Rachel's mother the night and tell her to get Rachel shifted back to Banchory as quick as possible, before my happy home is broken up."

His wife laughed. "Do you know who they are?" she said. "They're just two Banchory friends of Rachel's, and the one with the fancy waistcoat wants to marry her. He came here specially to ask her, and she says she will."

"Could he no' ask her up in Banchory?" asked Jimmy with surprise.

"No," said Mrs Swan; "not without her mother over-hearing. She was always there, and kept cracking Rachel up so much that the poor lad never got a chance to shove a word in telling his intentions."

"That's exactly what I thought!" said Mr Swan. "But what are you, at the age of over forty, comin' out so strong in the nutette[5] line for?"

"Just to cheer up and encourage Rachel; just to make

her think that married life's no' so dull as she would think if she saw me at my ordinary," said the amazing Mrs Swan.

## 18.  *A Poor Programme*

"You're the last landlord on this side of the Clyde to keep slippers for your guests," said Mr Swan. "It's not that I'm needin' them myself, but I like to see them; they're one of the few surviving relics of the age *de luxe* in the history of commercial travellin'."

"Do you know the way I manage to keep them, Mr Swan?" said the landlord of the Queen's. "I got them big! There's not a coffee-room pair of slippers here that's under easy number tens. It was a waiter, Alick Russell, put me up to't. I lost about a gross of slippers every year through gentlemen finding them so good a fit they thought they were their own. 'Whit ye want,' says Alick, 'is big and roomy yins they canna walk upstairs to their bedrooms wi'.' I went away at once and bought three dozen pair of number tens. The only man they ever fitted was a cattleman from Perth. The rest just leave them."

Mr Swan put on his own slippers.

"You're surely not in for the night?" said Mr Grant; "there's a Territorial concert[1] on."

Just for a moment Jimmy hesitated. "No," he said; "I'm bye wi' country concerts; they're too heatin' for my blood. If it was a swarry and a ball, or a Council meetin', I might risk it. That's the worst of bein' highly cultivated — I canna put up wi' 'Hitchy-Koo', and they're bound to have 'Hitchy-Koo' in Fochabers, especially wi' a Territorial concert. It's a hundred chances to one a Colour-Sergeant wi' a nearly tenor voice 'll stand up and give 'The Phantom Army', and as sure as daith I cannot stand 'The Phantom Army'. It was maybe good enough till the hundred thousandth time I heard it, but then it began to spoil my sleep. Forbye, 'The Phantom Army' 's no' a song for Territorials; it's far too personal."

"They have a lot of talent," said the landlord coaxingly.

"I know they'll have," said Mr Swan agreeably. "I notice in the country papers that they're always super-excellent. Did it ever occur to you, Mr Grant, that music's done in Scotland? I mean vocal music; of course there's aye the pianola. There are only two kinds o' singers now in Scotland — the real professional that needs an evening suit for't, and the young and healthy amateur who does 'Phil the Fluter's Ball' or 'No, John, No!' as if his life depended on it."

"The gramophone — " said Mr Grant.

"Of course! Quite right! The gramophone's the music-master now; whenever 'Everybody's Doing It' comes out in a Glasgow Pantomime, they wire at once from Fochabers to send a dozen records. No time is lost! The latest rag-time tune is up at Thurso wi' the mornin' post, and everybody's whistlin't by tea-time.

"Half the folk in the country's sick-tired o' music, and the other half's tryin' to be Clara Butts[2] and Harry Lauders — a thing that sounds quite easy when you hear it in a canister. Half the nice wee lassies that could sing like laverocks if they were content to sing the way that God intended them, fair sicken ye wi' tryin' to get cadenzas like the banker's Tetrazzini,[3] ten-and-six the double-breasted disc. The other half realise they could never do anything within a mile of it, and they never try; they just put up their hair another way, and tell the chap they're fond of cookin'."

"But still it's a very decent programme," said the landlord, producing it.

Mr Swan put on his glasses. "That's it! I knew it at once!" he said. "'The Prologue from Pagliacci, by Mr G. R. Williamson.' I don't ken Mr Williamson, but I'll bet ye he's a tall, thin, fair-haired chap in the Union Bank, and has a lisp. He'll be at least a light and easy baritone: he couldn't do't unless. Then there's 'A Wee Deoch an' Doruis' — I ken that, too! He'll likely be a gas collector, a smart wee blackavised chap wi' a comic kind o' face and a crackle up aboot the F. Comic singing is sappin' the manhood o' the nation; it's worse than cigarettes. 'Angus Macdonald,' by Miss — Oh! take it away and put it in the larder! The only thing I see on the programme worth a rap is 'God Save the King'; that's about the only chance that folk get now for singing.

"The place where people sing is Wales, and emulation o' the gramophone hasna spoiled them," said Mr Swan, warming to his subject. "Not being a solo vocalist myself, I always thought harmonic music was the best, and that's the notion o' the Welshmen. You see it gives a modest kind o' chap like me a chance. Thirty years ago there was some sense o' vocal music left in Scotland; there were choirs; now they think a choir is jist a special place for sittin' in the kirk. So long as there were choirs and glee parties there was some hope for us, though we maybe werena just exactly Covent Garden opera. We sang for singing's sake, and we didna try to beat the gramophone.

"There's two things worthwhile in this world — gettin' a Saturday to yoursel' and singin' bass in a choir that has a decent tenor. I never was happier! And music — genuine music — never got a better chance. So far as I'm aware there was never anything positively rotten put in harmony; quartet, glee, and catch were always decent. Three-fourths of the agony of life today is due to that ridiculous preference for the solo. When the average amateur soloist comes in leanin' heavily on himself wi' a couple o' music sheets — one for the poor soul at the instrument and the other for himself to hide his presentation watch-chain — I'm sorry for him.

"I'm all for choirs and a good bass part for willing gentlemen! It's only wi' part-singing that ye'll stem the tide of British musical decadence — what do you think of that for rhetoric at this early hour o' evening, Mr Grant?"

"I like 'O, Who Will O'er the Downs?' and 'Kate Dalrymple,'" said Mr Grant with modesty.

"Right you are!" said Mr Swan emphatically. "Your tastes are sound! They werena tripe — these songs — at any rate!"

"All these remarks o' mine," continued Mr Swan, "are due to the fact that at a Glasgow public dinner the other night there was a choir. I havena heard a choir at a Glasgow public dinner for twenty years, and I'm thinkin' neither did the company. The usual idea o' a Glasgow dinner now is that a dozen men spoil a' the fun wi' makin' speeches. You'll never convince the poor deluded creatures that they have not something really new to say, and that folk don't want to hear them. Nobody ever does. It just fair spoils the coffee and cigars.

"At this dinner some daring innovator introduced a choir, the speakin' was cut down to the assurance that the Navy was right and trade was boomin', and the choir took up the rest o' the evening makin' us really happy. If dinners were a' like that one, they would be my hobby."

"Then you're not coming?" said Mr Grant.

"Not me!" said Jimmy, lighting his pipe; "Be sure and lock the door when ye come back. And tell the Pagliacci gentleman he hasna't in him! Tell him to start a decent choir."

## 19. *Broderick's Shop*

JAMES SWAN went into an Argyle Street shop on Saturday to buy a knife. It is one of the oldest ironmongery shops[1] in town, but that was not the reason Jimmy went to it; antiquity of itself makes no appeal to him; he went to this particular shop because he knew the owner, who had for years been on the verge of losing money on it.

Elsewhere in Argyle Street[2] it was the busiest hour of the day. All the world seemed out for buying. Drapery warehouses were crowded to the doors, the grocery shops, which also advertise, appeared too small for the folk who wanted into them; the lust for giving money in exchange for something crowded the street itself with gutter merchants feverishly dispensing fruit, and flowers, and penny toys that last (with care) till Monday. Argyle Street blazed with light and roared with commerce; electric moons, refulgent, made it bright as day; a thousand windows gorgeously displayed their best; the pavements streamed with life, and every other person had a parcel.

"Beautiful!" said Jimmy to himself. "Tip-top! Lovely! And just to think that this was once a country lane!"

He felt a genuine pride in Glasgow, and a personal pride that he was an essential part in its commercial activities. It was with almost a paternal eye he stopped to look at a window with a dummy figure wearing one of C & M's 'Incomparable' Long-Busk Corsets, there because himself had thrown no little poetry into its recommendation.

To step from the street into Broderick's ironmongery shop, however, was to leave the roar of battle and get into a mausoleum. A solemn hush prevailed there. A customer was standing at the counter, plunged in the patient contemplation of long rows of rather dusty shelves with nothing more attractive to the eye on them than screw-nail packages. In parts behind two shopmen blew or flicked the dust from other packages; Broderick himself was on the ladder.

He came down at last, deliberately; gave a friendly nod to Jimmy; opened the parcel he had brought down with him, and found it was the wrong one. So he went up the ladder again, and in the course of time disposed of a key-ring to the customer for a penny. The customer gave sixpence for its payment. Mr Broderick picked the six-pence up and walked with dignity to some place far away in the back of his shop where he kept his cash-desk.

Jimmy took out his watch and held it in his hand.

The hum of the clamant, buying street came in, like some far murmur of a sea; below the wan, old-fashioned gas-light over Broderick's door ('Established 1812'), the multitude went skliffing past along the pavement, deigning not so much as a glance within. He hummed the funeral march from 'Saul' to himself, and felt exceedingly sorry for Alick Broderick.

When Broderick had got the change for sixpence and

dismissed his customer, he turned with a pathetic expansiveness to Jimmy.

"There's no' much profit aff a penny split ring, Jimmy," said he.

"I daresay no'," said Jimmy, snapping up his hunter watch with a last glance at the dial. "Show me a shilling knife, and then shut up this shop o' yours, and come out and ha'e a dram."

"Indeed," said Broderick, "I might well shut it up for a' that's daein'. I never saw things worse," and he took out a case of knives with great solemnity.

"Alick," said Mr Swan, "do ye mind the day ye blooded my nose in old Maclean's Academy?"

"Ay, fine!" said Mr Broderick. "Ye stole my jawry-bool."[3]

"Weel, I'm gaun to blood your nose the night," said Jimmy, smiling. "Ye better get oot your hanky. ... Ye say that things were never worse. Where are your ears and e'en? Take a daunder[4] alang the street and hear things humming. I could hardly get alang the pavement for folk fair daft to spend their money, and here are you sclimbin'[5] ladders and wearin' oot your shoon to get change for a customer that wants a penny ring. It took ye exactly one minute and forty-five seconds to go away back there to your cash-desk."

"For a' that's daein' —" started Mr Broderick.

"For a' that's daein' — fiddlesticks!" said Jimmy. "There's only six hundred minutes in a workin' day, and you have only the one pair o' legs on ye, and ye waste good minutes and good legs on the heid o' a penny ring. What ails ye at a cash railway, man? Or if ye canna hae a railway, can ye no' keep your cash beside your coonter? Naebody's gaun to pinch it on ye! When a customer sees ye makin' a North Pole expedition awa' back there wi' his penny, he thinks he has paid too much for the ring, and ye're away behind to dance the hoolichan."[6]

"There's naething to be done in business nooadays unless ye advertise," said Mr Broderick sadly; "and I never was in wi' advertisin'."

"Were ye no'?" said Jimmy, sharply. "What's your window for but advertisin'?"

"The cost's enormous," said Mr Broderick.

"Have ye ony money bye ye?" asked Jimmy, boldly.

"Thank God I have a little," said Mr Broderick.

"It would need to be a lot," said Jimmy, "for it's you that pays for other ironmongers' advertising, and nae thanks for it."

"I don't understand ye, Jimmy," said his friend. "How do I pay for other folks' advertisin'?"

"Who in heaven's name do ye think pays for't?" said Jimmy.

"The man that advertises."

"Not him! He doesna pay a penny. All he does is to lend a little capital in advertising, that comes back a hundredfold. The more he advertises, the bigger his profits at the end of the year. When did ye ever hear o' a big advertiser failin'? The thing's unknown, and advertisin's only in its infancy."

"Ay, but in the long run it's the customer that pays for advertisin'," said Mr Broderick.

"There, ye're wrang again!" said Jimmy. "What dae ye charge for this shilling knife?" and he picked up one that met his fancy.

"Just a shillin'," said Mr Broderick.

"Well, I can go to any ironmonger's shop in Gleska that advertises, and I'll get the same knife for a shillin'. Things are never ony dearer in a shop that advertises. So ye see it's neither the advertiser nor the customer that pays the newspapers."

"If it's no', wha is it, then?" asked Mr Broderick, with genuine interest. He had never studied the point before.

"It's you, and the like o' you!" said Jimmy. "Every customer you lose through no' advertisin', and every shop that goes doon through no' advertisin', swells the volume o' business in the shops that advertise, and indirectly pays for other folks' advertising. I never see your name in the papers, but when I read a splash o' Grant & Richards, I say to

mysel', 'There's some more o' Alick Broderick's money!'
… Take you my tip, Alick, blaw the stour aff them shelves,
and get a nice wee cash railway and a ladder that runs on
wheels, and hing oot some dacent lights, and advertise,
and ye'll no' complain o' naething daein'."

He paid for his knife and gave a genial chuckle. "Now
take out your hanky, lad!" he cried as he left the shop.

A hundred yards along the street he looked at a window
of Grant & Richards, in whose shop a roaring trade was
doing, and he saw a knife there priced at ninepence in
every respect the counterpart of the one he had bought
from Broderick.

"Stung!" he said to himself, with a humorous grin.
"Alick's got the best o' me again, and it's me that needs the
hanky."

## 20. *Gent's Attire*

THE UTMOST surprise was created last Friday in Campbell
& Macdonald's warehouse when Mr Swan appeared in a
familiar overcoat. In the memory of the oldest employee he
had never previously been known to inaugurate the winter
season in any other coat than one quite unmistakably fresh
from the tailor's hands. Nothing less would have seemed
becoming and appropriate to the oldest traveller for the oldest
soft goods firm in Glasgow. The tradition, long prevalent
among the warehouse staff of C & M, was that Jimmy
Swan owed much of his renown and success as a traveller
to the cut and fashion of his garments, always meticulously
fresh and trim, and worn with a certain distinction which
was the envy and despair of the younger travellers. They
also tried to dress like gentlemen, but only partially
succeeded, and always stuck at the halfway stage, where
the best that can be said of a wearer of clothes is that he is
a knut. They knew it themselves, when Jimmy's eyebrows
would lift at the sight of their heliotrope wood-fibre sox or
what they had fondly thought a stunning effect in waistcoats.

Yet here was Jimmy Swan in a last winter's greatcoat, ready to start on the northern journey through towns and villages to which, for years, he had been 'the glass of fashion and the mould of form'[1] — the seasonal inspiration and example of gent's styles as approved and passed in the Metropolis!

A lapse! A decided and disquieting lapse! It was inconceivable that the best shops in, say, Aberdeen, would give such orders as they used to do, to Jimmy Swan in a last year's topcoat, however cunningly cleaned and pressed to look like new.

"Excuse the liberty, Jimmy," said Carmichael the mantle-buyer, "but what's the matter wi' your tailor? Has your credit stopped?"

Mr Swan, puffing a little, rose from the case he was bent over, packing samples, and shrugged his shoulders.

"No," he answered. "If it's my coat you mean, it's just economy. Quite a good coat!"

"Ah! well," conceded Carmichael, "we have all to exercise some thrift or other these days."

"No' in the buyin' branch o' this establishment!" said Mr Swan; "Mr Macdonald's notions o' economy are concentrated in the meantime on the expenses o' the man who books the biggest orders for his firm, and — not to put too fine a point on it — that's me!"

"Good heavens! they're no' surely beginnin' to scrimp YOU, Jimmy?" ejaculated Carmichael, genuinely shocked; it was understood in the shop that, up to a pound a day, Mr Swan's bill for expenses passed the cashier unquestioned; that it was an historical right, like Magna Carta.

Mr Swan only smiled sadly. "Economy's a droll thing, Alick," he remarked; "It's like them Zeppelin bombs,[2] ye never ken where it'll licht, these days. Mr Macdonald has all of a sudden found oot that my buyin' a topcoat or a suit o' clothes noo and then from our country customers, involves us, someway, in the Corrupt Practices Act.[3] At least, it's the best excuse he could think o' for knocking a bit aff my expenses."

Carmichael looked surprised. "What does it matter to him where ye buy your clothes?" he asked. "But I never dreamt ye bought any in the country."

"Many and many a time!" said Jimmy. "But nobody can cast up to me that I ever wore them!"

He shut down the lid of his case, and strapped it tightly.

"If ever you had been on the road sellin'," he said, when that was done, "you would understand yoursel' what's meant by my auld topcoat, and Macdonald's new economy. Some o' you chaps get into the buyin' branch wi' little or nae education to speak o' in human nature. A buyer's cock-o'-the-walk; he doesna even need to study to be civil to the folk he deals wi'; it's very different wi' the bagman. I've seen me buy a Hielan' cape I wouldna be dragged oot o' the Clyde by Geordie Geddes[4] in, and wear it a couple o' days in Dornoch just to please a draper and tailor there I expected a thumpin' order frae."

"Great Scot!" said Carmichael, horrified at the very idea of Mr Swan in a Dornoch cape. "But do ye mean to say they passed the price o' a cape in your expenses?"

"No quite!" said Jimmy. "I sold it at a loss o' a pound when I got to Glasgow, and put the pound doon in my bill. This time last year old Macdonald himself would be the first to agree that it was a pound well spent on the Dornoch orders for fishermen's trousers I used to bring him. Do you know this, Carmichael? I one time went the length o' a suit o' kilts, complete even to the sporran! It was in Inverness, frae a customer that was awfu' namely for his kilts. But Mr Macdonald kicked at kilts; it cost me £2. 10s. to get rid o' them to a Hielandman that had a wee pub doon on the Broomielaw.

"It is the firmly rooted conviction o' the drapery trade in the rural districts o' Scotland that it's fit to tackle gents' attire," continued Mr Swan. "They get the designs and plans for spring lounge suits frae last year's *Tailor and Cutter* newspaper; heave a web o' tweed at their cutter the first fine day he's aff the spree, tell him the only change this season's in lapels, remind him that cotton lining's nae

langer bein' put in breeks, then press a lump o' chalk and a
fret-saw into his tremblin' hands, and order him to pro-
ceed.

"I've passed through the hands o' mair country cutters
than any other man in Scotland. Ye never catch me
wearin' onything but a genuine Glasgow suit, but for the
sake o' business I've had to order suits in lots o' places no'
the size o' Fochabers, where they put rabbit-pouches in
your jacket whether ye poach or no', and would palm off a
waistcoat wi' sleeves on ye if ye werena watchin'. There's
at least a score o' country clothiers in Scotland that expect
me to buy a suit or a topcoat frae them every year; the
goods is sometimes waitin' ready for me when I land; if
there's any difference in the length o' my sleeve since last
year, they're ready to tak' in a hem.

"What do I dae wi' the clothes? I sometimes put them
into my sample case and sell them in the next wee toon I
come to as a model garment fresh from London, goin' at a
dead-snip bargain. Some o' them I get rid o' in the packin'-
shop at fifteen shillin's or a pound less than I paid for
them; many a time I'm left wi' a Harris tweed the wife can
only use for cuttin' up to go under a runner carpet. But up
till now the firm has played fair horney,[5] and seen I didna
lose on my diplomatic stimulation o' the tailor trade in the
turnip districts."

"It's not fair!" said Carmichael emphatically.

"It is not!" agreed the traveller. "Macdonald's kickin'
aboot 30s. I honestly spent in pushin' business in Clachna-
cudden last October. I had aye to tak' a suit in Clach-
nacudden; Elshiner the draper seen to that. He had aye a
range o' home-dyed, homespun tweeds for the local cattle
show, and a cutter that took your measure a' wrang in
Gaelic wi' a piece o' string. I've got suits frae Elshiner I
could never sell onywhere at a third o' what they cost me;
they were that roary, and that defiant o' every law o' the
male anatomy.

"Last October, when Elshiner's cutter was passin' the
string all over my manly form, and stoppin' to tak' a snuff

each time that Elshiner put doon the Gaelic figures in a
pass-book, I says, 'Whit profit do ye expect to mak' aff this
suit, Mr Elshiner?'

"'Thirty shillin's or thereabouts,' says he.

"'Ah, well!' says I; 'don't bother makin' it; I'll pay the
30s. and we'll be a' square.'

"He took the thirty shillin's right enough, but his pride
was touched, for he someway jaloused I didna appreciate
his suits. And, if ye believe me, he has never given me an
order since! That's the way Macdonald's kickin'."

## 21. *Keeping up with Cochrane*

IT IS a stimulating thing to see a fellow-creature socially
climbing, and up to a certain point Mr James Swan was
quite delighted with the progress of his customer Watty
Cochrane. He had in a sense been the making of Watty. It
was he, nine years ago, who put Watty on to the excellent
opening there was for an up-to-date drapery shop in
Lairg.[1] He selected his first stock for him; got him a good
credit from C & M; put him up to the art of window-
dressing; and got him a wife with some sensible Glasgow
notions of a mantua department.

"She's doin' fine," said Mr Cochrane, after eighteen
months of married felicity. "She brought in last year £150
o' profit to the business, all out o' that bit room behind
there, where I used to keep my lumber. She calls it an
atelier, whatever that is; so far as I'm concerned she might
call it a fusilier, so long's she draws in business the way she
does in homespun costumes."

"The main thing is she's up to guarantee," said Jimmy
Swan. "I knew Kate Jardine was the sort to make a 'happy
fireside clime,'[2] and 'that's the true pathos and sublime o'
human life,' as Burns says."

"There's nothing pathetic about £150," said Cochrane;
"it's nearly £3 a week. But when ye speak about a fireside
climb, ye've hit the mark; Kate and me's started climbin',

and I lie awake at nichts sometimes wondering what I'll reach to if I keep my health. What would ye say to Provost Walter Cochrane, eh?" And the draper rubbed his palms together.

The traveller looked at him with a critical eye.

"'Well done!' I should say. 'Ye have fine shouthers for a chain, and the right sort o' chest for a door-knocker. But see and no' let your heid swell, Walter, or I'll be vexed I went and wasted Kate on ye!'"

After that, on every journey to the North he could see the climbing of Watty Cochrane. Mr Cochrane was made the Captain of the Golf Club, and immediately burst forth in knickerbocker suits. At the urgent solicitation of the citizens — at all events at the urgent solicitation of two of them, who were on his books — he went into the Town Council[3] and became assured of undying local fame as the introducer of the ash-bin cleansing system. He talked more about ash-bins and destructors to Jimmy Swan on his visits than about the drapery business.

"How's the mistress?" Jimmy asked him sometimes; she was never to be seen.

"Up to the ears in the atelier," would Walter say with pride; "she's thrang[4] on a weddin' job for Invershin."

"I hope," said Jimmy, "she's on the climb, too. There canna be much fun in sclimbin' if your wife's to stand at the foot a' the time and steady the ladder."

"I don't quite catch ye," said Councillor Walter Cochrane, convener of the Sanitary Committee.

"What I mean," said Jimmy, "is that if you're goin' to climb awa' up to the giddy heights o' social and civic eminence ye seem to have your mind set on, and leave her up to the ears in the atelier, which is just the French for workshop, I'll consider I did an ill turn by Kate Jardine when I put her in your road. So far as I can see, this climbin's a' in the interest o' Walter Cochrane. If ye go on the way ye're doing, she'll soon no' be able to look at ye except through a bit o' smoked gless, the same's ye were an eclipse. I thought it was a wife I got for ye, and no' a heid mantle-maker."

"Do you know what she made last year in the dressmakin'?" asked Councillor Cochrane.

"I don't know, and I don't care," said Jimmy bluntly. "I could get ye scores o' dressmakers just as good from Gleska, but no' another wife like Kate Jardine, and I'm feared ye're tryin' to smother her in selvedges."[5]

On Mr Swan's next journey to Lairg he was just in time to participate in a chippy little dinner given to a select stag company at the Inn to celebrate Councillor Cochrane's elevation to the bench of Justices of the Peace. The dinner was the new JP's. Councillor Cochrane was obviously becoming very fond of himself. He made three separate speeches in a newly acquired throaty kind of voice, which he seemed to consider incumbent on a JP Several times he took occasion to allude to his last interview with the Lord Lieutenant of the County.

"Who's he?" Jimmy took an opportunity of asking.

"The Duke, of course," said Councillor Cochrane.

"Which o' them?" asked Jimmy innocently. "I never can mind the names o' them unless I look up Orr's Penny Almanac."

"Sutherland," said the new JP. "He's the Lord Lieutenant o' the County, and makes all the JPs. At least, the names are put before him, and he signs the Commissions."

"Plucky chap!" said Jimmy. "Some men would bolt at the desperate responsibility. Listening to ye, there, Walter, I couldna help bein' sorry there's no' a uniform for JPs the same as for Lord-Lieutenants. That heid o' yours'll never get a chance until ye get a helmet."

The new JP considered the occasion incomplete without having his portrait done in oils, and he imported from Aberdeen a fearless young artist, who in five or six days achieved a masterpiece six feet high, wherein Councillor Cochrane was brilliantly revealed as the sort of man who is in the habit of sitting in a frock-coat suit, irrelevantly but firmly grasping a roll of vellum.

The consequence was that when Mr Swan returned to Lairg in autumn in the commercial interest of C & M, he found his customer had flitted to a grand new villa. The fact was intimated casually over a counter piled with Jimmy's samples.

"Keep it up!" said Jimmy with an air of resignation. "Lairg's gettin' ower small for ye. And how is she gettin' on, hersel', in the atelier?"

"Thronger than ever!" said Councillor Cochrane triumphantly. "Workin' till all hours since the shootin' started."

"Puir Kate!" said Jimmy. "She used to be the cheery yin when I kent her in Gleska. She used to hae her evenin's to hersel', and nae bother aboot a villa. What put the villa in your heid, Walter?"

"It was," said Councillor Cochrane, "the portrait to begin wi'. You see, in the old house the portrait was so big in the wee parlour it fair drowned everything else. Besides, in my position — " and he closed abruptly with a gesture which plainly indicated that the position of a JP with the prospects of further civic dignities demanded a reasonable area of domestic space to move about in. "What I want ye to do for me, now," he proceeded, "is to send me up from the Clyde a flag-pole for the front o' the house."

"What do ye want wi' a flag-pole?" said Jimmy with surprise. "Are ye goin' to start sclimbin' flagpoles next?"

"No," said Councillor Cochrane: "but a bit of a pole goes well wi' a villa. I see a lot o' them in the villas down at Inverness. Many a time a body wants to hoist a flag. A flag-pole gives a kind o' finish."

The flag-pole was duly ordered by Mr Swan, who had dreams of a greatly inflated Cochrane painfully sprawling up and sitting on the truck with Kate Jardine sitting making costumes at the foot. For months he had no communication with his soaring customer, but at last he got a letter asking him to keep his eye about for a couple of iron cannons, second-hand. The letter came to Jimmy one morning as he sat at home at breakfast, and he groaned as he perused it.

"What's the matter, Jimmy?" asked his wife.

"It's Watty Cochrane in Lairg," he told her. "He's goin'

to shoot himsel', and he thinks himsel' that big it needs a couple o' cannons to do the job."

"Nonsense!" said Mrs Swan

"No, I'm wrang!" said Jimmy, hastily, proceeding further with his reading of the letter "They're for the front of the villa; he wants them four feet lang and mounted, for he's noo a Bailie. I'll see him to the mischief first! I've troked[6] aboot for mony a droll thing for my customers, but I draw the line at cannons. What'll he be wantin' next if they mak' him Provost?"

Jimmy went up to Lairg on his next North journey with a plausible tale that there was a positive dearth of second-hand cannons in the West of Scotland, as they were all taken up by the Territorial artillery.

"It doesna matter," said Bailie Cochrane, looking slightly worried. "I thought they would make a kind of artistic finish to the villa, but I doubt I'll have to do without them. What I'm wantin' more's a forewoman. You would hear the news?"

"No," said Jimmy.

"The wife's given up the atelier. ... It's twins," said Bailie Cochrane.

## 22. *The Hen Crusade*

"Do ye mind yon hen ye were good enough to send my wife for her stall at the Bazaar?" asked Boyd the draper as Mr Swan was putting back his samples in their cases.

"Fine!" said Jimmy. "I hope it was all right?"

"It was right enough," said Mr Boyd, solemnly; "but it caused a lot o' ill-will among the customers," and Jimmy, bent above his cases, indulged in a crafty wink to himself.

"There wasn't a body came to that Bazaar," went on the draper, "that didn't want to buy the hen. There was what I might call a regular furore about her. And because one hen couldna be sold to four hundred different folk, they took the pet and went away without buyin' anything. I canna understand it; the folk in this place seem to be daft for poultry. ... What are ye laughing at, Mr Swan?"

"Was the Bazaar a success?" asked Jimmy.

"Indeed and it was not! They didna get half the money that they wanted, and I'm no' vexed; it wasna wi' my will that my wife gave countenance to a Bazaar to buy an organ; what we're needin's no' an organ, but a new minister; we're all fair sick o' Cameron. ... But what in a' the earth are ye grinnin' at, Mr Swan?"

"I'll tell ye that," said Jimmy; "I'm laughing at the continued triumph o' my Hen Crusade. You see I'm utterly against Bazaars, Mr Boyd. They're the worst form o' Sweatin' that we have in this country. They're blackleg labour. They're bad for the shopkeeper's business, and they're bad for my firm, C & M. If the craze for Bazaars went any further, I would soon be sellin' naething else but remnants, and folk would expect to get them gratis wi' a bonus ticket. Now, when a customer like yoursel' asks me for a trifle for his wife's stall, I darena well refuse, but I took a survey of the situation some time since, and I saw how I could please my customer and at the same time put a spoke in the Bazaar. The common hen, Mr Boyd, humble, unostentatious, and industrious in life, becomes, when dead, the valued friend o' British commerce."

"Yours was the only fowl in that Bazaar," said Mr Boyd, "and it fair upset it!"

"Exactly!" said Jimmy, rubbing his hands with the greatest satisfaction. "Works like a charm, every time! I'm strongly advising C & M to send a hen to every Bazaar that opens."

"Every person who came into that Bazaar made a dash at once for the produce stall and grabbed the hen, though it had a ticket 'Sold' on it before the door was opened."

"The wife, I suppose?" said Jimmy, innocently.

"Yes," said Mr Boyd, a little flushed. "It was a tidy hen; well worth the half-crown you put on it."

"I always fix the price as low as that," said Jimmy, "though that hen cost me exactly three-and-nine. If the price is low, the competition is the keener."

"At last my wife had to send the fowl home before it was torn to bits by exasperated customers; but all the same everybody coming into that place till the latest hour at night was asking for the hen. And because we didn't have table-loads o' half-croon hens they took the huff and went away, as I say, without buyin' anything. The funny thing is they all kent there was a hen before they came near the place."

"They always do!" said Jimmy. "The rumour of something really useful in a Bazaar goes round a town like this like a fiery cross, and that's the phenomenon I take advantage of in my Hen Crusade. You see, it has got this length wi' Bazaars that they're filled wi' fancy-work no rational mortal soul could fancy. The first thing a woman does in the way o' contributin' to a stall is to cut up something useful and turn it into something ornamental, and the poor misguided body who buys it and brings it home is chaffed a lot about it by her husband. Then, in addition, there's, at all Bazaars, a great bulk o' stuff that's never meant for either use or ornament — it's just Bazaar stuff, made for sellin'. The buyer takes it home and puts it out o' sight till the next Bazaar comes on, and makes it her contribution. It goes from Bazaar to Bazaar till it drops in pieces, or till folk canna guess what it was first intended for.

"It's some years now since the hen came to me as an inspiration. There's something about a hen wi' its heid thrawed[1] that strongly appeals to human nature. I thought to mysel' if I can introduce one fair good hen at a temptin' price to a Bazaar, the struggle for its possession will kill the interest in fancy-work that's far better bought from the retail shops that buy from C & M. It's sure to be bought at the very start by the lady who has it in her stall, and that in itself's annoyin' to the other customers. But, further than that, it's well enough known to every woman who goes about Bazaars that the only thing she can bring home from them to please her man is something he can eat. He has no use for home-made toffee, and he wouldna thank her for the minister's wife's conception o' a seed-cake. A fowl, on the other hand, will never go wrang wi' him, and that's the way ye'll notice that the rumour o' a hen for sale at a Bazaar brings up a queue o' women to the doors an hour before they're open. Half o' them have explicit orders from their husbands to buy that hen, and the other half are planning to give him a nice surprise.

"When the crowd find that the hen's awa' wi't already at half-a-crown to the lady at the stall, it goes home indignant without a glance at the table-centres, and that's another Bazaar burst! I'm tellin' you, Mr Boyd, it's aye weel worth a draper's while to make his contribution to a kirk bazaar a sonsy[2] hen marked down to a price that's temptin'. I've tried jucks, but jucks is no use; the public's dubious about jucks; ye can only rouse the spirit o' competition wi' a hen."

"You're an awfu' sly man, Mr Swan!" exclaimed the draper. "But I'm no vexed yon hen o' yours played havoc wi' the last Bazaar. I've quarrelled wi' the minister about that very organ, and now I havena any kirk to go to."

"It's surely no' for the want o' kirks," said Jimmy. "How many are there here for less than a thousand souls?"

"Five," said Mr Boyd sadly; "the Parish, the UF, which I belong to, the Episcopalian that belongs to Mr Snodgrass of Blairmaddy, and two different kinds o' Frees, the Wee Frees and the — "

"Oh! never mind goin' into that," said Jimmy, "just say assorted. I never could tell the difference o' one Free Kirk from another, and I've studied the thing minutely, even to the way they cut their hair. A customer up in Ullapool tells me it's a' in the way ye carry your hat in your hand goin' up the aisle; if ye happen to carry it upside down you're seen to be a slider,[3] and they fence the tables[4] against ye at the next Communion, so ye have to join the other body."

"The worst of it with me," said Mr Boyd, "is that there's

no' another body in the town I could take up wi' and respect myself. But I'm done wi' Cameron! He wants an organ and a lectern. It would suit him better if he stuck to the fundamentals."

"What exactly's that?" asked Jimmy gravely, fastening a strap.

Mr Boyd was content to wave his hands in the manner which indicates that words are quite inadequate to express ideas. "It's a bonny-like thing," said he, "that I have to go to Glasgow for Communion Sunday! I certainly will not go to the table under Cameron! Could you recommend a sound UF in Glasgow, Mr Swan? I'll take my wife and family."

"Cameron?" said Jimmy, turning something over in his mind. "The best kirk I can recommend's my ain, though ye'll have to thole the organ."

"I don't care!" said Mr Boyd, as he took a note of it. "Anything at all to get awa' from Cameron!"

Two weeks later all the family of Boyd came back from Glasgow looking rather downed. They had been to the Communion.

"What way did ye get on?" a customer asked the draper on the day that followed their return.

"I didna get on at all!" said Mr Boyd disgustedly. "A fair take-in! It cost us £2. 10s. to go the week-end to Glasgow, and we a' went to the kirk that Swan the traveller recommended. There we were sittin' expectin' a rousin' sermon from the Rev. Walter Spiers, and sure o' havin' the fundamentals. When the bell stopped ringin', I heard a skliff o' feet from the vestry that struck me as familiar, and when I looked up to see who the beadle was snibbin' in the pulpit, who was this but Cameron!"

## 23. *Linoleum*

MR JAMES Swan has lived for fifteen years in Ibrox.[1] For the
first six months he thought it horrible, and ever since he
has vexed himself to think how foolish he was not to have
gone there sooner. That is life. Men are like pot plants.
You shift a geranium into a new pot, and for weeks it wilts
disconsolate, till some fine sunny day it seems to realise
that other geraniums seem happy enough in the same sort
of pots, and that it isn't the pot that matters really. Where-
upon the geranium (which is actually a pelargonium)
strikes fresh roots into the soil, spreads out a broader leaf,
throws out a couple of blossoms, and delights in making
the best of it. It takes the first prize at the local flower show;
content is the best fertiliser. Jimmy Swan, after fifteen
years at Ibrox, thinks Ibrox is the centre of the solar
system. Take him to Langside or Partickhill, and he feels
chilly; at Dennistoun he feels himself a foreigner, and
looks at passing tramcars for the Southside as an exile from
Scotland, haunting the quays of Melbourne, looks at ships
from the Clyde with the names of Denny or Fairfield on
their brasses. Jimmy said to me the other day, "I canna
think how people can live onywhere else than Ibrox. It's
the best place in the world." "How?" I asked. "Well," said
he, "it's—it's—it's—it's Ibrox!" A little inconclusive, but I
quite understood. Nine-tenths of us have our Ibrox; the
people to be sympathised with are those who haven't.

But Jimmy got an awful start the other day! He came
home from the North journey on a Saturday very tired,
and exceedingly glad to see the familiar streets of Ibrox
again. Nothing had changed; the same ham was in the
grocery window, apparently only a slice the less, and he
had exactly the high tea he expected, but his wife was
different. She plainly nursed some secret discontent. Quite
nice, and interested in his journey, and all that, but still —

It turned out to be the linoleum. The lobby linoleum.
She put it to Jimmy if a lobby linoleum seven years old

could honestly be regarded as quite decent.

"Tuts! there's naething wrang wi' the linoleum," said her husband. "As nice a linoleum as anybody need ask for; I never tripped on't yet."

"The pattern's worn off half of it," said his wife; "Mrs Grant was in to-day, and I was black affronted. In her new house in Sibbald Terrace² they have Persia rugs."

"Kirkcaldy's³ good enough for us," said Jimmy; "Just you wait for a year or twa and ye'll see the fine new linoleum I'll get ye."

It was then that the shock came. Mrs Swan, having brooded for a while on the remoteness of a new linoleum, intimated with a calm that was almost inhuman that she had been looking at some of the houses to let in Sibbald Terrace. Their present house had become no longer possible. It had all the vices conceivable in any house built of human hands, and several others peculiar to itself, and evidently of their nature demoniac. It was cold, it was draughty, it was damp, it was dismal. Its chimneys did not draw properly; its doors were in the wrong places; its kitchen range was a heartbreak; its presses were inadequate, — she took ten minutes to expose all its inherent defects as a dwelling, and left her astonished listener in the feeling that he had been living for fifteen years in an orange-box without knowing it.

"We'll have to flit!" she said at last, determinedly.

"Sibbald Terrace is no' in Ibrox!" said her husband, astonished at her apparent overlook of this vital consideration.

"All the better o' that!" said the amazing woman. "I'm sick o' Ibrox! You can say what you like, James Swan; I'll no' stay another year in this hoose."

"Ye're fair fagged oot, Bella," said her husband, compassionately. "I doubt ye have been washin', efter all I told ye. Ye should stay in your bed the morn, and never mind the kirk. Sick o' Ibrox? Ye shouldna say things like that even in fun!"

It was at this stage, or a few days after it, I met Mr Swan. He was chuckling broadly to himself. "Did you ever flit?" he asked me.

"Once," I said.

"That's enough for a lifetime," said he. "Men would never flit any mair than they would change their sox if it wasna for their wives. The advantage o' an auld hoose is that ye aye ken where your pipe is. My wife took a great fancy to flit the other day, and I said it was a' right; that I would look oot for a new house. At the end o' three days I said I had a fair clinker — vestibule wi' cathedral glass in the doors, oriel windows in the parlour, fifteen by eight lobby, venetian blinds, bathroom h. and c., wash-hand basin, electric light, tiled close, and only five stairs up.

"She says, 'Do ye think I'm daft? Five stairs! Is it in the Municipal Buildin's?'

"'No,' says I; 'it's in Dalwhinnie Street.'

"'Where in a' the earth is Dalwhinnie Street?' says she.

"'It's a new street,' I said, 'near Ruchill. Ye take the car from aboot the foot o' Mitchell Street, come off at an apothecary's shop, and take the first turn to the right and ask a message-boy.'

"'I'll not go to any such street, James Swan!' she says; 'I would rather take a place!' And the dear lass was a' trimblin' wi' agitation."

"No wonder, Mr Swan," I said. "It sounded a very out-of-the-way locality. Where is Dalwhinnie Street?"

"There's no such street,"said Mr Swan; "At least if there is, I never heard o't. But ye see I wanted to put her aff the notion o' flittin'. And there was Bella, almost greetin'! I let on I was fair set on Dalwhinnie Street because it was so handy for the Northern Merchants' Social Club. But Dalwhinnie Street, right or wrong, she would not hear tell o', and I said I would take another look round."

Mr Swan cocked his head a little and looked slyly at me. "Ye're a married man, yoursel'," said he. "Ye know what wives are. They're no' such intellectual giants as we are, thank God! or else they would find us oot; but once they've set their minds on a thing, Napoleon himself couldna shift them. Some days after that I cam' hame from Renfrewshire wi' a great scheme for takin' a house in the country. I said I had seen the very house for us — half-way between Houston and Bridge-of-Weir."

"Whereabouts is Houston?' says the mistress in frigid tones, as they say in the novels.

"'It's half-way between the Caledonian and G and S-W lines,' says I, ' and if ye're in a hurry ye take a 'bus if it's there.'

"'What sort o' house is it?' she asked, turnin' the heel o' a stockin' as fast as lightning.

"'Tip-top!' I says. 'Nine rooms and a kitchen; fine flagged floor in the kitchen; spring water frae the pump in the garden; two-stall stable. Any amount o' room for hens; ye can keep hunders o' hens. The grocer's van passes the door every Thursday.'

"She began to greet. 'That's right!' she says. 'Put me awa' in the wilds among hens, so that I'll die, and ye'll can marry a young yin. But mind you this, James Swan; I'll no' shift a step oot o' Ibrox!'

"'Tuts, Bella!' I says, 'ye canna stay ony langer in this house; it's a' wrang thegither.'

"'There's naething wrang wi' the hoose,' says she, 'if I had jist some fresh linoleum.'

"'Well, well,' says I; ' ye'll get the linoleum' — and I was much relieved. 'I'll buy't to-morrow.' And I did. It cost me 4s. 6d. a yard."

"Your wife is a very clever lady, Mr Swan," I said; "She probably never thought of flitting, but badly wanted that linoleum."

"Of course!" said Jimmy Swan. "I kent that a' alang! But ye've got to compromise!"

## 24. *The Grauvat*[1] *King*

MOST PEOPLE — even in the dry-goods trade — think the Muffler that made Mildrynie Famous, and that great woollen factory which gives employment to thousands of people in Mildrynie, and has in ten years made a fortune

for the Drummonds, owed their conception wholly to
Peter Drummond. A great mistake! Peter Drummond, of
himself, never had any imagination, initiative, or enter-
prise; till this day (between ourselves) he is a pretty poor
fly, and his great national reputation as the Muffler King,
his grand Deeside estate, his superb collection of Old
Masters, his deputy-lieutenantship, and the marriage of
his daughter Cissy to Lord 'Tivitty' Beauchamp, are due
under Providence to Mr James Swan, traveller for the
Glasgow firm of Campbell & Macdonald. There is a marble timepiece of the most ponderous and depressing character in Mr Swan's parlour, with an inscription on it which
marks an epoch in the history of industrial Scotland. It
says —

To JAMES SWAN, Esq.,

FROM

HIS FAITHFUL FRIEND

PETER DRUMMOND.

*3 JUNE 1903.*

———

*"Lest we forget."*

The clock doesn't go; it hasn't gone for years; it is
merely a domestic monument — of ingratitude.

Peter Drummond, in 1903, was a customer of Jimmy
Swan's in Mildrynie. He and his brother Alick (now
Alexander Lloyd Drummond, Esq. of Ballochmawn) had
a tiny draper's shop in East Street, next door to a smiddy
which seemed to do nothing else from one end of the year
till the other but singe sheep's heads[2] for the inhabitants of
Mildrynie, who at that time numbered eight hundred souls
and two policemen.

One day Jimmy Swan turned up at the door with his
sample cases, and found the brothers much depressed.
They were doing wretched business. Their shop was off
the main street; the propinquity of the smiddy and its
perpetual odour of singed wool made the shopping public
avoid it; things were come to such a pass that the

Drummonds were contemplating closing up and going off to Canada.

"There's naething to be done in this hole o' a place," said Peter, who spoke Scotch in these days.

"There's plenty to be done in ony place if you're the kind o' man to do it," said Jimmy. "Mildrynie's no' much size; I've seen it missed a'thegither oot o' the maps; but for a' that it's a wonderful place, for it's fair in the middle o' the world. If it's a hole, as ye say, it's a hole to be respected, for it's like a hole in the middle o' a grindstane."

"Nonsense!" said Peter Drummond. "Aff the railway line, away up here in the North; it's oot o' the world a'thegither."

"Fair in the middle!" insisted Mr Swan. "Look you at a globe or a map o' the world, and ye'll see I'm richt. Every other place in the world's grouped roond aboot Mildrynie, just the same as if God had meant it to be great."

"Maybe that's so!" conceded Mr Drummond on reflection, "but my shop's no' in the middle o' Mildrynie, and so I whiles think I micht as weel ha'e my signboard up at the North Pole. That's the middle o' the world too."

"What do ye dae to attract customers?" asked Jimmy, adjusting his carnation.

"Just what everybody else does that keeps a shop," said Peter Drummond.

"Error No. 1," said Jimmy. "The way to attract customers is to dae what naebody else is daein'. That's where the profit as well as the fun comes in. I would get sick-tired daein' the same as everybody else; the only excuse ye have for bein' alive is that ye dae some things peculiarly in your own way."

"I carry a good stock, and I show everything at a reasonable price," said Peter Drummond.

"Error No. 2," said Jimmy, blandly. "Ye should start sellin' something at a quite unreasonable price."

"What dae ye mean?" asked Mr Drummond.

"Sell it at what it costs ye. Here's a new line I have in woollen mufflers, as cosy as a fur-lined coat, and fastens wi' a snap. They'll cost ye half-a-croon each from C & M, and that's even coontin' aff the discoont. The winter's comin' on; you make a splash wi' the Mildrynie Muffler at half-a-croon, and ye'll get the folk to your shop, for naebody else sells them for less than three shillings. Once ye have the folk buying your mufflers at cost price, it'll be gey droll if ye canna sell them other things at a reasonable profit."

"There's something in't!" said Peter Drummond.

On the next journey Mr Swan made to Mildrynie, he found that the half-crown muffler had moved the business slightly, but not enough to lift the spirits of the brothers Drummond. Their unpopular location and the smell of the smiddy were against a really popular and fashionable success.

"Do ye advertise?" asked Jimmy.

"No," said Peter; "naebody advertises here."

"My goodness! that's the very chance for you then!" exclaimed Mr Swan eagerly. "Chip in first before the others think o't. Advertise in the county paper — 'The Real and Original Mildrynie Muffler'; ye'll sell them like Forfar Rock!"

"But if naebody's wantin' mufflers?" said Peter, sadly.

"Naebody was wantin' Beecham's pills a hundred years ago, and noo they canna dae withoot them. Look at the way that soap's come into fashion, even in the country districts — a' the result o' advertisin'."

"It's the smell o' the smiddy next door that spoils this street," said Mr Drummond.

"Error No. 4642!" said Jimmy. "The smiddy 'll be a godsend if ye'll dae what I'm gaun to tell ye. Put you this advertisement in the local paper." — and he quickly drafted it out on a sheet of wrapping-paper —

THE MARVELLOUS MILDRYNIE MUFFLER,
ONLY HALF-A-CROWN.
DRUMMOND'S SHOP, 3 EAST STREET.
*Follow your Nose and the Smell of Sheep's Head Singeing.*

"I never saw an advertisement like that in a' my life," said Peter Drummond.

"Exactly!" said Jimmy. "That's the sort o' advertisement to advertise when ye're advertisin'."

On his next journey he found the Drummond business booming, and got an incredibly large order for Mildrynie mufflers at a price that left a reasonable profit for the retailer. But Peter was still a little depressed.

"There's money in't sure enough," said he; "but they ca' me the Grauvat King, and I don't like it."

"Nonsense!" said Jimmy. "It's just as fine to be the Grauvat King as the Oil King, or the Diamond King, or the Cattle King; it's a' the same to you so lang's ye get them on the neck. If you're the Grauvat King in Forfarshire, it's a' the easier for ye to be Muffler Monarch to the country at large. The Mildrynie Muffler's good enough to stand pushing just as far as Hielan' Whisky; you get a pickle money thegither and advertise the Rale and Original Mildrynie Half-croon Muffler in a' the papers in the country, and ye'll mak' a fortune. Tell them the Mildrynie Muffler's made aff pure hygienic wool that's grown on high-pedigree Hielan' sheep that graze on the heathery slopes o' the Grampian Mountains, the land where the eagle soars and the cataract flashes; that it's manufactured in the cottage homes o' the God-fearin', clean, and industrious native peasantry, and is recognised by the faculty as the one garment responsible for the sturdy health and universal longevity o' the Scottish race, and C & M'll keep ye supplied wi' a' ye want; there's plenty o' mills in bonny wee Gleska."

It was in recognition of this valuable tip that Peter Drummond, a twelvemonth later, gave Mr Swan the timepiece — a poor solatium to Mr Swan for his loss of Drummonds' muffler trade when they opened the enormous works of their own at Mildrynie.

## 25. *Jimmy's Sins Find Him Out*

MR JAMES Swan picked up a bunch of violets, which he had been refreshing in a tumbler while he wrote out his expenses for the week, and placed it in his buttonhole. From a pocket he took a small case-comb, and, borrowing from Pratt, the office 'knut', the little mirror which Pratt kept always in his desk to consult as often as the Ready Reckoner, he went to the window and combed his hair.

"What side are sheds worn on this season?" he asked Pratt, whom it was the joke of the office to treat with mock deference as arbiter of fashion, expert, and authority upon every giddy new twirl of the world of elegance.

"To the left," said Pratt, without a moment's hesitation, and with the utmost solemnity; the parting of his own hair was notoriously a matter of prayerful consideration. He was a lank lad with a long neck; it looked as if his Adam's apple was a green one and was shining through — a verdant phenomenon due to the fact that he had used the same brass stud for three years.

"Can't be done on the left," said Mr Swan. "That's the side I do my thinkin' on, and it's worn quite thin. I envy ye your head o' hair, Pratt; it'll last ye a life-time, no' like mine."

Pratt, with the mirror restored to him, put it back in his desk with a final glance at it to see that his necktie was as perfectly knotted as it was three minutes ago; put on his hat and bolted from the office.

"They're a' in a great hurry to be off the day," said Mr Swan to himself. "I wonder what they're up to?"

He was to find out in two minutes, to his own discomfiture.

At the foot of the stair which led to the upper warehouse he ran against Peter Grant of Aberdeen, who was in search of him.

"My jove!" said Grant, panting; "I'm in luck! I was sure ye would be awa' to't, and I ran doon the street like to break my legs."

"De-lighted to see ye, Mr Grant!" said Jimmy with a radiant visage. "This is indeed a pleasant surprise! But ye don't mean to tell me ye came from Aberdeen this mornin'?"

"Left at a quarter to seven," said Grant. "I made up my mind last night to come and see it. And I says to mysel', ' If I can just catch Mr Swan before he goes to the field, the thing's velvet!'"

"De-lighted!" said Jimmy, and shook his hand again. But the feeling of icy despair in his breast was enough to wilt his violets.

His sin had found him out! There was only one inference to be drawn from Peter Grant's excited appearance; he had carried out the threat of a dozen years to come and see a Glasgow football match, and expected the expert company and guidance of C & M's commercial traveller.

And Jimmy Swan had, so far as Grant was concerned, a reputation for football knowledge and enthusiasm it was impossible to justify in Glasgow, however plausible they seemed in a shop in Aberdeen. Grant, who had never seen a football match in his life, was a fanatic in his devotion to a game which for twenty years he followed in the newspapers. Jimmy in his first journeys to Aberdeen had discovered this fancy of his customer, and played up to it craftily with the aid of the 'Scottish Referee',[1] which he bought on each journey North for no other purpose, since he himself had never seen a football match since the last cap of Harry McNeill[2] of the 'Queen's',[3] in 1881.

The appalling ignorance of Jimmy regarding modern football, and his blank indifference to the same, were never suspected by his customer, who from the traveller's breezy and familiar comments upon matches scrappily read about an hour before, credited him with knowing all there was to know about the national pastime.

When Jimmy was in doubt about the next move in a conversation with Grant, he always mentioned Quinn, and called him 'good old Jimmy'. He let it be understood that the Saturday afternoons when he couldn't get to Ibrox were unhappy — which was perfectly true, since he lived in

Ibrox, though the Rangers' park was a place he never went near.

"I'll go and see a match some day!" Grant always said; he had said it for many years, and Jimmy always said, "Mind and let me know when ye're comin', and I'll show ye fitba'."

And now he was taken at his word!

What particular match could Grant have come for? Jimmy had lost sight of football, even in the papers, for the past three months.

With an inward sigh for a dinner spoiled at home, he took his customer to a restaurant for lunch.

"I want to see McMenemy,"[4] said Grant; "it was that that brought me; he's a clinker!"

"And he never was in better form," said Jimmy. "Playin' like a book! He says to me last Monday, 'We'll walk over them the same's we had a brass band in front of us, Mr Swan!'"

"Will they win, do ye think?" Grant asked with great anxiety; he was so keen, the lunch was thrown away on him.

"Win!" said Jimmy. "Hands down! The — the — the other chaps is shakin' in their shoes."

So far he moved in darkness. Who McMenemy was, and what match he was playing in that day, he had not the faintest idea, and he played for safety. It was probably some important match. The state of the streets as they had walked along to the restaurant suggested a great influx of young men visitors; it might be something at Celtic Park.

He looked at Grant's square-topped hat and had an inspiration.

"If ye'll take my advice, Mr Grant," said he, "ye'll go and buy a kep. A hat like that's no use at a Gleska fitba' match; ye need a hooker. If ye wear a square-topped hat it jist provokes them. I'm gaun round to the warehouse to change my ain hat for a bunnet; I'll leave ye in a hat shop on the road and then I'll jine ye."

"What fitba' match is on the day?" Jimmy asked a porter in the warehouse.

"Good Goad!" said the porter with amazement at him. "It's the International[5] against England."

"Where is it played?" asked Jimmy.

"Hampden, of course!"

"What way do ye get to't, and when does it start?"

"Red car to Mount Florida;[6] game starts at three; I wish to goodness I could get to't," said the porter.

Jimmy looked his watch. It was half-past one.

He found Grant with a headgear appropriate to the occasion, and wasted twenty minutes in depositing his hat at Buchanan Street left-luggage office. Another twenty minutes passed at the station bar, where Jimmy now discoursed with confidence on Scotland's chances, having bought an evening paper.

"Will ye no' need to hurry oot to the park?" Grant asked with some anxiety.[7] "There'll be an awfu' crood; twenty chaps wi' bunnets came on at Steenhive."[7]

"Lot's of time!" said Jimmy with assurance. "We'll tak' a car. Come awa', and I'll show ye a picture-palace."

It was fifteen minutes to three when they got to Hampden. A boiling mass of frantic people clamoured round the gates, which were shut against all further entrance, to the inner joy of Mr Swan, who lost his friend in the crowd and failed to find him.

"Where on earth were you till this time?" asked his wife when he got home to Ibrox two hours later.

"Out in the Queen's Park," said Jimmy truthfully.

"Wi' luck I lost a man outside a fitba' match, and spent an hour in Camphill — no' a soul in't but mysel' — listenin' to the birds whistlin'."

## 26. *A Wave of Temperance*

ONE DAY last week an hotel in Falkirk had six commercial travellers from Glasgow in its commercial room at dinner, the president and *doyen* of them Jimmy Swan, who unfeelingly depressed the company by drinking ginger ale. It was not so much his choice of this unorthodox beverage that saddened them as his evident enjoyment of it; he lingered over it, and smacked his lips upon it, and cocked his eye to look through the bubbling glass as if it were Clicquot, 1904. The others suddenly realised that this ostentatious gusto carried some reproach on their preference for bitter beer — so they defiantly ordered in another pewter each.

"You should try sour milk, Mr Swan," said that hardened satirist, Joe McGuire, the boot man; "It's said to be full o' the finest germs. If you drink sour dook you'll live to the age o' a hundred and fifty, and you'll well deserve it."

"Ginger," said flour man Wallace, "is all right in its own place. One time, I mind, I tried it — at the funeral o' an uncle o' mine who was a Rechabite; and I can tell you that so far as I was concerned that day he was sincerely mourned."

Jimmy Swan smiled blandly, and squinted again through his tumbler.

"Clean, wholesome, morally stimulatin', warmth-provokin', thirst-assuagin' — the nectar o' the gods!" he said with the eloquence of an advertisement. "What's good enough for the King and Kitchener[1] is good enough for me. You chaps should give it a trial; it would save ye a lot o' money in aromatic lozengers."

Five minutes after, the Crown Hotel commercial room was a debating club, with temperance and prohibition for its subjects. Mr Swan had by far the best of the argument, since none of the rest could agree upon what constituted the particular virtues or charm of alcohol, though they were unanimous in declaring their line of business made a judicious use of it absolutely indispensable.

"I've taken up that line mysel' in my unregenerate days — and that was up to a week ago," said Jimmy; "but to tell the truth, I took a dram because I liked it; my other reasons were a' palaver."

"But human geniality," said Peter Garvie (lubricating

oils), who was reputed on the road to have as little geniality as a haddock; "It wants a glass o' something stronger than ginger ale to bring men together. You couldna show your friendliness to a man unless you bought him a glass o' something."

"Ye could buy him a pair o' gallowses," suggested Jimmy, and saying so, he finished the last of his ginger ale hurriedly, and put down the glass with a bang. He had an inspiration.

A little later, six quite rational representatives of well-known wholesale Glasgow houses were, incredible though it may seem, in a solemn pact to suspend the ancient treating customs of their country for a week, eschew all the alcoholic beverages, and maintain 'the genial flow', as Jimmy called it, on a system more likely to benefit the sale of the goods they travelled in than standing rounds of beer or whisky-and-soda.

Two hours later McGuire met Jimmy in the High Street, beaming with satisfaction at a well-filled book of orders; his own success that day left no excuse for grumbling.

"It's a raw, cold day," said Jimmy, rubbing his hands. "Have ye any good in your mind?"

"I don't mind if I do," said McGuire, and absent-mindedly was making for the Blue Bell hostelry.

"Na! na!" said Jimmy. "Mind the pledge; there's nae-thing 'll cross my lips but a threepenny cheroot."

They went into a tobacconist's, and their cheroots were hardly lighted when Jimmy said, 'Hurry up and we'll hae another."

"No fears!" said the boot man firmly. "I never smoked two cigars a day in my life except on Sunday and I wouldna smoke this one noo if it hadna cost me threepence."

"Do ye feel the genial flow yet?" asked Jimmy, as they walked along the street.

"Not a bit!" said McGuire. "It's more like burned broon paper."

Jimmy chucked away his cigar and led him into a baker's shop.

"Two London buns, miss," said he, "the best, on draught"; leaned one arm elegantly on the counter; said, "Well, here's to us!" and ate his bun with a fair pretence at relish. McGuire, who was renowned for being able to eat anything at any time, was finished before him.

"Hurry up, Jimmy!" he said. "We'll jist have another one, for the good o' the house."

"All right!" said Jimmy. "Make it a small one this time, miss. No! I'll tell ye what — I'll split a parley[2] this time, Joe; I feel that bun in my heid already."

Wallace came round the corner just as they were leaving the baker's shop.

"Ye're just in time!" said Jimmy. "An hour till the train goes and we're on the batter." He was munching the last of the parley he had shared with McGuire, and Wallace dropped to the situation.

"What's it goin' to be?" he asked with something less than the usual convivial abandon expected with the question.

"They're no' half fly wi' their drapery shops in Fa'kirk," said Jimmy, twinkling. "They should ha'e a back-door to them. Slip in to this yin," and he led them into the premises of one of his oldest customers.

"Back again, ye see, Mr Ross," he said to the draper. "It's somebody's birthday, and we're on the fair ran-dan. What are ye goin' to have, gentlemen?"

"My shout!" said Wallace. "Give it a name."

"I think I'll just have a small pocket-hankey this time," said McGuire, and Jimmy Swan agreed that a pocket-hankey was the very thing he was thinking of having himself.

"We'll just have another!" he said when they had got them. "Just one more hankey 'll no' do ye a bit o' harm. I'm feelin' fine! A nasty raw cold day — ye need a hankey to cheer ye up."

McGuire, who pretended to be looking all round the floor for a spittoon, declared he couldn't find room for another handkerchief, but could be doing with a 16 collar.

"Collars all round let it be," said Jimmy; "We'll just make a night of it. But mind ye, McGuire, you're no' to start the singin'! When it comes to collars, I'm aye prood to say I can either take them or leave them. I'm no' one o' these chaps that's nip-nip-nippin awa' at collars a' day — the ruination o' the constitution and the breakin'-up o' mony a happy home. Three White Horse collars, Mr Ross, and what'll ye tak yoursel'?"

Mr Ross was a pawky gentleman himself, and had heard of the commercials' compact from the traveller earlier in the day. He turned his back on them, having put forth the collars, and scrutinised the shelves behind him with profound shrewdness.

"At this time o' day I never touch a collar," he remarked. "It doesna agree wi' me before my tea. I think, if you'll allow me, seeing it's so cold a day, I'll just have a Cardigan waistcoat, Mr Swan," and he pulled down a box of those garments.

## 27. *Country Journeys*

As THE train pulled out of Buchanan Street Station, Slymon, the tea man, drew off a fur-lined glove and put his hand inquiringly upon the foot-warmer.

"Feel that, Mr Swan!" he remarked, indignantly, and Jimmy did so.

"It's aff the bile, at any rate," he intimated cheerfully. "Or perhaps it's a new patent kind, like one of those Thermos flasks[1] my wife got a present of at Christmas, guaranteed to keep the heat for four-and-twenty hours. She wrapped it up in flannel, put it in the bed, and was awfully disappointed. 'Is that your feet?' she asked me at two o'clock in the morning. 'It is not,' says I. 'Then the shop that sold John Grant that bottle swindled him; it's an ice-cream freezer,' says the mistress.'

"A railway foot-warmer filled with liquid gas is no use to me," proceeded the indignant Slymon, and for the next ten minutes he said things about The True Line[2] which would have much distressed the directors of the Caledonian Railway had they been there to hear them.

Jimmy merely buttoned his coat a little tighter, tucked his rug more carefully round his legs, and looked compassionately upon his fellow-traveller.

"Man, Slymon," he remarked at last, "if you get so warm as that about the shortcomings of the Caley and every other system you'll work yourself into a perspiration that'll open all your pores, and get your death of cold when you go out at Larbert. It's your feet that's wrong to start with. Either your boots are tight or you're wearing the wrong kind of sox, or there's something up with your circulation. Thirty years ago the railways wouldn't even pretend to give us hot-water pans, and nobody in our line died of cold feet yet that I ever heard of."

"Travelling becomes more uncomfortable every year," said Slymon, irritably, and Jimmy snorted.

"Look here, Slymon!" he said. "You're making me feel old, and I don't like it. If you say travelling becomes more uncomfortable every year, I must be getting blind, or you must be thirty years younger than me, and I don't believe it. Here you are in a padded carriage — Third Class — fifty per cent better than the First we used to use in the days before the Firm took on Macauslane for a managing director. There's an electric light you can read your paper by without losing the sight of an eye, a thing you always risked when even Firsts were lit by oil. Here's an air-tight window that doesn't rattle, and a ventilator that works; here's a bogey carriage running so smoothly that you could drink a cup o' tea — if you thought of it — without spilling a drop, and in the old days you couldn't take a tot from the bottom of a flask, but had to bite on the neck of it, and drink between the dunts."

"Oh, I daresay things have a bit improved in your time," said Slymon, cooling down; "but even now they might be better."

"We might be better ourselves," said Jimmy Swan. "It's

a conviction of that kind that keeps me from kicking a lot of folk I meet.

"If you ask me," continued Jimmy, lighting his pipe, "there was far more fun on the road before cold feet came into fashion, and when the only kind of draught that did any harm was the kind you got in tumblers."

"Youth," suggested Mr Slymon, and Jimmy for a moment meditated.

"Ay, perhaps you're right," he said. "I sometimes envy the chaps that have it, and then again I'm vexed for them, knowing they'll never understand till it's bye what a jolly good thing it was. And whiles, again, I wonder if Youth in itself is ever half so fine as it's cracked up to be; it's maybe only nice to an old man's eye because it's out of reach. The young that have it, anyway, make an awful hash wi't. I did, myself. ... But all that has nothing to do with what we started out on — travelling.

"I've been on the road since the year the women wore the Dolly Vardens — d'ye mind the song? —

Come, dear, don't fear, let your ringlets curl,
If you're out of fashion, you better leave the world,
Your sweet and pretty face will wear a winning smile,
If you buy a hat and feather in the Dolly Varden style.

"Half my journeys then were made on gigs and wagonettes; none of your hot-water bottles and hairstuffed seats! And I tell you, my feet never got time to get cold. If it wasn't gigs, and taking the reins myself for half the journey because the postboy had been out all night at a kirn[3] or a coffining, it was cargo boats that started at six o'clock in the morning, and the first bell would be ringing before the Boots chapped at my door.

"I see chaps noo gaun aboot on bicycles wi' a sample box o' biscuits strapped behind," continued Jimmy, lapsing into the vernacular as his feelings warmed.

"They call themsel's Commercials, just like the rest o' us. I'm vexed for the chaps, do ye know; I never can see ony hope for them bein' comfortably married. It's the same wi' tea."

"Tea's done!" confessed Mr Slymon, lugubriously. "Between you and me. Everybody's selling it. I know ironmongers handling Cooper's packages. There's wholesale people going among the farmers selling 20 lb tins at what they call a wholesale rate, and never going near a grocer. I would sooner be on the road for specs or railway tunnels. Blended tea! — that's the wheeze! 'Fine silky liquor. ... Good body. ... Rich Darjeeling flavour. ... Soupcon of Pekoe gives it character ...' "

"I know," said Jimmy, sympathetically. "Worse than horse-cowpin'! The ordinary man kens nae mair aboot tea than I ken aboot shortbreid. And ye canna wonder at it; tea at the best's a skiddlin' thing ye tak' to wash doon breid and butter. The honestest thing ever I saw said aboot tea was in a grocer's window in Inverness — 'Our Unapproachable; 2s. 6d.'"

"Sooner be in specs, or railway tunnels," repeated Slymon, sadly.

"I see you're no' very keen on a line wi' a lot o' heavy cases, onyway," said Jimmy. "Noo, I wadna care to be without my cases. It's the stuff that talks! Stick it in their e'e! When I put oot my stuff in a wee bit shop in Grantown it makes it look like a bargain day in Sauchiehall Street, and the shopkeeper feels awfu' lonely and sees his place infernal bare when I pack up the traps again. So doon he claps his bonny wee order! ... The only thing that would gie me cauld feet would be travellin' withoot my cases. There's a moral weight in them as weel as avoirdupois. Man, on the quays and at the railway stations the porters ken them. 'That's C & M's,' they say — 'Auld Swan.' And when they're oot in the straun in front of a country shop, it's jist like a swatch o' Buchanan Street.

"I'll admit there's whiles when they're a nuisance, and that puts me in mind o' a time in the North when I got cauld feet richt enough.

"I had just got ower three weeks' rest at Christmas and New Year, a time I always used for packin' and postin' kind reminders to my customers. There was nae Secret

Commission Act then, and I tell ye I was a connoisseur at geese and turkeys, and the genuine F & F currant bun. I sent them by the score. I sent a hundred and twenty 'Chatterboxes'[4] every year to the children o' the drapery trade in the West o' Scotland. All I needed to be Santa Claus was a reindeer. Macauslane put an end to that; he found oot that the maist o' the weans that got the books belanged to customers a bit behind in the ledger.

"I got up to Golspie on a Hansel Monday,[5] did my business there in an 'oor or twa, and then ordered a machine for Brora. I couldna even get a barrow! Some minister was being inducted down at Dornoch, and every dacent trap in the place was aff to Dornoch wi' an elder.

"'We could run ye up wi' a shandry-dan,'[6] says the innkeeper, 'but then it wouldna haud your cases.'

"'I needna go to Brora wantin' cases,' says I. 'Shairly ye can dae something, Peter?'

"'There's naething in the yaird that would haud your cases except the hearse,' says Peter.

"'Well, oot wi' the hearse!' says I, and less than twenty meenutes efter I was on the road to Dornoch, sittin' beside the driver on a hearse, and the latest lines in C & M's Spring goods inside it. My jove, but it was cauld! We drove richt up to the shop o' auld Mr Sutherland. Doon I draps frae the dickey o' the hearse, and in I goes wi' a face like a fiddler, and asks for a yaird o' crape.

"'Dear me! Mr Swan, wha are ye buryin' the day?' says Mr Sutherland.

"'We're buryin' Annie,' says I.

"'Whatna Annie?' says Mr Sutherland.

"'Animosity,' says I — ony auld baur'll pass in Brora — and he laughed like a young yin, though I must alloo he yoked on me later for what he ca'd my sacrilege.

"It was the first and only time, sae far, I traivelled on a hearse, and I tell ye my feet were cauld!"

## 28. *Raising the Wind*

MR SWAN had the counter of Cameron's shop piled high
with the new season's samples of corsets, lingerie, hose,
lace, ribbons, and dress material. He handled them,
himself, as if they had been flowers — delicately, lovingly,
caressingly, and called attention to their qualities in the
ecstatic tones a dealer in pictorial art would use with a
customer for Raphaels. Cameron, on the other hand — a
rough, bluff, quite undraperish-looking man, who had
been a baker until he came to Perth from Glasgow twenty
years ago and married his cousin and her shop, had plainly
no artistic pleasure in the stuff displayed by the commercial traveller; he flung it about on the counter as if it had
been dough. It made the traveller squirm to see him.

"Bright colours, rich effects," said Jimmy; "that's the
season's note. Look at this cerise and tango — it makes ye
think o' a fine spring day and the birds whistling. It'll make
up beautiful!" He tossed it tenderly into billowy folds,
which showed in it the most entrancing shadows, aurifer-
ous glints, and the flush of cherries. "This stuff in stripes
(we call it 'peau-depeche' from the man that thought o't
first; he was a Frenchman) — it's the finest tailorin' stuff
I've ever handled, goin' to be a' the go when the King
comes to the Clyde."[1]

"Is he comin'?" Cameron asked with sudden interest.

"In July," said Jimmy. "There's a rush on flags already
oot at Coatbridge. It's goin' to be a drapery summer, I can
tell ye! Ye'll feel it even up in Perth."

And Cameron sighed.

"Na," said he; "we'll no' feel't in Perth. We never feel
onything here but cattle shows. We just kind o' driddle on
frae yin year's end to the ither, and read about splendid
things in the papers. I never see ye strappin' up your boxes,
Mr Swan, but I wish ye would strap me up wi' them and
take me back wi' ye to Gleska."

Cameron, in twenty years, since he had left St Mungo,[2]

had never returned to it even on the shortest visit. He spoke of it now with a sentimental air, and expressed a firm intention to go down and see the gaieties of July.

"I'll see a lot o' changes on Gleska," he said. "Twenty years! It looks like a lifetime ! What would ye say yoursel', Mr Swan, was changed the most in Gleska in twenty years?"

Jimmy puckered up his brows and chewed a pencil, lost in thought.

"Well," said he, "there's the picture-palaces, where ye can get everything now except a dram and a bed for the night — they'll be new to ye. And then there's the Central Station;³ ye've never seen the Central since they altered it, have ye?"

"No," said Cameron sadly. "What's it like, noo?"

"Oh, it's beyond words!" said Jimmy, rolling ribbons up. "Ye could put the whole o' the folk in Perth between the bookstalls, and they would just look like a fitba' team. It's got the biggest, brawest, nameliest lavatory in Europe, doon a stair, where ye can get your hair cut, and a bath for sixpence. Lots o' men go down for baths and barberin', stayin' down for hours if they think their wives are lookin' for them."

Cameron laughed. "What do ye want wi' a bath in a station?" said he.

"I've kent o't bein' used for a bank," said Jimmy; "At least it served the purpose o' a bank in a way, for it got twa chaps I ken some money when they couldna get it otherwise."

"How that?" asked Cameron.

"It happened this way. Twa packers in our warehouse — Dan MacGhie and Willie Lovatt — got on the scatter a year ago at the Gleska Fair. They spent the half o' the day goin' round the town in search of the perfect schooner that was goin' to be the last, and they found their joint re-sources down to a single shilling. A shilling's a lot o' money in Gleska if it's tramway rides you're buying, but it doesna go far in the purchase o' liquid joy, and they were sore distressed. A' the banks were shut, but that didna matter;

they hadna ony money in the banks onyway. And the notion o' goin' hame at three o'clock was naturally horrible.

"Dan MacGhie's such a fool in the packin' business, ye would fancy the only way he could think o' keepin' his socks up would be to stand on his heid, but on this occasion he was pretty 'cute. 'I'll tell ye what, Willie,' said he. 'You'll hae a nice hot bath at the Central Station.'

"'What dae I want wi' a bath?' says Willie. 'I had yin a while ago.'

"'That's all right!' says Dan. 'You'll go down and have a nice wee bath to yoursel'. It'll cost ye sixpence, and ye'll take your time. Ye'll slip your coat and waistcoat oot to me. I'll go, like lightning, and put them in a fine wee pawn for a pound, and buy ye an alpaca jacket for three-and-six, and we'll have a' the odds. See? Phizz!'

"'But ye'll be sure to come back?' says Willie. 'I have no notion o' goin' out the New City Road in my galluses.'

"'Right oh!' says Dan, and Willie went down wi' him and trysted[4] a bath, and slips his coat and waistcoat oot to Dan.

"Dan takes the coat and waistcoat in an awfu' hurry down to Oswald Street, and into a nice wee pawn, and asks a pound on them. The man in the pawn ripes the pouches,[5] and says he couldna gie more than seven-and-six.

"'Seven-and-six!' says Dan. 'They belang to a landed gentleman!'

"'I don't care if they belanged to Lloyd George,' says the man in the pawn, 'seven-and-six is the value, and that's no' includin' the price o' the ticket.'

"Dan took the seven-and-odd-pence-ha'penny, after switherin' a wee, and went awa' doon the stair and along Argyle Street. He was disappointed. If he bought a lustre jacket[6] for Willie, there wasna goin' to be much left for fun. A dishonest man would have just spent the money and gone awa' hame withoot botherin' aboot Willie, but Dan MacGhie wasna a chap o' that sort; he had the true British spirit.

"He goes alang the street till he comes to a shop window where there were clocks on the instalment system. If ye paid the first instalment o' half-a-crown, ye got the nock wi' ye, the notion bein' that ye paid the other seventeen-and-six in monthly instalments. Dan goes in as bold as brass and asks to see a nock. The man produced a fair clinker, fitted up wi' an alarm that would waken ye even on a Sunday. Dan tried the alarm, and made it birl, and said he thought it would dae, although he would have preferred yin a little quicker and louder in the action. He paid down half-a-crown and signed his name and address for the rest o' the instalments, and awa' oot, like the mischief, to the Trongate.

"He went into a pawn in the Trongate and pledged the nock. 'I want fifteen shillin's on that,' says he. 'It's a Kew-tested, genuine, repeater nock, jewelled in every hole.' The pawnbroker opened it wi' a knife the same's it was an oyster, and looked inside it. 'I'll gie ten shillin's on't!' says he.

"'My mither's nock!' says Dan, and him near greetin'. 'It cost five-pound-ten the year o' the *Daphne* disaster.'[7]

"'Half-a-quid !' says the pawnbroker. 'Take it or leave it!'

"Dan took the ten shillin's; looked at the time on the pawnshop clock, and ran like a lamplighter awa' back to Oswald Street. He kent fine that Willie would be vexed waitin' in the bath a' wet.

"He goes back to the first pawn and lifted Willie's coat and waiscoat, payin' back the seven-and-six and interest.

"'Ye havena been lang!' says the pawnbroker, surprised to see him.

"'No,' says Dan; 'I forgot about a funeral I'm booked for this afternoon, and I need my coat.'

"He got Willie's coat and waistcoat, and bunks awa' up to the Central Station and doon the stairs to the lavatory, and chaps at the door.

"'Is that you, Dan?' says Willie.

"'It is,' says Dan, and slips him in his clothes.

"'My goodness!' says Willie, 'and I was gettin' cauld! I was sure ye had forgotten all aboot me! What speed did ye come?'

"'Tip-top!' says Dan. 'I started wi' sixpence, and I've three shillin's. Come on oot and we'll have a pint!'

"That's Gleska!" said Jimmy Swan. "Oh, it's changed a lot since you were there last, Mr Cameron! And now, this shell-pink moire velours, just look at the style that's in it — "

"Ye're a terrible man," said Cameron.

## 29. *Roses, Roses, All the Way*

FROM THE 1st of May till well on in October no one for years has seen James Swan in business hours without a flower in his coat lapel. Any old kind of cigar is good enough for him, though his preference runs to black Burmese cheroots that look like bits of walking-stick; but when it comes to button-holes, he is a fastidious connoisseur. If the Karl Droschki rose is ever to have a perfume, you will find that Jimmy will anticipate the florists' shops by a week or two; he likes his buttonholes large and redolent, and a scented Karl Droschki the size of a rhododendron is a joy he sometimes dreams of. In town he gets his daily flower by some arrangement with commercial friends in the neighbourhood of the Bazaar; on his business journeys he is rather unhappy anywhere out of the reach of fresh carnations, sweet peas, roses, or camelias; but even there he can make shift with a spray of lilac or of wallflower culled from vases in the coffee-rooms of the hotels.

"The button-hole is getting a bit out o' fashion," he told me recently; "but I don't mind; it will aye go very well in the coat of a middle-aged commercial gentleman with the right breadth in the chest for it. Give me a clean shave and a carnation, and I feel as cheery as a chap that earns his bread by singing. A flower in the coat goes a long way to conceal yon tired feeling in the morning; it's a kind o' moral pick-me-up."

"I fancy," said I, "that it's also not without some beneficial effect on business," and Jimmy slyly chuckled.

"You may be sure o' that!" said he. "Make your buttonhole big enough, and the business man behind it's almost lost to sight; there's wee shops yonder in the East End where they look on me and my carnations like a kind o' glimpse o' the country, where the mavie whistles and the milk comes from. They sniff as if it was the sea-breeze down at Millport — I tell you it puts a lot o' them in mind o' their mothers' gardens! Give me that kind o' country sentiment, and I'll be busy wi' my wee bit book!"

But Jimmy was not always a wearer of *boutonnières* and a connoisseur in cut flowers. Fifteen years ago, as he told me once, he would as soon have worn a wedding-ring or a Glengarry bonnet, and the only thing he knew about flowers was that certain ones were roses and the others weren't. His wife's pathetic struggles for bloom in a tiny front plot near the Paisley Road never, in these days, roused his slightest interest in horticulture. He is still inclined to regard flowers as a product best procured in shops, but his knowledge of them at the marketable age is now extensive. It began with an experience he had in Kirkcaldy.

For two years he had made the most valiant but unsuccessful efforts to get an order from a Kirkcaldy draper, who appeared to cherish the distressing delusion that he was well enough served by other wholesale firms than C & M. Mr Dimister was the hardest nut Jimmy had ever tried to crack. At any hour of the day he was called on he was always too desperately busy to look at anything, and never by any luck was he to be got with a vacancy in his stock that Mr Swan could replenish.

"Man, he was a dour yin!" Jimmy said to me, narrating the circumstances. "I don't object to a dour yin in reason, for once ye nab a dour yin he's as dour to stop ye as he was to start ye; forbye it's aye a feather in your bonnet. But Dimister was a perfect he'rt-break; he had nae mair come-and-go in him than Nelson's Monument — my jove! the baurs I wasted on that man! I got the length o' jottin' the heids o' my newest stories doon in a penny diary just to be sure o' ticklin' him wi' something fresh, but devil the haet[1] would tickle Dimister; he had nae mair sense o' humour than a jyle door. There's folk like that.

"Ye have nae idea o' the patience I showed wi' the body! I tried him on the majestic line, the same's I was sellin' peerages, and I tried him on the meek or at least as near on the meek as I could manage wi' half a ton o' cases from C & M in a couple o' barrows at the door. It was a' the same to Dimister — he had nae mair interest in me than if I was selling sheep-dip or railway sleepers. I tried him wi' kirk affairs, put oot a feeler now and then on politics, and gave him a' the grips in Masonry; but it was nae use: he just hotched on his stool, glowered ower his specs at me, and let me ken there was naething doin'. For a' that was in the cratur's business at the time, it wasna worth my while to bother wi' him; but my pride was up, and I swore I would have him, even if I had to take a gun to't.

"One day I asked the landlord o' the hotel I was puttin' up at where Dimister stayed, and went oot to look at the ootside o' his hoose. It was a nice enough bit villa, wi' a gairden fu' o' floo'ers and a great big greenhoose. A letter-carrier passin' told me Dimister was the champion rose-grower and tomato hand in Fife.

"'I have ye noo!' says I to mysel', and wired to my friend in the Bazaar to send me oot three o' the finest roses in Gleska by the first train, even if they cost a pound. They came in the aifternoon — fair champions! — I stuck them in my coat and went to call on Dimister.

"'Very sorry,' he says as usual; 'I'm not needin'' — and then his eyes fell on my button-hole. It was the first time I ever saw a gleam o' human interest in the body's face. His eyes fair goggled.

"'That's a good rose,' he says, and came forward and looked at them closer. 'A Margaret Dickson; splendid form!'

"'No' a bad rose!' I says, aff-hand. 'It's aye worth the trouble growin' a good one when ye're at it,' and I passed them over to him wi' my compliments. Ye would hardly believe it, but he was mair pleased than many a man would be wi' a box o' cigars.

"'I didna know ye were a fancier,' says he. 'That's a first-rate hybrid perpetual.'

"'The craze o' my life !' says I, quite smart. 'What's better than a bit o' gairden and an intelligent interest in the works o' Nature?'

"'Nature!' says he, wi' a girn. 'If Nature had her will o' roses, they would a' be back at the briar or killed wi' mildew and green-fly. But I needna tell you the fecht we hae wi' the randy[2] — you that can sport a bloom like that!'

"The lang and the short o't was that I got a first-rate order there and then frae Dimister, and promised to go to his gairden next time I was roond and give him the benefit o' my experience wi' hybrid perpetuals. Me! I didna ken a hybrid perpetual frae a horseradish! But I had my man! And I have him yet, there's no' a draper in the East o' Scotland that's mair glad to see me. When I had a day to mysel' in Gleska I went to my friend at the Bazaar, and learned as much aboot the rose trade in a couple o' hours as would keep me gaun in talk wi' Dimister for days. I bought a shillin' book on gairdenin', laid in a stock o' seedsmen's catalogues, and noo I ken far mair aboot the rose as a commercial plant than Dimister, though I never grew yin a' my days. What's the use? What's shops for? But every time I went to Dimister's, I aye had a button-hole that dazzled him. The droll thing is that havin' a button-hole grew into a habit; I started it to get roon' auld Sandy Dimister, and noo I'd sooner go without my watch."

## 30. *Citizen Soldier*

MR JAMES SWAN sat at his Saturday dinner-table, and was about to draw his customary bottle of beer, when, on reflection, he put down the corkscrew and filled up his glass with water.

"Bilious, Jimmy?" said his wife.

"No," he answered. "I'll wager there's no' a bilious man this day in the Citizen Corps.[1] Two hours' route-merchin' on the Fenwick Road is the best anti-bilious pill I ken; if it could be put up in boxes and sold in the apothecary shops, it would fetch a guinea a dozen. But ye couldna put Sergeant Watson in a box, and he's the main ingredient o' the route-merch pill. Watson's a fine, big, upstandin' chap, and it's a treat to see him handle his legs and arms the same's they were kahouchy, and double up a hill without a pech from him, but I wish he would mind at times our corps's no' made up o' gladiators or Græco-Roman wrestlers, that we're just plain business men, off and on about five-and-forty in the shade, wi' twenty years o' tramway travellin' and elevator lifts, and easy-chairs, bad air and beer in our constitution. It's no' to be expected we can pelt up braes on the Fenwick Road like a lot o' laddies."

"I hope you'll not hurt yoursel'," said Mrs Swan anxiously.

"Hurt mysel'! I'm sore all over! Sergeant Watson sees to that! It's no' the Madame Pomeroy treatment for the skin he's givin' us, nor learnin' us the dummy alphabet; he wouldna get a wink o' sleep this night if he thought we werena sore all over. 'The sorer ye feel,' says he, 'the sooner ye'll be fit.' I tell you he's a daisy! I never knew I had calves to my legs nor muscles to my back before I joined this army. ... My goodness, Bell, is that all the meat ye have the day? That's no' a sodger's dinner."

"At any rate," said Mrs Swan, "I never saw you looking better or eating more."

"I don't know about my looks," said Mr Swan, "and that bit doesna matter, for I suppose the Germans are no great Adonises themselves, but I wish to Peter they had my legs!" And he bent to rub them tenderly. "I've learned something in the last month, Bell — that a body's body's no' just a thing for hangin' shirts and stockings on — the same's it was a pair o' winter-dykes.[2] For twenty years I have been that intent on cultivatin' my intellect and the West Coast trade of C & M, and dodgin' any kind o' physical effort that would spoil my touch wi' the country drapers, that I was turnin' into a daud o' creash,[3] and slitherin' down this vale o' tears as if the seat o' my breeks were soaped. Do ye ken what Watson said to me one day, just the week I joined? He saw me pechin', and had the decency to call a halt. 'Are ye all right?' says he; and I told him I had the doctor's word for it that all my internal organs were in first-rate order, and as strong as a lion's. 'Since that's the case,' says he, 'it's a pity we canna flype ye, for the ootside's been deplorably neglected.'"

"The idea!" said Mrs Swan, bridling.

"Oh, the man was right enough; a bonny job I could have made last month o' any German that came down the Drive wi' his bayonet fixed to look for beer! I wouldna have the strength to hand him out a bottle. But let him try't now! — Oh, michty, but I'm sore across the back!"

"I hope you haven't racked yourself?" his wife said, anxious again.

"The only thing I've racked's my braces. Just lie you down on your hands and toes, face down, wi' your body stiff, and see how often ye can touch the floor wi' your chin."

"Indeed and I'll do nothing of the kind!" said Mrs Swan. "I don't see what good that sort of thing's going to do if you have to fight the Germans. It's surely not on your hands and toes you're going to tackle them, James Swan?"

Her husband laughed. "No," said he; "and I'm no' expectin' to have to fight them even standing on the soles o' my feet, for the only Germans ye'll see in Scotland after this'll come when their trouble's bye, wi' a pack, selling Christmas toys; their whiskers'll be dyed for a disguise, and they'll call themselves Maclachlans."

"And what on earth are you drilling for?" said his wife. "I'm sure I wish you were on the road again. Since ever you were back in the shop six weeks ago, it's been nothing but darning socks for me, with your marching and parades."

Mr James Swan sighed, as he was helped to a man's size portion of the pie, which, to an appetite sharpened by his military duties, seemed quite inadequate.

"If ye want to know," said he, "I'm drilling mainly to make up the average for myself and for the country. The idea that the Black Watch and the Gordon Highlanders at a shilling or two a day per man were enough to keep us safe and let us carry on fine soft-goods businesses, allowing reasonable time for golf and football, was a slight mistake. It would have worked all right if the other chaps across the North Sea did the same, but you see they dinna. Instead of goin' in, like us, for a rare good time wi' athletic sports at half-a-crown for the grandstand seats, for tango dancin' and ke-hoi, the silly nyafs went, for a penny a day, into the army. So far as I can make out from the papers, they're all as tough as nails, and they cornered the toy trade too, and a lot o' other lines that's the inalienable right of the British business man. 'Our mistake, Maria!' said the Countess. All Britain is divided into two parts — the flabby-bellied and the fit; I don't expect to have the luck to shoot a German, but at least I'm no' goin' to be flabby."

"Then it's just for your health you're away parading?" said Mrs Swan.

"No," said her husband. "For self-respect. Sergeant Watson's system's gey sore on the muscles for a week or two, but it's most morally elevatin'. Four weeks ago if I had attempted to lean on mysel' wi' any weight I would have crumpled up like a taper; I'm sore all over just at present, but I feel that I could take a cow by the tail and swing it round my head. ... What you want in this house, Bella, is more beef, and a more generous sense of what is meant by dinner. Are ye not aware, my dear, that a sodger gets a pound a day of beef without bone? So far as I can judge, he needs it — every ounce!"

"Man, ye're just a great big laddie!" said Mrs Swan, with a shake of her husband's shoulder.

He shook his head. "That's just the worst of it, Bella," said he; "I'm no'! The greatest luck in the world just now is to be a lad of twenty. When I was young there was hanged-all happened in the world to waken me in the morning, sure that I was needed to do something: it was just, every day, a trivial wee world of business, and feeding, and playing, and sleeping; no drums nor bugles in't, and nothing big enough to bother to roll my sleeves up for a blow at. ... James Swan, Commercial Traveller. ... Sold stays! ... There was a destiny for ye! And I go along the streets just now and I see a hundred thousand men in the prime o' life who haven't the slightest notion of their luck and the chance they're missing."

"What chance?" asked Mrs Swan.

"To make a better, cleaner world of it; to help to save a nation; make themselves a name that, even if they perished, would be honoured by their people generations after. ... Pass the water, Bella, please."

"Are you not going to take your beer?" asked Mrs Swan.

"No," said Jimmy firmly.

"Why that?" she asked.

"Because I want to," he answered. "When we were doubling along the Fenwick Road I thought of that beer all the time. I could feel the very taste o't! But the oddest thing about Sergeant Watson's system is that it's learned me this — that the thing you're not particularly keen to do is the thing to do, and pays in the long-run best. So I'll just take water."

## 31. *The Adventures of a Country Customer*[1]

NOW THAT the Exhibition has the gravel nicely spread, and the voice of the cuckoo is adding to the monotony of a rural life, there is going to be a large and immediate influx of soft-goods men from places like Borgue in Kincardineshire and Lochinver in the North. They will come into town on the Friday trains at Exhibition excursion rates; leave their leatherette Gladstone bags at Carmichael's Temperance Hotel or the YMCA Club, have a wash-up for the sake of our fine soft Glasgow water; take a bite, perhaps, and sally forth to the Wholesale House of Campbell & MacDonald (Ltd) ostensibly to see what can be done in cashmere hose, summer-weight underwear, and a large discount on the winter bill. Strictly speaking they know nothing about Campbell & MacDonald, having never seen them, even if they have any existence, which is doubtful; the party they are going to lean on is Mr Swan the traveller, who covers Lochinver and Borgue two or three times a year, and is all the Campbell & MacDonald that the rural merchants know.

Mr Swan came through our two former Exhibitions[2] with no apparent casualties beyond a slight chronic glow in the countenance and a chubby tendency in the space between the waistcoat pockets where he keeps his aromatic lozenges and little liver pills respectively. For an hour's convivial sprint through the various Scottish blends with a hurried customer in from Paisley, or a real sustained effort of four-and-twenty hours with a Perthshire man who is good for a £250 order, Mr Swan is still the most reliable man in Campbell & MacDonald's. He can hold his own even with big strong drapers from the distillery districts of the Spey; help them to take off their boots and wind their watches for them and yet turn up at the warehouse in the morning fresh as the ocean breeze, with an expenses bill of £3. 10s. 4½d which the manager will pass without the blink of an eye-lash. The City of Glasgow, for the heads of the retail soft goods trade in Kirkudbrightshire and the North, is practically Jimmy Swan and a number of delightfully interesting streets radiating round him. In Borgue and Lochinver he has been recognised affectionately since the 'Groveries'[3] year as a Regular Corker and Only Official Guide to Glasgow, and no one knew better than himself when the turf was turned up again in Kelvingrove, just when the grass was taking root, that 1911 was going to be a strenuous year.

"I feel I'm getting a little too old for the game," he said to his wife with a sigh.

"You ought to have got out of the rut long ago, Jimmy,"

said Mrs Swan. "It isn't good for your health."

"A rut that's thirty years deep isn't a tramway rail, Bella," he rejoined, "and anyhow, I'm not in it for the fun of the thing, but mainly because I like to see you in a sealskin coat. But mark my words! this is going to be a naughty summer for your little Jimmy; every customer I have from Gretna to Thurso is going to have some excuse to be in Glasgow sometime when the Fairy Fountain's[4] on."

The first of the important country customers turned up on Friday afternoon. He came from Galloway, and ran all the way from the station to the warehouse so as not to lose any time in seeing Mr Swan, who was just going out for a cup of tea. "Why! Mr MacWatters! Delighted to see you!" said Jimmy, with a radiant smile, kneading the customer's left arm all over as if he were feeling for a fracture. "Come right in and see our manager! He was just saying yesterday, 'We never see Mr MacWatters' own self,' and I said: 'No, Mr Simpson, but I'll bet you see his cheques as prompt as the cheques of any man in Campbell & MacDonald's books!' I had him there, Mac, had him there!"

The manager was exceedingly affable to Mr Mac-Watters, but vexed that he had not sent a post-card to say he was coming. "I should have liked," he said, "to take you out to the Exhibition, but unfortunately I have a Board meeting at three o'clock — of course I could have the meeting postponed."

"Not at all! Not on my account!" said the Galloway customer with genuine alarm and a wistful glance at Jimmy. "I just want to look over some lines and leave an order, and then —"

"But my dear Mr MacWatters, you must see the Exhibition, and you must have a bit of dinner, and — Perhaps Mr Swan would take my place?"

"Delighted!" said Jimmy, heartily.

Mr MacWatters was introduced to some attractive lines in foulards, Ceylons, blouses, and the like, and said he would think it over and give Mr Swan his order at his leisure.

"Very good!" said the manager, shaking him by the hand at leaving. "I'm sure you'll have a pleasant evening and enjoy the Exhibition. You will be immensely struck by the Historical section: it will show you what an intensely interesting past we have had; and I'll wager you'll be delighted with the picture gallery. Then there's Sir Henry Wood's[5] Orchestra — I wish I could be with you. But Mr Swan will show you everything; you can depend on Mr Swan."

Five minutes later Jimmy and his country customer sat on tall stools in a lovely mahogany salon, and Jimmy was calling the country customer Bob, an affability which greatly pleased any man from Galloway. It was Bob's first experience of the mahogany salon; his business relations with the firm of Campbell & MacDonald didn't go back to the 'Groveries', and he had so far only the assurance of the soft-goods trade in Galloway that in Glasgow Jimmy was decidedly a good man to know.

In Galloway it is drunk out of a plain thick glass, with a little water, and it is always the same old stuff. In this mahogany salon, Jimmy appeared to control magical artesian wells from which the most beautiful ladies, with incredibly abundant hair, drew variegated and aromatic beverages into long thin glasses that tinkled melodiously when you brought them against your teeth. Jimmy gave his assurance that they were quite safe, and the very thing for an appetiser, and the man from Galloway said he never dreamt you could get the like of that anywhere except on the Continent. He added, reflectively, that he really must take home a small bottle. Pleased with his approval, Jimmy prescribed another kind called a Manhattan Cocktail[6], and the country customer enjoyed it so much that he started feeling his hip-pocket for his purse that he might buy another. But Jimmy said, "On no account, old man! Leave this to me, it happens to be the centenary of the firm." So the country customer carefully buttoned up his hip-pocket again, and consented to have another cocktail solely out of respect for the firm.

It was now decided by Jimmy that they could safely have a snack upstairs where the band was, and the country customer, being a corporal in the Territorials, walked upstairs carefully keeping time to the music, but somewhat chagrined that he had not divested himself, somewhere, of his yellow leggings.

They began with 'Hors d'oeuvres', which tasted exactly like sardines, then they had soup, of which the country customer had a second helping after which he looked round for his cap and was preparing to go. But Jimmy laughingly said the thing was just starting, and a banquet followed which reminded the country customer of the one they had had at the Solway Arms Hotel in 1903 when the Grand Lodge deputation visited the local brethren.[7]

When the fish had passed, Jimmy picked up a List Price card or catalogue affair and said something about a bottle of 'buzz-water'. Concealing his disappointment, the country customer, who never had cared for lemonade, said he didn't mind. It turned out to be quite a large bottle with a gilt neck, and except for a singular tendency to go up the nose, it was the most pleasant kind of lemonade he had ever tasted. He was surprised that Jimmy hadn't ordered two bottles and said so, and Jimmy, begging his pardon, promptly did so.

This stage of the proceedings terminated with cups of black coffee and two absurdly minute glasses of a most soothing green syrup strongly recommended by Jimmy as an aid to digestion. There was also a large cigar.

"I think," said Jimmy, in dulcet tones, with the flush of health upon his countenance, and a roguish eye, "I think we will be getting a move on, and as one might say, divagating towards the Grove of Gladness."

They had just one more, seeing it really was the centenary of the firm, and the country customer, as he walked downstairs, was struck by the beautiful convoluted design of the marble balustrade.

In the very next moment the country customer asked, "What is this?" and Jimmy responded, "It is the Scenic

Railway. Feel the refreshing breeze upon your brow!"[8] They were dashing with considerable celerity past a mountain tarn, and the country customer expressed a desire to stop for a moment that he might have his fevered temples in the water. Far off a band was playing a dreamy waltz. A myriad lamps were shining in the night, and restlessly flitting from place to place. The air had a curious balminess that is not felt in Galloway. It was borne home to the country customer that he must there and then tell Mr Swan — good old Jimmy Swan! — about Jean Dykes in Girvan, and how he loved her and meant to marry her if he could get another extension of the lease of his shop at present terms, but before he could lead up to this subject with the necessary delicacy, he found himself on a balcony looking down on an enormous crescent of humanity, confronted by a bandstand and a tumbler.

"The firm," Jimmy was saying solemnly, "has always appreciated your custom. Our Mr Simpson says over and over again, 'Give me the Galloway men; they know what they want, and they always see that they get it!' He says, 'Whatever you do, Mr Swan, pay particular attention to Mr MacWatters, and put him on bedrock prices.' I have always done so; Galloway has been, as you might say, the guiding-star of my business life."

The country customer, profoundly moved, shook Jimmy by the hand.

"Where are we now?" he asked and the balcony began to revolve rapidly. He steadied it with one hand, and tried to count the myriad lights with the other. They, too, were swinging round terrifically, and he realised that they must be stopped. He became cunning. He would pretend indifference to them as they swung round him, and then spring on them when they were off their guard. "Where are we now?" he repeated.

"The Garden Club," said the voice of Jimmy, coming out of the distance. "Try and sit up and have this soda-water."

Next morning, sharp at nine, Mr Swan came into the warehouse with a sparkling eye, a jaunty step, a voice as mellifluous as a silver bell and a camelia in his button-hole.

"Morning! Morning!" he cheerily said to the Ribbons Department, as he passed to the manager's room.

"Old Swan's looking pretty chirpy," said the Ribbons enviously. "He's been having a day at Turnberry[9] or the Coast."

Jimmy laid a substantial order for Autumn goods for Galloway and a bill of expenses for £3 9s. before the manager.

"Ah! just so!" said the manager. "And how did Mr MacWatters like the Exhibition?"

"Immensely impressed!" said Jimmy.

"It is bound to have a great educative influence. Great! And such a noble object — Chair of History![10] What did Mr MacWatters think of the Art and Historical sections?"

"He was greatly pleased with them particularly," said Jimmy. "I have just seen him off in the train, and he said he would never forget it."

The manager placed his initials at the foot of the expenses bill and handed it back to Jimmy who proceeded at once to the cashier's department.

"£3 9s.," said the manager to himself. "Art and History in Kelvingrove appear to come a little high, but it's a good order. And there's only one Jimmy Swan."


## 32. *The Radiant James Swan*[1]


MR SWAN, with a white piqué waistcoat, a one-button morning coat, an absolutely perfect crease down his discreet grey cambric trousers, the sauciest of silk hats just faintly tilted to the right (a weakness he could never get out of) and an orchid in his button-hole, went round his own samples-cases, piled up in the hall of the hotel, as if he had never seen them in his life before. He shook hands ceremoniously with the lady clerk in the office, put down his name in the flourish of his signature, and mentioned to the clerkess in a tone that was almost a caress that he had never seen her looking better.

"It's this salubrious air you have here, I suppose," he added. "I really must send my wife down for a holiday ... How is the fishing doing?"

Several obvious anglers were lounging in the hall; their presence accounted for Mr Swan's failure to recognise his own sample-cases.

"Some good catches were got yesterday," said the clerkess, paling down again to her natural colour.

"Ah!" said Mr Swan, delightedly, rubbing his hands. "That's good! I hope we have a little rain tonight; then we must see about the river tomorrow." The ecstasy of the ardent angler was in his eye, though, to tell the truth, his honest conviction always was that the noblest of the fish species, and the only one worth getting up early for, was the brandered finnan haddock.

He moved in a stately way round the corner, tapped at the landlord's private door; opened it on a cry from within, put in his head, and said, "Scene Two — Mountain Glade. Cave of the Mountain Robbers. In centre Chief of the Mountain Robbers lying in wait for the defenceless traveller. Sound of Muffled Cocoa-Nuts in the distance ... How's a' wi' ye, Mr Coats?"

"Good heavens, Mr Swan!" said the landlord. "Is that really you? You're the greatest nut yourself I've seen this season. Where's your wee pea-jacket?"

"From scenes like these, Auld Scotia's grandeur springs!" said Mr Swan, posing majestically in the middle of the sanctum. "Cast your eye on this coat — fits like the peeling o' a plum! In waistcoats, now, have you ever seen anything so judiciously evading vulgar ostentation while yet arresting to the eye of taste? Genuine orchid — cypripedium, something-or-other, secured at great expense from Watty Grant in the Bazaar this morning; silk hat the latest touch; look at the brim of it! You haven't a hat like that in Banchory. Solomon, sir, at his best, would look like a remnant sale if brought in here for comparison.[2] ... I'm tired, Mr Coats; I've been on the road since six o'clock this morning," and he sat down wearily on a chair. "I'm gettin' too old, Robert, for any protracted performance in the role of tailor's dummy, but if you ask me, that's a jolly smart hat!" and he surveyed it at arm's length with approval.

"You're going to Rachel Thorpe's[3] wedding to-morrow, I suppose?" said the landlord, juggling with some bottles behind and putting out two glasses containing an amber fluid.

"You'll mak' a mistake wi' these bottles some day, and gie me the cauld tea yin," said Jimmy. "However, here's tae ye! And ye're right about Rachel; her mother fixed the wedding to suit my journey; she says I found the man for Rachel — a' nonsense! Rachel had the chap picked and settled on before he jaloused anything himself. But this is my last weddin' in the way o' business; after this I'm only goin' to the weddin's o' folk I have a spite to."

"You've launched a lot in your time," said the landlord.

"For twenty years," said Jimmy, "I was the champion thrower of the rice in the West of Scotland, and held the record for heaving bowl-money[4] in the rural districts till the sport went oot o' fashion. I've put in a luscious bass to 'The Voice that Breathed O'er Eden,' and proposed 'The Ladies' oftener than any other man in Britain. But I'm no' goin' to dae it ony mair; I don't need! I doubt, indeed, if my bein' the ever-joyous Aye-Ready paid me or my firm in the long run. Now I'm goin' to settle down and enjoy mysel', and tell all kind inquirin' friends more or less connected wi' the drapery trade that I've the doctor's orders no' to go oot at night, or excite mysel' at public functions. The heart, Mr Coats! The heart!" — and Jimmy slightly tragically rose and tapped himself on the place where he keeps his pocket-book.

"You're not giving up bowling!" said the landlord with genuine distress. "We expected to have you out at the green to-night."

"Bowls is off!" said Jimmy firmly, "I aye hated bowlin', but kept it up to please my customers. Same wi' curlin'; since they stopped lang kale soup there's nothin' in the roarin' game for me. But the lang and the short o't is that

I've learned my trade, paid my 'prentice fees, and can now afford to dae what I like."

"Lucky man!" said the landlord. "They're making me a Baillie!"

"Do you know?" said Mr Swan, "twenty to thirty years o' my bright young life was wasted o' the cultivation o' the social side o' business? When I came first on the road for C & M, the man that took me roond and introduced me said that nine-tenths o' the customers would be no use to me unless they got the length o' callin' me 'Jimmy' and saw me wi' their own e'en ride a goat.[5] It was Big Campbell — ye mind o' him? — The Prince? He was somethin' devilish fancy in the Royal Arch[6] and he got me made a Mason in Inverness to please a customer that was RWM.[7] Next year at Aberdeen, I got the Mark, to please a tailor and clothier chap who took some tweed from me and took my measure for a knickerbocker suit the time he was puttin' me through the grips and passwords!

"I laid mysel' oot to be the most widely-kent and popular man in the wholesale dry-goods trade. I was an Ancient Shepherd in Kirkcudbright, wi' a six-foot crook and a bunnet the width o' a barrel, and I wouldna ken a yowe from a ram if I saw them in a park. I was a Royal Forester in Alloway — me that never planted a tree in my life! I was affiliated to six Gardeners' Lodges[8] north o' the Forth. If there had been an Ancient and Royal Order o' Sanitary Engineers, I would have been one like winkin'.

"Every time I struck a town in the way o' business, they skirmished roond and got some poor sowl to put through the First, and Brother Swan was the life and soul of the succeeding harmony. My boxes were no sooner clapped aff the train than a bill was up in the baker's window callin' an emergency meetin' o' the Gardeners, or the Shepherds, or the Foresters, or the Oddfellows. If they had nae other excuse for the meetin', they had some doleful cause o' an afflicted brother, lyin' ill in the infirmary, and I was aye at the top o' the subscription sheet.

"There's ony number o' football clubs goin' to stop this

summer because James Swan, Esq. is no longer goin' to be a Patron — "

"But you were a great football enthusiast!" said Mr Coats, with surprise.

"Me! I'm just as keen on the game o' moshy![9] I got mixed up wi' football in the country because I sometimes do a line in strippit jerseys. Oh! I tell you, Robert, my reputation for affability and high spirits cost me some trouble and a lot o' sundries that werena covered by C & M's pound a day.

"I drank when I didna want to drink; I took tickets for balls and concerts and subscription o' sales that were nae mair interest to me than the Balkan Imbroglio or the Pan-Germanic Conference. I drove to weddin's or walked to funerals o' folk I never kent; I took the chair or sung at concerts when I should be in my bed. Never again, Robert, never again!"

"How's that, Jimmy?"

"Doctor's orders!" said Mr Swan. "A quiet life. No undue exertion. Forbye, it doesn't pay. I doubt if in the last twelve years it got me a single order; this is no' an age for the cultivation o' the social side in business; it's the stuff ye sell, and the terms, that talk, and the right sort o' crack across a counter goes far further than the Mark Degree and 'Out on the Deep when the Sun is Low' at the local smokin'-concert. ... Is it No. 20, Mr Coats?"

## 33. *Jimmy Swan's German Spy*[1]

THE LANDLORD of the Cross-Keys Inn filled up his evening schedule[2] for the Sergeant of Police — the names and addresses of his guests; when they had arrived,      and when they meant to go away; their nationality, and their business. There were only three or four, and the last entry was 'James Swan, Commercial Traveller, Glasgow'.

Mr Swan himself, with his slippers on, and his pipe going, looked over the landlord's shoulder.

"There's no a German spy in that bunch, anyway, Mr Grant," he said. "Two Macs and a Fisher; and as for the name o' Swan it's so reassurin' to the police that whenever they see't on a hotel list now they gang hame to their beds for the nicht."

The landlord of the Cross-Key Inn apparently had no comment to make. He completed his filling-in of the daily report with his signed testimony on soul and conscience that it was correct so far as he knew. He looked at Mr Swan a little curiously, and then without a word went out on the verandah. It was a perfect night, of mildly frosty moon-shine; a flock of sheep was bleating on the golf-course, and someone with a winking light was moving about the first hole.

Mr Grant, having watched the light a while, came in and took up his schedule again.

"You don't happen to know any Samuel Fisher in Strathbungo[3], Mr Swan?" he asked. "In the ship chandler business."

"No," said Jimmy on reflection. "Whoever he is, he's been done in the eye, for there's no river Bungo, and there's no fish and no ship-chandlin' there either. Is Fisher the sandy-haired wee bald young yin wi' the crimson cardigan waistcoat?"

"Yes," said Mr Grant, who appeared to be a little nervous. "I never saw him before. He drove in just at the gloamin', with a droll kind of box, and when I asked him all about himself, as we have to do now, and what his business was, he looked quite startled."

"It would startle onybody that had no experience before o' wartime conditions in Hielan' hotels, Mr Grant. Very few o' us could come through the test without a sudden sinkin' at the he'rt, for fear we were discovered at last. What's the worst that ye suspect him of?"

"There is something in his look," said Mr Grant.

"I know!" said Jimmy; "I noticed it — a kind o' vacancy. It's a kind o' look that aye goes wi' the higher branches o' ship-chandlin".

"And there's something in his manner o' speech," continued the landlord. "His accent's no English, and it's no' Scotch, and it's no' Irish."

"I have it!" said Jimmy, snapping his fingers. "It'll be Hydropathic."

"And he's been out there for the last half-hour wi' a light on the golf course, signallin'," proceeded Mr Grant's indictment.

At the suggestion of Mr Swan they went into the hall and had a look at the mysterious Fisher's box.

"H'm!" said Jimmy, pursing his mouth and rubbing his chin. "Damnin' fact to start wi'; it's a wooden box! it's painted broon, and it's locked — that shows the owner has something to conceal. There's no doot, Mr Grant, that we're on the track o' a big thing here. 'S.L.F.' is painted on the lid — a pure blind!"

It was a long, narrow box, apparently quite new; Mr Grant took hold of it by handle which was on the top for convenience of carriage, and shook it. There was no sound.

"Thirty years in the trade," said the hotel-keeper, significantly; "I never saw a box in this house exactly like that before."

"What do you think it'll be?" asked Jimmy, solemnly. "Airoplanes?"

"Oh, no," said Mr Grant, a little surprised at Jimmy's innocence; "It couldn't be airoplanes — not in that space. The engines alone — "

"True!" said Jimmy, hurriedly.

"True! It might be bombs, if we could think o' onything that could be done aboot here wi' bombs except blaw up the gas-works, and considerin' the quality o' your gas, Mr Grant, I think that could be considered no unfriendly action. … Again, it might be wireless telegraphy."

"That would mean big masts," suggested the innkeeper who knew science.

"Not the latest," said Jimmy. "Rhones. Ye can get the effect wi' rhones."

"When I think," said Mr Grant, piteously, "of the hundreds o' German waiters I've had here, payin' them the best wages, I must say I consider I should be the last man to be harassed … "

"Harassed!" said Jimmy. "They wouldna hesitate to harass onybody; it's a fair delight to them."

Mr Grant was getting more nervous and agitated every minute. He went out to the verandah and looked towards the golf course again; no light was to be seen. "I will not put up with it!" he came back crying. "I'll have no filthy German spies about my place; out he goes this very evening, box and baggage."

Mr Swan, however, pointed out that this would be a great mistake; if Mr Fisher was able to prove his innocence, he could claim substantial damages for being thrown out of his hotel at night. On the other hand, if he were a spy, the crafty thing for them to do was to pretend he was not suspected, and keep an eye on him till he could be discovered in the act.

When Mr Fisher came in from his belated ramblings round a golf course which had not seen a player for five months, he got quite an affable 'good night' from the landlord and Mr Swan as he passed upstairs to his bedroom.

Next morning, when Mr Grant came down to breakfast, he found Mr Swan in the hall before him contemplating the mysterious box, which was now unlocked and empty.

"He's gone!" said Jimmy, gravely.

"Gone!" said the landlord; "When?"

"More than an hour ago," said Jimmy, "whenever it was light. I heard the front door bang, and I looked out at my bedroom window, and there was the bold Fisher sneaking up the road, hiding something under his topcoat. Guilt was in every step o' him; the sparks were fleein' from the very tackets in his boots. Whenever I understood what he was up to I opened my window, and cries — 'Ah, Mr Fisher! Mr Fisher! Ye think ye're not observed, but God sees ye!' "

"The ruffian!" exclaimed Mr Grant, all trembling; "I wish you had warned me, and we could have had him stopped."

"Oh, he'll be back for breakfast," said Mr Swan. "Then ye can have it oot wi' him."

"Back for breakfast," said Mr Grant, bewildered. "If he's a spy … "

"Tuts!" said Jimmy, chuckling. "He's no a spy; he's the last that's left o' the young Glasgow golfers, and he's here incognito as a chandileer. You see he daurna, at his age,[4] be seen near Glasgow wi' a golf bag, so he puts it in a box and hies him as far as he can into the country where he thinks he'll no be noticed."

## 34. *Jimmy Swan in Warm Weather*[1]

As A classy dresser, James Swan, the traveller for Macdonald and Campbell[2], leaves nothing to be desired. You cannot be two minutes in his company without an uneasy feeling that you ought really to have shaved this morning, and that the right sort of hat or necktie actually does contribute to an impressive human personality. Mr Swan always looks like my idea of a thoroughly well-dressed man — a retired colonel with a smart little place in the country, two setter dogs, and a whole row of boot-trees. The sort of man whose trousers for the day are dictated by the barograph, and who would not be found dead in a bow-tie with a turn-over collar.

He looked exceptionally smart on Friday coming home from his Aberdeen journey, not a superfluous crease in his garments. The dove-grey spats, the ash-grey bowler hat, the unsoiled creamy gloves, the lustrous footwear of the same leather as the best dukes' cigar-cases are made of, the ebony walking-cane, the faintly-spotted foulard necktie, and the handkerchief en suite would have gained him an entrance to the Royal enclosure at Ascot without a ticket.

The rest of us were sweltering with the heat, feeling sticky underneath, horribly baggy at the knees, caught in a tropic atmosphere with semi-winter clothes on.[3] He looked as cool and clean as the Sound of Kerrera.

"How do you manage it, Jimmy?" I asked, indicating the perfect sartorial ensemble and the air of 45 Fahrenheit.

"Thought," he answered, lighting a cigar. "Profound and unremitting thought. Considering that I put on my clothes only once a day except on Sundays I feel justified in putting my mind into the job. Most people in this town have souls far above trivial considerations of that sort; they're so taken up with the Ruhr situation,[4] poetry, the rising bank rate or the tennis tournament that they would go to their work without a waistcoat if their wives didn't watch them. But I'm a humble, low-browed sort of chap, and I feel that I'm not depriving my fellow-creatures of any priceless contribution to human thought if I concentrate my attention for a wee while every morning on my personal appearance."

"Yet I fancy some crafty consideration of the effect of clothes on business comes into the question too," I suggested.

He chuckled. "Ye may be sure o' that!" he admitted, a little relinquishing the fastidious English that usually goes with a flower in his coat. "When I went first on the road I thought it didn't matter a hang what I wore or the way I wore it so long as my samples were attractive and the prices right. If plus-fours[5] had been invented then I would have had them. Yes I'd have had the neck to try to sell two-piece tennis suits, fancy Shetland wool hip panels in contrastin' colours on a day as hot as this with me in Harris tweeds! I had no sense! Not an iota of sense.

"Now if here's one thing a traveller in the dry goods line should study it's the human mind as often seen in drapers. Ye may tell them the funniest Gleska bawrs[6] and show them Jap schappes and silk marocains there's no the like o' offered north o' Perth, at prices fair ridiculous, but if the suit ye're wearin' yoursel' is scuffed and your hat's the least bit chafed it's domino for big orders.

"Ye have no idea o' the effect o' a good silk hat and nae dandruff on the retail trade. It fair dazzles shopkeepers in the rural belt that never themselves wear anything but a hooker-doon[7], and aye look as if they shed their hair wi' a curry-comb.

"It was our late Mr Williams who put me up to it first, after I had been six months goin' round the country tryin' to sell the daintiest ladies' wear in a D.B. navy blue suit that gathered a' the dust and one o' yon 1880 waterproof coats made oot o' the same kind o' rubber as hose-pipes and hot-water bottles.

"'Mr Swan,' he says one day, 'did it ever occur to you ye should look like the stuff you're sellin'. It's no' a sheep dip firm ye represent; for one thing, ye havena the whiskers for't, and ye have no great head for drink. Ye may think these people in Dornoch don't care a rap even if ye came to them in a kilt and a suit o' oilskins, but ye're wrong. Dornoch's a long way from Buchanan Street, but even in Dornoch they don't like a glass o' champagne offered to them on a porridge plate; they have an intuition that it should be a silver salver. Dress like the season, dress like your samples, dress like a pound a day expenses, and for God's sake don't wear cuffs that need clippin' wi' a pair o' shears.'

"He was a great man, William Campbell — by George, he knew his business! I never forgot what he said — 'Look like the stuff you're sellin', look like the season.'

"There's no' one man in a hundred in Glasgow dresses like the weather. Even men in a good way o' business go through the year in winter-weight underwear and havena a thin flannel suit in their repertoire. Look at yoursel', for instance, wearin' on a day like this a thick tweed suit adapted for the January fishin' on Loch Tay. No wonder you're so glossy about the face and pechin' aboot sultry weather and relaxin' climates. Ye would be far better wi' an alpaca jacket. If I went into a customer's shop perspirin' that way, I doubt he would let me open up a single case.

Half my care in life is keepin' cool when other folks are moppin' their silly heids wi' naipkins and in lookin' snug and cosy when it's frost.

"In dull grey weather I'm the little ray of sunshine. If I'm doin' Oban in November, they put the time I spend in the town in their statistics, and report 'Sunshine 6 hours', to be upsides wi' Bournemouth or Torquay. All this week, in the North, my aim was to be like an evenin' breeze from the sea blowin' through a tailor's workshop.

"A draper in Dingwall on Monday says to me, 'Man, Mr Swan, ye put me in mind o' a plate o' ice-cream at a night's dancin'.' He had the humid hand o' a herrin'-curer, and generally looked parboiled, wi' a big bottle o' lime juice and a carafe o' water constant on his desk. Just to keep me by him for the coolness I brought into his wee bit shop he gave me the biggest order ever I had from him."

"It's all very well, Jimmy," I said, "but in a variable climate like this your psychology must sometimes get you into trouble."

He laughed. "Quite right! But I have to risk it. I once went up to Elgin in the month o' June in swelterin' weather, wi' not so much as an umbrella, wi' a panama hat, a white piqué waistcoat, patent-leather shoes, and a bottle o' midge lotion. The very day I landed it started to snow! 'James Swan,' I says to mysel', 'ye're in the soup!' If I had tried to go through my customers in my Isle o' Man turn-out, in weather like thon, heaven pity Macdonald and Campbell! What I did was this — I got fearful ill in the hotel wi' threatened peritonitis, whatever that is; went to my bed in a sample pair of Jap silk pyjamas, broad stripe effect, and sent word round to my customers that I was poorly.

"They came in droves to my bedroom; I ordered in a drop o' spirits, sat up in bed in the tastiest gentleman's night attire that was ever seen in Elgin, no countin' the shootin' tenants, and I booked bumper orders."

# 35. *The Tall Hat*[1]

FOR A dozen years at least I have not seen Jimmy Swan wear a tall silk hat. When he started a bowler, even on his Northern journeys, I recognised it was a portent, and that 'lums' were doomed. For at least quarter of a century before that, his silk hats, in sauciness and gloss, made him conspicuous among all the commercial travellers who do business for Glasgow firms in these country towns where they still ring curfew bells and have shutters on shop windows.

"I was getting into a rut with my topper hat," he explained to me when he made the change to bowlers, "and for any man on the road in the soft goods line that's fatal. Wearing a top hat all the time left me with no latitude for rising to what you might call a supreme occasion. A top hat is the acme, the ne plus ultra of ceremonial garb for gents; you can put on nothing more respectful to the departed or more consoling to the victims of a weddin'. But wearing a topper always, as I did in the way of business, I felt no special moral uplift or elation at a wedding or a funeral; it was just like being there in my working clothes. The commonest country stone-mason on these occasions, with a mid-Victorian 'lum' and crape on it experienced a satisfaction with himself that was denied to me.

"Forbye," he added, more colloquially, "the top hat, as a regular head-dress, dates a commercial man and puts him in the septuagenarian class. You might as well go about wi' a brocaded waistcoat and carry a snuff-box. It's held in a certain respect, I admit, but it's apt to be the same respect as folk have for the ruins o' Tillietudlem Castle."[2]

Mr Swan, when I met him the other day, had the jauntiest of bowler hats — a perfectly priceless shade of Cuban brown.

"Then the topper's gone for good?" I remarked to him.

"Completely!" he replied, with emphasis. "I'd as soon wear a fireman's helmet — except it was for a Royal garden party. I flatter mysel' I was one o' the first in the national movement for its abolition. It was a species o' hat never right adapted for Gleska heids. It cast a gloom o' its own on the Scottish Sabbath, for ye daurna cock it, and imposed the most cruel physical restraint on the right enjoyment o' a weddin'.

"When I went in to business first, tile hats were at their zenith. They were held as heirlooms in a family, and descended from father to son. It took the wearer years to get used to them; ye had to learn them like the fiddle. But, all the same, they had an air o' money in the bank and strict sobriety. On the strength o' a well-brushed topper hat, wi' nothing inside but hair, many a Gleska business was built up, that's now been ruined by sons that go in for velours and Homburgs."

"You have never gone in for the velour or Homburg yourself," I remarked.

"I have more gumption that that," replied Jimmy. "As head-gears they are far too flippant and don't-give-a-damn, if ye follow me. A soft hat's all right for the Fair at Rothesay, for a man in the rural districts wi' a bit o' shooting, or for a chap like yoursel' that's steeped to the neck in the newspaper business; but a man in commerce wi' a soft hat on in his business moments always raises doubts about his strict integrity. When one o' my customers starts the soft hat habit in the streets o' Gleska I keep my eye on Stubbs[3] for the earliest mention o' his name.

"No, the bowler's the thing! Ye'll still see a lot o' reckless young men that came out o' the Army carryin' on wi' more-or-less velours that they have down on their ears like a jelly-bag, but they're far astray. The head o' the firm says nothing to them about it, but in his mind he says 'billiards or the palais de danse,' and goes sniffin' about the warehouse lookin' for surreptitious golf-bags. To any young chap comin' from the country to start his career in Gleska, unless it's in the police force or tramways, I would say, 'learn Double Entry and aye wear a bowler hat.'

"Unless ye stick it on the back o' your head and have cobwebs on it, the bowler hat never gives ye away. It's equally good for a Temperance festival or a football match;

a Corporation banquet or a rally in the Stock Exchange. If you're anyway over fifty, your bowler hat should be just a trifle square on the top; there's no' a surer sign of solvency and earnest endeavour.

"Look at the photographic group o' the Hammermen[4] or any other prosperous group o' incorporated merchant princes — all square-topped bowler hats. I aye put on a square one when I go to Aberdeen."

"But one sees an occasional topper still in Glasgow," I pointed out.

"I admit ye do," said Jimmy, "but it's at its last kick. A businessman is apt still to keep one in the office for goin' to a funeral or to see about an overdraft, but he daurna take it home for fear o' his wife and family if they're anyway free and easy wi' him. The man who keeps a top-hat in the office may escape the frightful ordeal o' wearin' it in the train or on a tram-car, but ye can tell by his look when it's on his mind that he has to go through the office wi' it. The very thought of it makes him haggard.

"I can tell when our senior — old Macdonald — has a funeral engagement. He rampages all forenoon round the office, findin' fault wi' everything, and when it's gettin' near time for the obsequies he keeps talkin' wi' me just to secure my company as far as St. George's Church[5], where the mournin' cars are. Ye'll never see a Gleska man walkin' his lone through the streets wi' a topper on; he must always have somebody wi' him to share the blame wi'.

"Everybody looks at him and wonders who's deid. It's universally recognised as a thing he wouldna be wearin' if he could help it, and so there's a certain amount o' popular sympathy that keeps even boys from throwin' snowballs at him. He knows himself that it doesna fit him; he is harrowed by the thought that, bein' twelve years old, it's likely out o' date; he canna keep his mind off it, and it spoils his day. As a matter of fact, the art of wearin' a tile-hat as unconsciously as a watch-chain is practically forgotten in Scotland except in places like Milngavie[6] where ye can smoke a pipe wi't and forget your trouble."

## 36. *The Groveries in Retrospect*[1]

JIMMY SWAN put down his evening paper with an air of
finality, took off his spectacles and wiped them carefully.
"It looks to me," he remarked "as if it might be a toss-up
between a new Municipal Buildings altogether or an International Exhibition. It's ominous that they've started
already on the Municipal Buildings; at least they have the
plans prepared for another big extension. I doubt that
means postponing the Exhibition till I'm too frail for diver-
sion on the switchback railway. We're due an Exhibition![2]
There's hundreds of young chaps in Glasgow wi' their
education incomplete; they never saw the fairy fountain
going at Kelvingrove, nor heard the joyous squeals of the
summer flapper skooshing down the water chute. They've
got to the age of manhood oblivious of what can be done
with stucco, bands, bright lights and balloon ascents to
make Glasgow really jolly. Lots of them think, no doubt,
that the West End Park[3] is fine the way it is, with snow-
drops in it, a rockery, a duck pond, seats for the aged and
bowling greens. They have no conception what we used to
do with it when they were babies. Mighty! when I mind o'
the gondolas, the Clanneries[4], the Royal visits[5], the athletic
competitions, the fireworks, the fairy lamps, the Russians[6],
and the champion cornet player of the world that played
'The Lost Chord' every night to a populace that sat round
holding each other's hands, full of pathos to the last degree, I am vexed for the present generation."

"There was also the educational effect," I said — "the
Art Sections, if you remember, and the Palaces of Industry
and Engineering."

"Quite right!" said Jimmy Swan. "I mind that fine — the
machinery for making sweeties and the pictures — miles of
them! But I was thinking more of the general uplifting
effect of the Exhibitions, their social hilarity. A season-
ticket for the Groveries was as good as a year of foreign
travel; you saw life.

"I don't suppose we'll ever have another Exhibition at Kelvingrove; there's not the room for it now, but I can hardly imagine an Exhibition in Glasgow anywhere else.[7] Do you mind the first one — 1888? Wasn't it a corker? It changed the habits of the whole community. Folk began to put on their Sunday clothes every other day in the week, and the joys of daundering down the Kelvin-side were rediscovered for the first time in a hundred years. It was found that it didn't hurt in the least to have the band of the Grenadier Guards playing 'The Departure of a Troopship' outside the place where you took your tea. Great times! Everybody was young then. I don't think it ever rained that Summer, and there was no Income-tax — at least I never had to pay it. The Chesterfield covert coat was the vogue for all smart young gentlemen, and the smart young women carried themselves well in front to make up the loss of the bustle that had just gone out of fashion.

"You could take your lunch at the Clanneries any day with all the stars of the Italian Opera Company at the next table to you, and if you wanted Science to the utmost limit you had only to go out to Hamilton Park and see Baldwin[8] drop in a parachute from his balloon. The idea was that in a few months afterwards we would all have parachutes and the bicycle would be extinct. When the last night of the Groveries of 1888 came on November 11th with the summer still going strong the turnstiles clicked for an attendance of 117,904, and there wasn't a tumbler left on the place that wasn't pinched for a souvenir.

"Everybody was bit older when the next Exhibition came in 1901, but, thanks to that indomitable Scottish thrift that makes us the people we are, we had all saved a little money, and Gray Street was jammed every night with season-ticket holders. The whangee cane of 1888 was out of fashion, and the bowler hat was giving way to the Homburg or the straw basher, but the lads o' the old brigade were still the same stout fellows who wrecked the Clanneries on the last night thirteen years before. And we beat all the 1888 records in attendance, mirth, vivacity.

"There was the Dome, and in below it the piazza — I tell you strolling the piazza was worth the money itself! The Grosvenor and the Royal Bungalow and the Princes Restaurant — the Russian pavilions, the Indian Theatre, the Japanese, the fireworks and the searchlights, the — "

"The new Art Galleries," I suggested. "They were, I think, what we called the 'clou' of that Exhibition. I remember the Rodin sculptures."

"Quite!" said Jimmy, cheerfully. "Most artistic! We must always keep Art going but do you mind the gondolas on the river? Genuine Venetian! there was another marine delight, outside the Exhibition, where the Mitchell Library is now[9], called the 'Hidden Rivers'. You sat in a boat singing 'Funiculi Funicula,'[10] and sailed through tunnels opening up every now and then on foreign scenery as in Hamilton's Diorama. Great!

"But some of the survivors of 1888 never right caught the old abandon — especially if they were married, and I mind an old maid's poem of the time that went:

There's no such music now as that the Blue
        Hungarians[11] played,
When fiddles thrilled to fingers skilled in Kelvin's
        greenwood shade,
No eager swain will wait for me an hour beneath
        the Dome,
And now sit and watch the game and cannot feel elate,
The girls in socks and baby frocks in 1888
Are having all the innings now, and getting all the fun —
I've only got the memory of Groveries No. 1

"The 1911 Exhibition at Kelvingrove still found the natural appetite of Glasgow for art, education, and a high old time unabated; but I had to miss a lot of the attractions for the sake of my commercial reputation. Would you believe me? — I never went on the Aerial Railway or the Joy Wheel; I thought they didn't comport wi' my dignity and now I'm vexed for it. The Mountain Scenic Railway was my favourite touch. But everything else was educative to a degree — the Historical collection, the Africa and Esquimaux villages, the Laplanders with their reindeer, the 'Auld Toon[12]' and 'The Clachan'[13].

"And then there was the music! The Blue Hungarian Band again; the Berlin Philharmonic, the Italian Carabinieri; the Roumanian Orchestra, the Scottish Orchestra with Mlynarksi; Pachman, Kubelik, Backhaus, Marchesi; the Queen's Hall Orchestra under Sir Henry Wood, and all the best bands in the British Army! ... It's certainly time we had another Exhibition!"

## 37. *Selling Shoes*[1]

THE LATEST device of the retail boot trade to ensure a perfect fit for the customer and eliminate all risk of corns, bunions, fallen arch, hammer-toe and ingrowing nails, is an adaptation of the Rontgen[2] rays. A shadow image of the feet, inside the boot, is thrown on a fluorescent screen, revealing all points of pressure or distortion. The customer may go away with a strong conviction that his new boots pinch him across the instep, but it is impossible to argue with an X-ray instrument.

I was speaking about this beneficent new appliance on Saturday to Mr James Swan, the doyen of commercial travellers in the West of Scotland soft goods world, and found him unusually sardonic.

"We'll have a Chair of Bootmaking at Gilmorehill[3] before long," he remarked drily. "It only wants a start from Sir Daniel Stevenson.[4] We'll have a professor of Pedology; special classes in Anatomy, the French Heel, Brogues in the Middle Ages, Slippers for Sedentary Gents, and Comparative Physiology of the Hack and Chilblain.

"There's sure to be travelling scholarships; the champion student of the year will get three years tourin' abroad to inspect the lark or laverock heel of the native African races, the Chinese club-foot, and the American extra-wide welt. No man'll get a responsisble job in a bootshop unless he has the B.Sc. and a Rontgen Ray diploma. He'll be called a Pedologist or a Bootician, wear horn-rim specs, and have a wee place of his own in the shop, hung round wi' charts and photographs o' the leading feet among the Crowned Heads in Europe.

"There is no trade in the country with more go in it than the shoemakers," continued Mr Swan; "It started humbly as a cottage industry when the first roads were made, and the native tribes were gettin' their feet all cut wi' broken bottles. The man that made the first pair of shoes is supposed to have been a chap in Fintry. He killed a cow and made from the hide of it a rough kind of leather socks for himself and his family. Ye'll see a pair in the Kelvingrove Museum — no heels, the hair inside — fine for dancin' the Hoolachan!

"For centuries every man made his own shoes wi' a knife or a hatchet, and history says the human foot was then at its highest perfection. When they started heels and water-tights the job became more complicated. Men that were sick of ploughing in dirty weather took up shoemakin' as a trade and made money of it.

"When I was a lump of a lad, the ploughman-snab[5] was at his zenith. In my native place, you went into his workshop for a pair of either trysted or ready made. If you wanted them made to measure, he went over you wi' an inch-tape, chewin' away at a rossety-end[6] and your shoes were ready for you by the next Fast Day. But if ye had only the money for ready-mades, he took the first pair he laid hands on from a boxful made in Glasgow, squeezed them on to you, fastened them up in a hurry wi' porpoise laces; tied a knot on them you could hardly loosen in a fortnight, and sent ye off hirplin'.

"No tact, you notice! No Salesmanship! The word 'psychology' was unknown. A man had no inducement to buy boots unless he was absolutely needin' them.

"For generations, the public bought its boots wi' as little concern about fittin' as if they were buyin' coffins. There were only two species of them — them with sparrables or tackets, and Sunday boots wi' a squeak in them, usually 'lastic-sided. The boot-seller was no help to you at all; he just flung them at ye, and you could take them or leave them.

"Look at the art that's put into the sale of boots and shoes to-day! A shoe-shop window's a perfect treat; when you look at it you're black affronted wi' yon shabby old bauchles, and make up your mind to have the perfect shoe at last and be a gentleman.

"You go in wi' your heart in your mouth to a grand saloon wi' Persian carpets and no' a shoe in sight, but the walls all piled round wi' cardboard boxes.

"There is a solemn hush in the place, and a faint, religious aroma of Nugget Polish. It might be a Savings Bank. A fine up-standin', nicespoken young gentleman comes up to you and puts you in a seat. With some chatty discourse about the weather, he takes off one of your shoes and looks closely at it. You can see at once he does not think much of it, unless it was bought in his own shop. You're just as much ashamed of your shoes as of the hole in your sock.

"Wi' the practised hand of the expert, he takes the length of your foot wi' a calliper foot-rule; says 'nine and five-eighths,' but that's not, seemingly, close enough, so he uses a micrometer. Havin' looked at your foot from every angle, and grasped, as you feel sure, its every short-comin', he glides up a ladder and takes down a box. Reverently openin' it, he produces the shoe of your dreams!

"Such elegance! Such smooth unwrinkled leather! Such lustre! Such a delightful nut-brown tone! And what a pleasant leathery smell! Such shoes, you feel, would make you a really good man, and distract attention from your hat or the baggin' at your knees.

"He coaxes your foot into one, almost without your knowin' it, as if it was a New Year's Honour, laces it up deftly with a 'love-knot'; stands back wi' his head to the side like a landscape painter and says, 'Now that's a sound shoe!'

"It doesn't seem to you extravagant praise for a shoe that not only looks delightful, but feels as easy-fittin' as a slipper, and you make up your mind immediately that it will do. But the art of salesmanship in the shoe trade calls for more subtlety than letting you away wi' a first pair you try on.

"The young scientist discerns a small degree of tightness o'er the instep, or a narrowness at the toe. He fondles your foot all over again, applies another pair of callipers; feels every joint, like a bonesetter; then up the ladder again like a whitterick and down wi' another pair that looks the identical.

"He may try on you half-a-dozen pair before he's pleased, but you go away wi' the first pair you tried on, convinced that for the first time in your life you have had scientific treatment. But shoes never look so splendid as in the shop where they're for sale. Perhaps the X-ray treatment will put this right."

# Notes

**1 Stars to Push**
1 A fictitious location used for many of these tales.
2 A somewhat pretentious term for a commercial traveller.
3 A commercial traveller. So called because, like Jimmy Swan, they normally carried samples of their wares in bags and cases.
4 A soft silk fabric originating from the Chinese northern coastal province of the same name.

**2 On the Road**
1 A card game similar to whist in which players undertake to win a certain number of tricks.
2 An unconvincing disguise for the well-known firm of Gray Dunn, who had a large biscuit factory at Kinning Park on the South Side of Glasgow.
3 An Ayrshire town noted for its textile industry.
4 The identity of this trade rival is unclear. Glasgow, however, had a great range of such firms and the reader may select from such famous names as Copland & Lye or Trerons.
5 Jimmy Swan's employers have been tentatively identified with the major Glasgow manufacturing and wholesale warehouse firm of Stewart and MacDonald. This concern had clothing factories in Glasgow, Leeds and Strabane, with warehouses in Mitchell Street, Argyle Street and Buchanan Street in Glasgow. Seventy travellers represented the firm in territories as diverse as Sweden and Australia. In a curious case of life imitating art the company later changed its name to Campbell, Stewart & MacDonald.
6 Baillie. A senior councillor in a Scottish town or city with a legal function as an *ex-officio* justice of the Peace.
7 Social evening at a Masonic lodge.

**3 The Fatal Clock**
1 No establishment of this name appears in the Glasgow Post Office Directory for 1913, the year of publication of this story.

2  Tall chest of drawers.
3  The Glasgow underground system was completed in 1896.
4  The Glasgow Necropolis was one of the city's most famous burying-places and from its establishment in 1833 was extensively used by Glasgow's industrial and commercial elite. The Southern Necropolis in the Hutchesontown area of the Gorbals was a later creation.
5  The United Free Church, formed by a union in 1901.
6  A popular total abstinence movement. The Rechabites, apart from their campaign against drink had an important role as a major friendly society with over 200,000 members. The movement's name comes from Jeremiah Ch. 35 vv 5 & 6 —"And I set before the sons of the house of the Rechabites pots full of wine, and cups, and I said unto them, drink ye wine. But they said, we will drink no wine: for Jonadab the son of Rechab our Father commanded us, saying ye shall drink no wine, neither ye, nor your sons for ever."
7  At this time (1911) still a novelty. The first vacuum cleaner, a large machine mounted on wheels and operated from outside the house, had been invented by the Scot, Herbert Cecil Booth, in 1901.
8  Bankruptcy.

## 4  A Spree

1  An open, four-wheeled carriage with an inward-facing bench seat along each side.
2  Turned inside out.
3  Wandering.
4  Dried fish, such as whiting or haddock.
5  The United Presbyterian Church was formed in 1847 from a union of the Secession and Relief Churches. In 1901 the U.P. Church merged with the Free Church to form the United Free Church. As a result this building was surplus to requirements and had become the established Church of Scotland's Church Hall.
6  Not a reference to aged farmers. The Loyal Order of Ancient Shepherds was a popular friendly society. A Royal Commission in the 1870s had reported it to have 46,000 members organised in local lodges. The coming together of the Established and U.F. Church choirs for the Shepherds' Church parade is indicative of better relationships between the presbyterian denominations at this time. The United Free Church and the Church of Scotland were finally to sink their differences and unite in 1929.
7  At the end of the nineteenth century and in the early years of the twentieth century many Italians emigrated to Scotland. Large numbers of them entered the catering industry and came to dominate the two key areas of the fried fish trade and the ice cream parlour. Glasgow and the seaside resorts of the West of Scotland would have been unimaginable without the presence of these early fast-food operations.
8  The 100th Metrical Psalm "All People that on Earth do Dwell". With its familiar tune "Old 100th" taken from the Franco-Genevan Psalter of 1551, it was probably second only to the 23rd Psalm in the affections of Scots worshippers.

9   The American evangelist D. L. Moody and I. D. Sankey published
    two collections of gospel hymns in the 1870s. These were highly
    popular, though obviously not with the traditionalist Jimmy Swan.
10  The North British Railway's routes included a branch line through the
    Stirlingshire town of Slamannan.

## 5   His "Bête Noir"

1   Many of the leading Glasgow drapers and outfitters such as Copland
    and Lye and Trerons had build magnificent stores, with, as Jimmy
    suggests, attractive catering facilities to restore their customer's
    strength. In a much later piece in his "Looker-On" column which
    discussed Glasgow restaurants and their innovations Munro has a
    Scot returning to this native city after many years in America remark
        "But say! That's a nifty dodge of the Department Stores to start up
    restaurants and get the dames warmed up and replete with wholesome
    soup and sundaes before they go over the top and attack the bargain
    counters."
2   An opera by Vincent Wallace, first produced in 1845.
3   Franz Lehar's operetta, first produced in Vienna in 1909 as "Der Graf
    von Luxemburg", opened in London in English translation in May
    1911. Its popularity ensured a wide and speedy circulation for the
    music.
4   Glasgow's unique series of Exhibitions included the 1901 Interna-
    tional Exhibition and 1911 Scottish National Exhibition held at
    Kelvingrove Park in the west end of the city. Still an obviously topical
    reference when this story first appeared in the *Glasgow Evening News*
    in December 1912.
5   A London institution dedicated to the sport of boxing.
6   The women's suffrage movement, as represented by organisations
    such as Emmeline Pankhurst's Women's Social and Political Move-
    ment, was actively campaigning for their cause in the years before the
    First World War. As Jimmy's comment suggest, these campaigns
    became increasingly given to direct action.

## 6   From Fort William

1   The home ground of Queen's Park Football Club and Scotland's
    national football stadium.
2   Elsewhere, Gower Street is described as being in Glasgow's Ibrox
    District. However street maps show it situated between Bellahouston
    and Pollokshields, about a third of a mile south of what might
    normally be thought of as Ibrox.
3   This story was first published in 1912, a time when the cinema craze
    was a matter of regular press comment.
4   The citizens of Fort William had only gained the benefits of rail travel
    in 1894 when the West Highland Railway, running from Glasgow's
    Queen Street station to an initial terminus in Fort William was
    opened. The line was later extended to Mallaig in 1901, doubtless
    extending still further Jimmy's Mazeppa cigar zone.
5   A once popular product of the great Dundonian publishing empire of
    D. C. Thomson.

**7   Jimmy's Silver Wedding**
1   A superior neighbourhood in the fashionable Kelvinside district of Glasgow's West End.
2   So sleepy is the village of Kirkfinn that it has quite escaped the attention of the Ordnance Survey.
3   The first Tay Railway Bridge was destroyed in a severe gale in December 1879 with the loss of 77 lives of crew and passengers on a train from Edinburgh to Dundee.

**8   A Matrimonial Order**
1   A high quality woollen fabric used for women's dresses. From the French *de laine* — of wool.
2   A dyeing process for calico. A main centre of the industry was in the Vale of Leven, Dumbartonshire, some 20 miles from Glasgow.
3   Tips, pours, cascades.
4   J. H. Haverly (Munro miss-spells the name) was the manager of "Haverly's Mastodon Minstrels" the first of the large-scale American minstrel troupes. The Haverly Minstrels were disbanded in 1896.
5   The Hengler family were prominent in British entertainment from the 18th century. Among their many enterprises were permanent circuses in London, Dublin, Hull and Glasgow. Their Glasgow circus was located in Wellington Street from 1885-1903 and re-opened in the Hippodrome Building in Sauchiehall Street in 1904.

**9   A Great Night**
1   While we noted in the first story that Birrelton is fictitious, it is also curiously protean. Its characteristics change in a quite alarming way. In this tale Dawson's is described as the only draper's shop in Birrelton, and Jimmy, as we will be told, spends the night there for the first time due to bad weather and a foundered horse. In "His Bete Noir", also set in Birrelton we are told that Jimmy puts off his visit to Joseph Jago's shop till the very last, having "swept up all the other soft-goods orders of the town." In "Stars to Push" he is staying overnight at the "Buck's Head" Hotel in Birrelton and is on terms of familiarity with the residents of the community — experience surely hard to come by if he only made a brief visit to Birrelton. Even more curiously in the present story we are told that Birrelton is only of significance in that it is on the road to several other places of importance. In "Stars to Push" (written a year and half after "A Great Night") Birrelton has become a sea-port from which Jimmy is to sail the next morning. Curious! Can there be two Birreltons?
2   Ignace Jan Paderewski (1860-1941) Polish violin virtuoso and advocate of Polish independence. Briefly Prime Minister of Poland in 1919.
3   Nellie Melba. Stage name of Helen Porter Mitchell (1861-1931), an Australian soprano of Scots descent who specialised in the Italian operatic repertoire. Created Dame Commander of the Order of the British Empire in 1927.
4   Scottish music hall singer and composer. Lauder (1870-1950) was an active recruiter and troop entertainer during the First World War and

was knighted for his services in 1919. Lauder and Munro were friends
and Lauder attended Munro's funeral in 1930.

## 10 Rankine's Rookery
1  A Perthshire village situated at the junction of a number of important
   transport routes. In particular it was an interchange point between the
   West Highland Railway and the Callander and Oban Railway.
2  David Lloyd George (1853-1944), Liberal politician. In June 1912
   when this story appeared he was Chancellor of the Exchequer in
   Asquith's administration.
3  A famously fertile stretch of land on the North bank of the Tay
   between Perth and Dundee. Anywhere less like Rannoch Moor, an
   infertile and inhospitable acid peat-bog lying at an average height of
   300 metres in the West Highlands, is hard to imagine.
4  A tenement property of flats.
5  Jimmy is talking of the second Tay Rail Bridge, completed in 1887
   and Europe's longest railway bridge.
6  A public park donated to the City of Dundee in 1863 by Sir David
   Baxter, a local jute magnate.
7  Bonnethill was a district to the North of Dundee's city centre largely
   settled in earlier centuries by the makers of knitted woollen bonnets.
8  The Scouring-burn is a small stream running into a creek in the centre
   of Dundee and which may have formed the site of the first harbour of
   the town.
9  A property manager responsible for collecting rents.

## 11 Dignity
1  Confectionery — acid drops.
2  Raeberry Street is situated off Maryhill Road, Glasgow.
3  Trouser braces.
4  Like all the best stories this one is set in the country of the imagination — Auchentee has escaped the map-makers.
5  A street-gutter, or the drain and cover in such a gutter.

## 12 Universal Provider
1  This story first appeared in April 1912, just as the results of the 1911
   Census would have been in the news.
2  Jimmy's customer need hardly have feared exposure in the "Northern
   Star", a paper circulating in Wick in the 1830's. A more probable
   source of home-town embarrassment would have been the Golspie-
   based "Northern Times".
3  One of the great issue in Scottish church history was the fight to
   abolish patronage (the presentation to a clerical vacancy by the Crown
   or a local landowner) and to ensure for the local congregation the
   right to choose their own minister.
4  The black preaching gown worn by ministers of the reformed
   churches.
5  One of the great Victorian hero-figures, Field Marshal Roberts
   (1832-1914) first came to prominence by winning the Victoria Cross
   during the Indian Mutiny. In 1880 he marched through Afghanistan

to relieve Kandahar. Later Roberts was Commander-in-Chief in India. During the 2nd Boer War "Our Bobs", as he was knicknamed, was sent out to South Africa to take command and relieved Kimberley and marched on Pretoria. Created Earl Roberts of Kandahar in 1901.

## 13  The Commercial Room

1  This Fifeshire inn is not to be confused with the Birrelton "Buck's Head".
2  A room in a hotel set aside for the use of commercial travellers.
3  Oddly enough all the Boots in hotels patronised by Jimmy Swan appear to have been called Willie. Perhaps the name went with the position.
4  Slimmer.
5  Lively, cheerful.
6  In a later story (No. 20 "Gent's Attire") we will learn the definition of a pound-a-day man. "… it was understood in the shop that up to a pound-a-day Mr Swan's bill for expenses passed the cashier unquestioned; that it was an historical right, like Magna Charta."
7  To broil on a griddle.
8  Finnan haddock; a cured haddock. The name is usually held to derive from the Kincardineshire village of Findon, some six miles south of Aberdeen. The *Concise Scots Dictionary* suggest that the alternative form "Findram Haddie" may arise from a confusion with the Morayshire village of Findhorn.

## 14  The Changed Man

1  A reference to fusel-oil, an undesirable by-product of spirit distillation.
2  A popular range of souvenir china — either plates or vases with a town's coat of arms or models of famous buildings; a particularly popular example of the latter being J. M. Barrie's house in Kirriemuir "A Window in Thrums".
3  Popularised after a newspaper cartoon in 1902 showed President Theodore "Teddy" Roosevelt with a bear cub.
4  William Thomson (1824-1907) was a Scottish physicist and mathematician who was professor at Glasgow University for over 50 years; advised on the laying of the first transatlantic telegraph cable, developed the Kelvin or absolute temperature scale and carried out a wide range of pioneering work in theoretical and applied physics, electricity and hydrodynamics. Created 1st Baron Kelvin in 1892.
5  Sadly, though unsurprisingly this distinguished ornament of the Heidelberg faculty and his novel theory seem both to be fictitious.
6  John Gough (1817-1886) was an English-born temperance reformer who, having emigrated to the United States at the age of 12 and succumbing to alcohol, later became one of the leading figures in the temperance movement in both the USA and Britain.

## 15  Vitalising the Gloomy Grants

1  "The store" was the usual popular term for a Co-operative society shop.
2  Captain Kettle was a Welsh sea-captain with a red beard and the hero

of a successful series of novels by C. J. Cutcliffe Hynd which appeared between 1898 and 1932.

3  The Franco-Prussian War commenced in July 1870 and ended with the fall of Paris in January 1871.

4  Song thrush (*Turdus ericetorum*)

5  In the metrical version in the Scottish Psalter this psalm opens:
> "The Lord's my light and saving health,
> who shall make me dismayed.
> My life's strength is the Lord of whom
> then shall I be afraid?"

The tune "Dunfermline" comes from the Scottish Psalter of 1615.

## 16  Blate Rachel

1  Shy, backward.

2  Having a squint (strabismus) in one eye.

3  Hydropathic establishments set up as spa hotels and specialising in the treatment of minor, or perhaps imaginary disorders by one form or another of water treatment — sea bathing, medicinal springs etc.

4  Literally someone who is deaf or hard of hearing, but used here in a pejorative sense to indicate someone who is generally dull or backward.

## 17  Rachel Comes to Town

1  Small town in Kincardineshire, 18 miles east of Aberdeen.

2  Resort on the Cowal Peninsula on the Firth of Clyde.

3  A popular dance of the period.

4  Armpit.

5  A female nut. A nut or knut was a period term for a dandy.

## 18  A Poor Programme

1  The Territorial Force was created in 1908 as a citizen's army to replace the earlier Volunteers. The Territorial Army, as it was later re-named, was designed as a home service force but could, and did during the First World War, volunteer for foreign service.

2  Clara Butt (1873-1936) was an English contralto whose chief fame was won on the concert platform rather than in opera; a specialisation perhaps resulting from her statuesque build and height of 6'2". Created Dame Commander of the Order of the British Empire in 1920.

3  Louisa Tetrazzini (1871-1940); Italian soprano. She made her London debut as Violetta in Verdi's "La Traviata" in 1902.

## 19  Broderick's Shop

1  Neil Munro had a continuing interest in the ironmonger's trade. As a young man coming to Glasgow to seek his fortune he started work in an ironmongers' shop in the Trongate — an eastward extension of Argyle Street. In one of his articles reprinted in *Brave Days* he wrote: "My passion was, as it still remains, the windows of toolshops and ironmongers, and MacHaffie and Colquhoun's, next door to "Pie Smith's" at the corner of Maxwell Street, particularly intrigued me. It

proclaimed itself the oldest ironmongers's firm, wholesale and retail, in the city, and it looked it."

He later wrote of the closure of what seems to have been the same shop, though this time using the name Macaulay and Buchanan, and this piece is preserved in another posthumous collection of his journalism, *News from the North*.

2 "We came to "Glasgow of the Steeples" from the hills, expecting from generations of Gaelic tradition to find Argyle Street the most amazing thoroughfare in Scotland, and we were not disappointed." Neil Munro *Brave Days*.

3 An earthenware ball used in the childrens' game of marbles.

4 Stroll.

5 Climbing.

6 A reel. The *Concise Scots Dictionary* points out that this word specifically relates to the "Reel of Tulloch" being a corruption of the Gaelic for Tulloch — Thulachain.

## 20 Gent's Attire

1 A quotation from *Hamlet* Act 3 Sc.1 Ophelia says of the apparently deranged Hamlet:
> "O, what a noble mind is here o'erthrown!
> The courtier's, soldier's, scholar's, eye, tongue, sword;
> The expectancy and rose of the fair state,
> The glass of fashion and the mould of form
> The observ'd of all observers…"

2 The German armed forces had developed airships to a considerable extent between 1900 and the outbreak of the World War. They were named after Ferdinand, Count von Zeppelin, the German soldier who had pioneered their military use. This story was published in September 1915, some months after the first Zeppelin raid on Yarmouth.

3 The Prevention of Corruption Act (6 Edward VII Ch. 32) of 1906.

4 George Geddes II was employed by the Glasgow Humane Society as their officer between 1889 and 1932 and was responsible for many rescues from the River Clyde as well as the less rewarding task of recovering corpses from the river.

5 Fair play.

## 21 Keeping up with Cochrane

1 Sutherlandshire village strategically situated at the intersection of the main North/South and East/West routes through the County.

2 Jimmy is quoting from Burns's poem *To Dr Blacklock*
> "To make a happy fire-side clime to weans and wife
> That's the true pathos and sublime of human life."

3 Despite Jimmy's convincing tale Lairg was never more than a village, so never had a Town Council and could never have offered a civic career to Watty Cochrane.

4 Busy.

5 The finished edges of a piece of fabric.

6 Busied one's self.

## 22  The Hen Crusade
1  Wrung.
2  Amply proportioned.
3  Backslider, reprobate.
4  Bar from the Sacrament of Holy Communion.

## 23  Linoleum
1  See No. 6 for discussion of the location of Jimmy's Gower Street residence.
2  So select is Sibbald Terrace that it does not appear in the Glasgow street atlas.
3  The Fife town of Kirkcaldy was recognised as the centre of the linoleum industry. Its fame, and the characteristic smell of the process was celebrated in the poem "The Boy in the Train" by Munro's contemporary M. C. Smith, with its final two lines:
    "For I ken mysel' by the queer-like smell
    That the next stop's Kirkcaddy!"

## 24  The Grauvat King
1  Cravat, scarf or muffler.
2  To prepare a sheep's head for the popular Scottish delicacy of sheep's head broth.

## 25  Jimmy's Sins Find Him Out
1  A popular sporting paper published between 1888 and November 1914.
2  Harold MacNeill of Queen's Park won ten international caps between 1874 and 1881.
3  Queen's Park Football Club.
4  Jimmy McMenemy of Celtic and Patrick Thistle amassed a total of 503 Scottish League appearances. He also represented Scotland 12 times between 1905 and 1920.
5  This story was published on Monday, 6th April 1914, the International match against England at Hampden having been played on Saturday 4th. The 3-1 victory for Scotland doubtless pleased the majority of the 105,000 crowd.
6  Internationals were played at Hampden Park, situated in this Southside suburb.
7  Stonehaven, the county town of Kincardineshire, some 12 miles south of Aberdeen.

## 26  A Wave of Temperance
1  This war-time story, first published in May 1915, reflects something of the austerity and temperance movements which were encouraged as part of the war effort. King George V had announced in April 1915 that the Royal Household would cease to drink beer, wine or spirits for the duration. Horatio Hubert Kitchener (1850-1916) 1st Earl Kitchener of Khartoum, had been Secretary of State for War from August 1914.
2  Ginger biscuit (from Parliamentary cake).

**27  Country Journeys**
1  The Thermos flask, invented by Sir James Dewar, was patented in 1904, so would still be something of a novelty when this story appeared in January 1912.
2  A slogan used by the Caledonian Railway in their advertising at this time.
3  Harvest-home.
4  A once-popular children's magazine.
5  The first Monday of the New Year–a traditional time for the exchange of gifts.
6  A type of light chaise, but often used as a term of mockery for any old or rickety coach or carriage.

**28  Raising the Wind**
1  The Royal visit to Scotland in July 1914 was indeed an extensive one. King George V visited Edinburgh, Glasgow, Clydebank & Dumbarton, Coatbridge & Hamilton, Dundee & Perth, Dunblane & Stirling.
2  The patron saint of Glasgow, here used metonymically for the city itself.
3  Glasgow Central Railway Station, built for the Caledonian railway and opened in 1879, was, as Jimmy suggests, greatly extended between 1899 and 1906.
4  Booked.
5  Searches the pockets.
6  A jacket of a wool, or wool and cotton mix, with a shiny finish.
7  The *Daphne* steamer was launched on 3rd July 1883 from the Clydeside yard of Alexander Stephen & Sons. On entering the water she turned turtle and sank with the loss of 124 lives. The inherent instability of *Daphne's* design, combined with loose machinery and the rapid inflow of water through a boiler access hole in the main deck contributed to this disaster.

**29  Roses, Roses All The Way**
1  Not an iota.
2  A generalised term of disapprobation indicative of coarseness, rowdiness, etc. and frequently used of women; not necessarily with the sense of sexual looseness.

**30  Citizen Soldier**
1  This war-time story (first published in December 1914) sees Jimmy enlisted in the Citizen Training Force, formed in October to provide the First World War equivalent of the Home Guard. Two drill parades a week and battalion exercise every second Saturday gave basic training to men over the age for military service or otherwise disqualified.
2  Frames for the indoor drying of clothes.
3  A piece of grease or fat.

**31  The Adventures of a Country Customer**
1  This previously uncollected story first appeared in the Glasgow Evening News of 8th May 1911.

2  Glasgow had held major Exhibitions in Kelvingrove Park in 1888 and
   1901. The 1888 International Exhibition had as one of its aims the
   funding of a new Civic Art Gallery and Museum. The 1901 Glasgow
   International Exhibition was designed, in part to inaugurate this new
   civic treasure.
3  "The Groveries" was a popular, if unofficial, name for the
   Kelvingrove Exhibitions. However Munro was unimpressed with this
   term and wrote elsewhere "On Saturday, 10th November, 1888, 'The
   Groveries' — silly name for an International Exhibition — had
   closed..." *The Brave Days* p. 64
4  A Fairy Fountain, a large central water feature illuminated by
   coloured electric light, was a feature of both the 1888 and 1911
   Exhibitions.
5  Sir Henry Wood (1869–1944) is of course otherwise best remembered
   as the originator of the Promenade Concerts.
6  A Manhattan Cocktail consists of bourbon or rye whiskey, vermouth
   & bitters.
7  One of a number of references to freemasonry in these stories.
8  The mile-long Mountain Scenic Ride was one of the most popular·
   features of the Exhibition.
9  A seaside resort in Ayrshire much frequented by golfers and the
   location of a luxury hotel.
10 The 1911 Scottish Exhibition of National History, Art and Industry,
   raised £15,000 to endow a Chair of Scottish History at Glasgow
   University.

## 32  The Radiant James Swan
1  This previously uncollected story first appeared in the Glasgow
   Evening News on 21st July 1913.
2  "Consider the lilies of the field, how they grow; they toil not, neither
   do they spin: And yet I say unto you, That even Solomon in all his
   glory was not arrayed like one of these" Matthew Ch 6 vv 28–29.
3  See no. 16 "Blate Rachel' and no. 17 "Rachel Comes to Town" for
   the earlier adventures of Jimmy Swan and Rachel Thorpe.
4  Money scattered to the crowd at a wedding to ensure good fortune
   and prosperity for the newly married couple.
5  A reference to the rituals of freemasonry.
6  The Royal Arch is a higher order of freemasonry.
7  Right Worshipful Master, the chief officer of a masonic lodge.
8  Jimmy is referring to various Friendly Societies which were active in
   the period.
9  Marbles.

## 33  Jimmy Swan's German Spy
1  This previously uncollected story first appeared in the Glasgow
   Evening News on January 18th 1915.
2  As part of the security precautions during the First World War,
   introduced under the Defence of the Realm Act, hoteliers had to
   register guests and notify new arrivals to the local police.
3  Strathbungo is a select residential district on the South Side of Glasgow.

4  Mr Fisher, as a young man of military age, would not wish to be seen
   engaging in a frivolous pursuit like golf, lest questions be raised about
   his failure to volunteer for service. Compulsory conscription was not
   introduced until January 1916.

## 34  Jimmy Swan in Warm Weather

1  This previously uncollected story first appeared in the Glasgow
   Evening News on 9th July 1923.
2  The attentive reader will have noted that Mr Swan's employers have
   undergone an unaccountable change of name in the eight years since
   the previous Jimmy Swan story appeared. In all the other stories the
   company's name was Campbell & Macdonald. Readers may choose to
   believe in either an internal power struggle within the firm and a
   consequent re-naming of the company or in a fit of forgetfulness on
   the part of Neil Munro.
3  At the time of first publication Scotland was enjoying a remarkable
   heatwave.
4  In January 1923 French and Belgian troops had occupied the Ruhr
   following the failure of the German government to pay reparations
   demanded under the Treaty of Versailles.
5  Plus fours, a type of baggy trouser favoured by golfers, became
   fashionable around 1920.
6  A joke, tale or anecdote. An all purpose word (often spelled "baur")
   more often associated with Jimmy Swan's sea-going contemporary
   Para Handy.

## 35  The Tall Hat

1  This previously uncollected story first appeared in the Glasgow
   Evening News on August 13th 1923
2  Tillietudlem (the Evening News spells it Tul111etudlem) Castle features
   in Walter Scott's *Old Mortality* and is identified with Craignethan
   Castle in the parish of Lesmahagow, Lanarkshire.
3  A publication listing bankruptcy actions.
4  The Incorporation of Hammermen is one of the fourteen trade
   incorporations of Glasgow. Originally a craft guild, by the time of this
   story the member's proficiency in the manual skills of blacksmith and
   engineer had become somewhat attenuated.
5  St George's Tron Church in Buchanan Street. A conspicuous city
   centre landmark designed by William Stark and built in 1807-9.
6  Milngavie is a small town a few miles north west of Glasgow favoured
   by city businessmen as a residential area. It has never been noted as a
   centre of the avant-garde.

## 36  The Groveries in Retrospect

1  This previously uncollected story first appeared in the Glasgow
   Evening News on February 11th 1924.
2  Despite such views Glasgow had to wait until 1938 for its next
   Exhibition.
3  Kelvingrove, or West End Park, was the site of the 1888, 1901 &
   1911 Exhibitions.

4   Dining rooms decorated in clan tartans.
5   The 1888 Exhibition was opened by the Prince & Princess of Wales
    and visited by Queen Victoria in August.
6   The Russian section in the 1901 Exhibition was the largest of the
    foreign contributions.
7   Despite the strength of Jimmy's views the 1938 Exhibition was held at
    Bellahouston Park on the South-Side of Glasgow.
8   Captain Thomas Scott Baldwin, American balloonist, parachute
    jumper and pioneer aviator. Munro, as so often was the case, made
    repeated use of his memories and experiences. His other account of
    Baldwin dropping in to Hamilton Park appears in *The Brave Days* and
    gives a flavour of the excitement of these days of pioneer aviators:
    "On September 25th a performance of his [Baldwin's] at Hamilton
    Park proved a serious rival to the fascinations of Kelvingrove. Special
    trains were run to Hamilton; the curious flocked from all parts of
    midland Scotland to see a man risk his life in a dive from a balloon
    at 4000 feet.
    When I got to the race-course, myself, I found Baldwin in the centre
    of a vast concourse gathered about his balloon, already inflated. His
    wife, a fragile little woman, who was said to have made the para-
    chute, was standing anxiously by while the husband finally scruti-
    nised her handiwork. He crawled out of sight inside the parachute to
    make certain that the rain which had fallen in the morning had not
    handicapped its chance of opening out in the air when the crucial
    moment came.
    Fifteen minutes later, a tinselled circus acrobat, he was swinging
    from a trapeze below the balloon and waving flags. We took his word
    for it, later, that he reached an altitude of 4000 feet before he dived
    with the parachute strapped to him. It opened after a vertiginous
    second or two and soon he was on terra firma with Mrs Baldwin
    kissing him. The balloon, ripped open by a cord control at the
    moment of the dive, sailed into a neighbouring parish. We didn't go
    to look for it. We had got the worth of our money in the gasp of
    apprehension before the umbrella opened out."
9   "The River", an aquatic panorama, invented by Captain Paul Boyton,
    and premiered in New York, was presented in Berkeley Street,
    Charing Cross. The Mitchell Library, the city's major reference
    library, was built between 1906 and 1911.
10  A popular song by the Neapolitan composer Luigi Denza (1846-
    1922).
11  Herr Wilhelm Morgan's Blue Hungarian Band was a leading conti-
    nental ensemble and regular visitors to Glasgow exhibitions. They
    were the subject of a well-known painting by the Glasgow artist Sir
    John Lavery.
12  A recreation of Scottish urban vernacular architecture.
13  A feature of the 1911 exhibition was a reconstruction of a Highland
    village or clachan with Highlanders practising various crafts and
    domestic activities, singing in Gaelic and wearing the national dress.

**37  Selling Shoes**
1    This previously uncollected story first appeared in the Glasgow
     Evening News on January 4th 1926.
2    Now more commonly known as X-Rays. Named after their discov-
     erer, Wilhelm Konrad von Rontgen (1845-1923), the Nobel prize-
     winning German physicist.
3    The location of the University of Glasgow.
4    Daniel Macaulay Stevenson (1851-1944) was a Glasgow merchant
     and philanthropist who was a major benefactor of Glasgow University,
     endowing the Chairs of Italian and Spanish among many other
     benefactions. He was given an Honorary Doctorate of Law by the
     University in 1934. He was Lord Provost of Glasgow from 1911-1914
     having served on the City Council since 1892.
5    Cobbler or bootmaker. Also often used in the form "snob".
6    A rosin-treated thread used in bootmaking.